Not the Norm
A Small Town Story

Lorraine M. Harris

Copyright © 2012 by Lorraine M. Harris

All rights reserved. No part of this book may be reproduced, stored in a retrieval system or transmitted in any form or by any means without prior written permission of the author, except by a reviewer who may quote brief passages in the review to be printed in a magazine, newspaper or journal.

The story is a work of fiction but. All of the characters, names, incidents, organizations, and dialogue in this novel are either the products of the author's imagination or used fictitiously. However, information quoted is factual.

ISBN: 13:978-1480249189

ISBN 10: 1480249181

LCCN: 2008942491

Other Works by Lorraine M. Harris

Novels

Sunday Golf

After Bowling

Golf Course View

Casserole Parade

Casserole Surprise

It Could Happen To Your Child

Intuition, co-authored with Deborah Seibert

Self-Help Books

Marketing Tips for Self-Published Authors

Seniors Learn Mah Jongg, Guaranteed

For more information about Lorraine, visit her website, www.lorrainemharris.com

DEDICATION

This book is dedicated to my husband, Lamont C. Harris, who saw something unique about Connellsville, Pennsylvania. This book was written because of Lamont and our daughters, Nicole and Natalie, who encouraged and inspired me. Thank you for your unconditional love and for believing that I could capture the essence of my home town.

None of this would have happened without the love and support of my parents, my later father, Cornelius A. Mockabee and my mother, Dorothy Marilla Mockabee. They inspired me by stating that you can do anything with God and hard work. I am also grateful for my loving and supportive sisters, Doris Marilla Lee, Patty Mockabee White, Nancy Mockabee Murrell, and Janice Mockabee Cunningham.

Every black American born, raised and educated in Connellsville are special and you made a difference. You are the reason why I created this book and for that, thank you.

ACKNOWLEDGEMENTS

When you acknowledge individuals, you run the risk of forgetting someone. I could not possibly list everyone who shared or provided me with a photo. Just know how much I appreciated your time and support. Words cannot express my gratitude. Your stories and pictures added authenticity to my words.

For everyone not mentioned in the book, I apologize. Your accomplishments were important, but either I did not now about your story or I found out after the book was published.

My sincere thanks to the individuals who helped in finalizing this book and they are Gloria (Gigi) Hey, Jo Jones and Don Whipp.

CHAPTER 1

A hint of a cool breeze hit my face as I opened the sliding glass door to the lanai. Carrying a glass of iced tea in my hand, I stepped outside. My plan was to watch the magnificent colors of yellow, orange, and red fill the sky. Sunsets reminded me of artists painting on a blank canvas, blending an array of colors with each result different.

As I thought about it, I watched Mother Nature create her own picture, splashing the blue sky with varying shades of light grey to black. All I could think about was how the gloomy atmosphere was the ideal setting for the start of a bloodcurdling movie.

Within minutes, large rain drops were hitting against the lanai's acrylic windows. Speeding down the street was a stream of golf carts. With the heavy downpour and lightning striking in the far distance, I hoped each person would arrive home safely.

Keeping an eye on the weather and sipping tea, my mind filled with flashbacks of when I met my husband, Lamont, and how and why we ended up in central

Florida.

When I started dating Lamont, marriage was the last thing on my mind. After several months of seeing one another, I discovered that Lamont and I were not on the same page regarding our relationship. One evening, in the car, before we left for our date, Lamont turned towards me and stated firmly, "We need to talk."

Taken off guard, I didn't know what to say as he picked up my hand. As I looked at him, his expression was somber and his tone was serious as he started speaking. As I listened, my stomach began churning, not knowing where the conversation was going.

As I withdrew my sweaty hand from Lamont's light hold, I was apprehensive. My shoulders straightened as I prepared myself for the blow. Folding my hands in my lap, I sat and waited. His voice was slow and deliberate as he shared in detail his goals, dreams and the future.

Intently, I listened to his words that were open, honest, and heart-felt expressions of love. My eyes were tear-filled when he once again picked up my hand. These probably weren't his exact words, but he said something similar to—"Lorraine, I want you to marry me and become my wife and lifelong partner."

Before I could answer, he added, "Before you agree to marry me, there are two conditions."

Wide-eyed, I glanced at him. My heart was pounding against my chest, wondering what kind of conditions he wanted to tell me. I prayed they weren't things I couldn't live with such as not wanting religion in our life, being a nudist, or wanting more than two children.

No sooner had he said the word *"conditions"* before he began enumerating them. "Number one, I want to retire as soon as I'm eligible." He let out a nervous laugh and added, "That means I'll retire as young as possible." He cleared his throat and ended with, secondly, we must retire somewhere warm, where the sun shines every day."

We were living the American dream—marriage, two children, fulfilling careers, luxury cars and a five-bedroom house in the Washington, D.C. suburbs. One highlight of our life was planning vacations, visiting relatives and going to places of interest.

In our forties, while planning an upcoming vacation, Lamont gave me a friendly reminder. "It's time we start researching places where we might retire. Most of all, the place must be warm and sunny."

I said nothing while recalling my agreement to his conditions as we started mapping out what we thought would meet his requirements. We didn't rule out any state, but after much research and consideration for where our daughters lived, we decided to retire on the east coast. Our search began with trips to cities in the states of Virginia, the Carolinas, and Georgia.

To all of these states, Lamont's response was a "no."

The roadside signs were a reminder to Lamont why these places were unacceptable. "It's not warm enough. As long as it says bridge freezes before road surface that means the possibility of ice or snow." He would shake his head and add, "We're not far enough south."

When we reached Florida, Lamont beamed. "This is it! Did you notice there were no signs about bridges freezing over? And, did you see the welcome sign's logo—the sunshine state?"

After visiting many retirement communities in Florida, we made our decision and shared our plans with relatives and friends. The majority of them was in disbelief and confused about our choice.

Their responses were similar in nature. "But you don't know anyone in Florida. Why would you move away from friends and family? Do you realize that Florida has more seniors than any other state? What will you do?"

We listened to our family and friends' concerns and had long debates about the advantages and disadvantages of living in Florida. The discussions always ended in an impasse, but in the end our minds could not be changed. We believed that anyone visiting us would have a better appreciation and understanding why we had chosen Florida as our retirement home.

###

Our move was from the Washington, D.C. Metropolitan area to The Villages located northwest of Orlando. Up until the move, our friends' and relatives' kept expressing their concerns about us being young and vibrate and how would we adjust to being around people using walkers and playing shuffle board and bingo.

What our relatives and friends didn't know was that we had found a unique Florida retirement community. The lifestyle was probably similar to those that are wealthy. The difference is that most people on a fixed income can afford The Villages' standard of living.

Some of our friends accused us of sounding like a commercial. We would laugh, but understood how they reached that conclusion. Our faces lit up like nightlights when talking about the *"free"* nightly entertainment, no annual or monthly country clubs fees, the variety of restaurants, movie theaters, and town squares.

Another concern of our friends was that we didn't golf, yet we moved to a golfing community. That didn't concern us because we took lessons and like so many others, we were hooked on chasing that little white ball. Besides, how could we not golf living in The Villages when it's basically *"free"* when playing on executive courses? Like any other golfing community, the championship golf courses cost, but with a membership, the fee becomes reduced.

Initially The Villages caught Lamont's attention because of the two bowling centers. Being an avid bowler, he was excited about the number of sanctioned leagues he could join as well as the array of bowling tournaments offered.

As we settled into our lifestyle, I began noticing that Lamont seemed anxious about something, but I didn't know what. Taking my time, I finally asked him.

"What's wrong? Don't you like living here?"

"Oh, no. I love it, but I never envisioned the possibility of not watching my favorite football team, the Washington Redskins, playing on Sundays."

From his expression, I could tell the thought of it was agonizing.

As we discussed the issue, I suggested, "Why not buy the cable television football package?" I paused and added, "Then, you won't miss a single game."

"That's an option but..." His voice drifted off. "I can't justify spending that kind of money."

"Why not? You only live once?"

"That may be, but we're on a fixed income and when I spend that amount of money I want something tangible in return."

Before I could dispute what he was saying, I noticed his shining bright eyes followed by a chuckle. "Maybe I can find someone who's already bought the package and they'll invite me to watch the game with them."

Before he got too carried away, I asked, "And if you don't find this person?"

"Then, I'll consider buying the package, but not until I explore all my options."

I teased, "I have an idea. You can always pick a Florida team to cheer for." My comment met by Lamont's glaring stare.

CHAPTER 2

During the next several weeks, Lamont was either wearing a sign on his shirt or he had become a human magnet. Everywhere we went—church, grocery stores, restaurants, and movies, we met someone from Virginia, Maryland or Washington, D.C.

Enthusiasm and friendliness were the two words to describe Lamont when he introduced himself to these individuals. The second the small talk of where did you live, work, and why did you move to The Villages ended, he moved on to the real topic that interested him.

Each time, I braced myself, but nothing kept me from cringing when he asked his question, "Do you like professional football?"

Hearing the word, "yes" he would go for the jugular. "By any chance do you root for the Washington Redskins?"

Again, if the answer was "yes," I watched his fist by his side when he gave it a slight pump while trying to keep his emotions in check. Then, in a casual tone, he would ask, "Do you know where a fan can watch the televised Redskins' games?"

As he waited for the answer, I could see him crossing his fingers, hoping to hear the individual say that he or she had purchased the cable or satellite football package. When Lamont heard the negative response, a plastered smile covered his face, trying to hide his disappointment.

Over the next several weeks, Lamont encountered lots of Redskins' fans, but not one of them had purchased the football package. In addition, none of these fans knew where they might watch the televised NFL games not shown on the regular television channels. Lamont flinched at those willing to becoming a fan of the Miami Dolphins or the Tampa Bay Buccaneers.

With the football season fast approaching, Lamont was anxious, fearing he would have to break down and purchase the football ticket. About two weeks before the season started, Lamont told one of our neighbors about his football dilemma. The unexpected happened when the neighbor shared some incredible information.

"At the Fiesta Bowling Center, a restaurant, called Crazy Gringo's shows all the NFL games." To make sure he had heard right, Lamont asked, "Do they show the Redskins?"

The neighbor laughed. "Yes, every Sunday, Gringo's shows all the NFL games."

###

The football season began and all was well. Lamont could watch his beloved Redskins.

The following Sunday, we attended the eight o'clock church service, went home, changed into our Redskins shirts, and headed to Gringo's. Not knowing what to expect we arrived at the Fiesta Bowling Center about an hour before the one o'clock kickoff time.

We drove around the bowling center several times before finding a parking space. The lack of parking concerned us until we entered the bowling center and saw that a league was bowling. Since we were early and had no worries about Gringo's being crowded, we strolled down the bowling center aisle, stopping, watching, and chatting with some of the bowlers.

At one of the lanes, we paused after watching a bowler we knew throw his fourth strike in a row. As we cheered him on, the strikes ended in the seventh frame so we continued our stroll.

Lamont glanced at his watch. "It's getting late. We better go." When Lamont opened the door, our mouths dropped open. As we stood glancing around the restaurant, we found ourselves in a packed filled room of football fans. No matter where we looked, people were dressed in NFL team gear. The boisterous voices matched the blaring televisions that were showing pregame shows.

Lamont glimpsed at his watch, leaned down and whispered in my ear, "I guess we were wrong about all the cars in the parking lot. What time do you think these people got here?"

I shrugged. "We shouldn't be surprised. After all, this is The Villages and people arrive early for almost any event—the movies, craft shows, parades, or concerts."

As we turned to leave, I yelled and pointed. "Over there are two empty chairs." Squeezing our way through the narrow passageway, we made our way to the seats and sat down.

Introductions were made. "Hi, I'm Lamont Harris and this is my wife, Lorraine." Before we could ask the names of the people at the table, a waitress appeared, taking our drink and food orders.

"Is it always this crowded?" My voice shrieking as I asked the woman sitting across the table from me.

She shouted back, "Yeah, this is pretty typical of most Sundays. The Green Bay Packers' and the Cleveland Browns' fans take up most of the seats. The Browns' fans have priority because they're recognized as an official NFL fan club."

"Are you kidding me?"

"I'm serious."

Lamont leaned over to one of the Browns' fans and yelled, "Have you ever heard of Robert "Bo" Scott?"

"Uh…yeah, he's from Columbus, Ohio and played

for the Browns back in the late 60's and early 70's."

"You have the right Bo Scott, but he's from Connellsville, Pennsylvania."

"Are you sure?"

Proudly Lamont pointed a finger at me. "Yes, he's my wife's cousin."

Before anything else was said, the games started and the fans' voices were bouncing off the walls shouting, "Tackle him." "Don't let him score." "Touch down."

During a commercial, a man in his mid-to-late seventies leaned across the table and bellowed. "Did you say you were from Connellsville?"

Yelling back, I said, "Yes, I did. Why? Do you know where it is?"

"You won't believe this, but I was born and raised there."

Instead of responding, I sat with my mouth ajar. Once I gathered my wits and was about to ask him a question, the man had turned his attention back to the game.

I had lost interest in the game as I thought, "What a small world? What were the chances of meeting someone in The Villages from my small town?"

During the fourth quarter with ten minutes left of the Redskins' game, I excused myself and went to the Ladies' Room. When I returned to the table, I stood, scanning it and then the room.

As I sat down, I leaned into Lamont. "What happened to the couple that was sitting over there?"

"I don't know. When you went to the Ladies' Room, I was right behind you. When I returned, they were gone."

CHAPTER 3

Finding the disappearing man was like looking on a milk carton for a missing person. Lamont and I had no idea how to find him. No matter what we discussed, our conversation returned to the mystery man. I was disappointed that I had not obtained one vital piece of information about the man. Not to mention, I could have given him one of our business cards with our name, address, and telephone number.

When Lamont questioned me about it, my only explanation was, "My focus was on meeting him being from Connellsville which caused me to forget about anything else. By the time I recovered from the shock of hearing what he had said, he was gone."

He smiled and slapped his forehead. "Why didn't we think of this before? I bet he and his wife are regulars at Gringo's. We'll probably be able to find them there on Sunday."

"Lamont, you're right. I don't know what took us so long to realize it."

"Well, the main thing is that all is not lost. This might

have been a missed opportunity if we couldn't locate him. What a wonderful resource this man will be while you're writing the Connellsville book. To obtain the viewpoint of a man in his seventies would be invaluable as well as interesting."

My voice was firm. "Wait a minute. You mean if I write the book."

Lamont's voice laced with confidence said, "I'll wear you down with my charm and …." He raised his right eyebrow and teased, "And, I have some persuasive means to make you write the book."
I made a face. "You think."

"I'm sure of it. Sooner or later, you'll grow tired of me asking you about it."

He taunted. "You know I'm right. The only reason you're being stubborn about it is because you'll have to admit that I've been right all these years."

Playfully, he patted my behind and added, "Besides, you hate being wrong."
I opened my mouth and started to disagree, but I refused to debate the pros and cons again of the book. I changed the subject. "I thought you were going to wash the car?"

Laughter was mixed with Lamont's reply. "While I do manual labor what may I ask are you going to do?"

The question didn't deserve a response. I turned my back and focused on the computer as it booted up. I heard the door close.

As I sat typing, something appeared in my peripheral

vision. Standing at the den's doorway was Lamont, out of breath.

His twinkling eyes matched the exhilaration of his facial expression. "I just discovered the most amazing thing and you're not going to believe what it is." He halted, stared at me and gave me a wide grin. He blurted out. "I found your mystery man."

"Who are you talking about?"

"The man you met from Connellsville." My eyes widened as I heard Lamont say, "He lives across the street, four houses down."

"Are you kidding me?"

"No. I talked to him and his wife. They invited us to come over to their house, tonight."

I could hardly wait. I had all kinds of questions: How long did he live in Connellsville? How had Connellsville changed from the time when he was born? Does he still visit Connellsville?

CHAPTER 4

On our way to our neighbors' house, the humidity combined with my nervous anxiety made beads of sweat form on my forehead and upper lip. It was seven o'clock in the evening, but the temperature was still in the ninety's. The short walk seemed longer than what it was.

As happy as I was to walk to their house, apprehension filled my body. Lamont rang the doorbell and there the man stood. He was taller and heavier than I realized, but his smile was welcoming.

"Please come in." He extended his hand to me. "My name is Vinnie Deyerchek." After we shook, he motioned toward the short woman standing beside him. "This is my wife, Dot."

She smiled. "We're so happy to meet you."

Vinnie and Lamont shook hands. "I'm glad to see you again. Please, please come in. Can I get you something to drink?"

Lamont and I declined. Everyone sat down and the conversation began with how each of us ended up in The Villages. Vinnie and his wife moved to The Villages from Maryland. Another coincidence, we had lived approximately twenty miles apart. They had lived in Waldorf and our home had been in Fort Washington.

I was amazed at how many people had moved to The Villages and had found relatives, co-workers, childhood friends, military buddies, or high school and college classmates. After we concluded our conversation about these fascinating stories, we began talking about Connellsville.

Our conversation about the town was in generalities—the new Wal-Mart, the closing of stores in town, and the lack of viable employment.

I didn't want to rush Vinnie, but I had some specific questions I wanted to ask him. I was curious to hear from an older white man about his opinions and impressions of being born, raised, and educated in Connellsville.

With gusto, Vinnie's voice was loud as he stated, "I'm not trying to impress you, but I'm Zachariah Connell's descendant. He was my great-great-great grandfather."

My mouth dropped open. Recovering from his statement, I uttered, "You mean Connellsville's founder?"

"Yes, the Zachariah Connell."

Despite Vinnie's disclaimer, I was in awe. What were the odds of me meeting my hometown's founder's descendant, and he lived across the street?

Both Vinnie and I laughed and excitedly reminisced

about the good old days living in Connellsville. I noticed Lamont squirming in his seat. Several times, he tried jumping into the conversation, but without luck.

When Vinnie and I fell silent, Lamont asked quickly. "What was it like when you grew up in Connellsville?"

Vinnie cocked his head to the side as he answered, "I don't know what you mean?"

Lamont's expression seemed thoughtful. All eyes were on him, waiting for an explanation. "From an historical viewpoint, what was Connellsville like?"

"I don't know how to answer you and I certainly don't want to bore you with historical facts."

Lamont said nothing as Vinnie continued, "The original inhabitants were Native American Indians. You can double check, but I believe the tribes were the Iroquois, Delaware, and Kanawha."

When Vinnie finished Lamont stated, "Any facts you might have will be helpful to Lorraine because she's writing a book about Connellsville."

My nostrils flared and if I had been a cartoon character, steam would have been coming out of my ears. I wanted to strangle him. If he thought by telling people I was writing a book about Connellsville would make it happen, he was mistaken.

Vinnie inquired, "I would hope you wouldn't write anything negative about Connellsville. What would you write about?"

I tried to hide my annoyance. After all, my anger

had nothing to do with Vinnie. I exhaled, giving myself a few minutes to calm down. When I responded, I hoped my voice was pleasant. "I'm not sure. I'm still doing research."

After Lamont's outburst, I was ready to leave. I glared at him as I stood up. Reluctantly, he followed my lead.

A frown covered Vinnie's face and his voice sad. "Do you have to leave so soon?"

I pasted a smile on my face. "We've taken up enough of your time." I paused and teased. "I know where you live and we'll be back. Besides, I'm amazed and overwhelmed knowing I've met someone from Connellsville, living here in The Villages. I'm trying to absorb it all."

Vinnie nodded. "I know what you mean."

"Thank you again for inviting us over. I appreciate your willingness to answer our questions."

"No problem. I enjoyed your company. Please come back any time." Then, he added, "If nothing else, Dot and I will see you Sunday at Gringo's."

We walked down the sidewalk and glanced around when we heard Vinnie yell, "Go Skins." We watched as he pumped his fist in the air.

Lamont yelled back. "Go Skins. We'll see you Sunday at Gringo's."

CHAPTER 5

The evening had been a success until Lamont opened his big mouth about me writing a book. While Lamont was exchanging cheers with Vinnie I had hurried across the street. Although I had a head start it only took Lamont several long strides to catch up with me. He attempted to grab my hand, but I pulled away.

Peeping over my shoulder, I noticed Vinnie and Dot were still standing outside their house. When he reached for my hand again, I relented. As angry as I was at Lamont, I didn't want my emotions to erupt in front of them. The remaining walk home was quick, tense, and silent.

Despite Lamont's outburst it didn't diminish my excitement about having a neighbor living across the street who was from my hometown. What a treat? The only opportunity to reminisce about Connellsville is when I visit my parents, talk to one of my sisters, or see an old friend.

Once we were inside our house, Lamont's face was as bright as a lightning bug. His voice was high-pitched as he exclaimed, "What a discovery! Vinnie's knowledge will be invaluable to you."

I listened and added nothing as Lamont rambled on about Vinnie and how I might use his expertise when writing the book.

My response to Lamont's exhilaration was a series of grunts and groans. It took him a while to realize that the conversation had been one-sided. As he was in the middle of a sentence, he stopped. "Honey, what's wrong?"

"What's wrong?"

With narrowed eyes, I glared at Lamont. "Why did you tell Vinnie and his wife I was writing a book about Connellsville? When did I agree to do that?"

He shrugged. "Well, since you've completed the research I thought you were pretty much committed to doing it." He added, "I thought the reason you had not started it was because of your other writing commitments."

I shook my head. "You're impossible."

Lamont grabbed me and put me in a tight embrace. "Come on. You know you love me. Give me a smile. Don't be mad."

I looked into his dark brown eyes. That was a mistake. I melted and slowly a smiled covered my face.

My voice was low as I said, "Please don't tell anyone else I'm writing a book about my hometown. I haven't decided."

Sh-sh-sh. Lamont kissed me and held me tight. I leaned against his chest and let him comfort me.

Lamont kissed my forehead and whispered. "Let's go to bed. It's been a long day.

###

Several weeks later neither Lamont nor I mentioned the book. Instead, we concentrated on yard work, painting the inside of the house, and relaxed by going to the pool, golfing, and going to happy hour at the Spanish Springs Town Square.

One morning, Lamont and I were walking through the neighborhood when we saw Vinnie working in the yard.

"Good morning."

We returned his greeting. Vinnie waved and motioned us to come over. He said, good morning again. "You're out early. You're wise to try and get your exercise out of the way before it gets too hot." Before we could respond, he hurried on. "What are you doing later?"

We glanced at each other. We said we were free and asked why.

"Dot and I would love for you all to come over for dinner."

I answered, "That would be nice. What time

should we come over?"

"What about six?"

After agreeing to dinner, I began to panic, wondering, "Would there be anything for me to eat?" I probably should have mentioned that I have Celiac Disease (someone who cannot eat anything with gluten and wheat), but I didn't want Vinnie's wife to worry about cooking something special for me.

When we arrived at Vinnie's for dinner, I was relieved when Dot served grilled steaks, corn, and a green salad. Dinner conversation covered a variety of subjects involving The Villages—the amenities increase, new restaurants and new executive golf course openings. Dessert was cake and ice cream. Rather than discuss my disease I declined dessert saying, "I was watching my weight."

After I helped Dot clean the kitchen we joined Vinnie and Lamont who were sitting on the lanai. As we took a seat, Vinnie turned toward me and asked, "How's the book coming along?"

I took a deep breath and said, "I'm still gathering information."

Vinnie's brown eyes were shining like new pennies. "Maybe I can help."

Before I could respond, Lamont had eased forward in his seat and was saying. "That's exactly what I told Lorraine."

Vinnie looked at me and said, "But, I want an assurance that you'll write only the good things about Connellsville."

CHAPTER 6

I smiled as I thought about Lamont's endless questions. For someone who wasn't interested in Connellsville's churches, he sure had a lot of questions. "Mom didn't know where the Baptist congregation met. She indicated that it was possible that blacks continued to worship with the white congregations."

"When did you say the A.M.E church was built again?"

"Uh…let's see. In 1878, the A.M.E church was built and located between Sixth and Seventh Streets on the West side of town. The first church structure was a one-frame house." I felt a sense of excitement as I handed Lamont the picture.

He looked at it and asked, "Who gave you this picture?"

"Miss Elsie…Mrs. Elsie Webster Haley, the Payne A.M.E Church Secretary Vinnie's statement puzzled me and I wanted to ask for clarification, but Lamont was already asking him another question.

"When you were growing up in Connellsville what was the African American population?"

Unexpected tension crept into room. In addition, deep furrows filled Vinnie's forehead before he answered. "I honestly don't know. I mean it's a lot like living in The Villages. We know you're here but...." His voice faded away as Dot placed her hand on his knee.

From Lamont's next question I could tell he had not noticed how the mood in the room had changed. "Do you know whether or not Connellsville had slaves?"

Vinnie cleared his throat. He murmured his answer. "Like most cities...uh...in the early settlement, there were slaves. If I remember correctly, Pennsylvania passed an Act in 1780 abolishing slavery."

Lamont leaned forward making a tent with his fingers while lowering his voice. "I guess I'm not making myself clear. What I'm asking is whether there were slaves among the original inhabitants?"

Vinnie was a seventy something white man and his taut jaw and frowning expression made it apparent that the question made him uncomfortable. Instead of changing the subject, I stood up.

"Thanks for having us for dinner, but I think we should be going."

Lamont did not follow my lead. As I stood fidgeting, Vinnie continued grimacing.

Vinnie waved his hand. "Please sit back down. Don't go. I'm thinking." He paused before continuing.

"Uh...Connellsville's original ethnic population was primarily from Italy and Poland."

Abruptly Vinnie stood up. "Excuse me for a minute."

I was ill at ease and the room seemed to have taken on my nervousness. I glanced at Dot. She was wringing her hands in a continuous motion. Lamont was crossing and uncrossing his legs. With no one talking, the quiet made the room even more intense. The word "agonizing" would best describe the wait for Vinnie.

Finally, Vinnie reappeared, carrying a tattered, worn leather black book, similar in size and shape to a large Bible. Close to his chest, he held it, as if he feared one of us would take it from him. From his posture, you could tell he treasured it. Vinnie didn't say and I didn't ask, but the book might have been an old family heirloom passed down from generation to generation.

With great care Vinnie protected his prize possession, turning the book's frayed pages, making sure no one could see inside of it but him. Finally locating what he was searching for, he peeped over the imposing book, directing his attention to Lamont.

"To answer your question, yes, Connellsville had slaves." He cleared his throat, his voice hoarse. "According to my great-great-great grandfather's records, he had slaves."

Vinnie hurried on, sounding like a little boy, as he added, "But, he wasn't the only one. Let's see, William Crawford and his brother, the Presbyterian minister and his brother, all had slaves. That's it with regard to who owned slaves in Connellsville."

Lamont asked, "Who is William Crawford? Is he someone who was important in Connellsville's history?"

Vinnie seemed pleased with himself as he provided information about the town's history. "Crawford worked as a land surveyor for President George Washington. He also fought in the French and Indian War as well as the American Revolutionary War. After which time he settled in what is now Connellsville. His cabin was reconstructed and is one of the town's historical landmarks."

After answering Lamont's question, Vinnie buried his face back inside of the book. Occasionally, he glanced up at us and returned his attention back to the book. He turned several pages before settling on one. "Getting back to the slaves, unfortunately nothing is written about how long they kept their slaves or when they freed them. I'm sorry."

Vinnie's last comment caused silence followed by an unexplained awkwardness. I could not help but notice how the mood of the room kept changing depending on the topic of discussion.

I bent my head and coughed several times. My subtle hint for Lamont to stop the questioning went over his head. I didn't want him asking any more sensitive questions. I could tell from the tightness along Vinnie's jaw line when he talked about the slavery questions that it was difficult for him to discuss and caused him considerable anguish.

Vinnie and Dot had invited us into their home and I didn't want to appear unappreciative.

CHAPTER 7

To my disappointment, I winced as Lamont continued with another question. "Is there anything in your book about other African Americans who migrated to Connellsville? Since there were only a few slaves does that mean the other blacks living there were free?"

Vinnie shrugged. "I don't know. I can only tell you what information I have." He paused and thoughtfully added, "I think there might have been free slaves because the coal mining companies visited different states recruiting white and black men to work in the coal and coke mines."

Lamont was biting his lower lip. As he opened his mouth to ask another question, Vinnie began talking.

"During the 1900's, Connellsville was a thriving city." He paused and was grinning from ear to ear with his chest puffed out. "When I was a small boy, the town had hotels, theaters, streetcars and according to most folks and records, the town had more millionaires than any other place during that era."

He clapped his hands and said, "Would you believe

at one point, the population soared to more than 13,000?"

Lamont nodded his head and pressed Vinnie about the town's minorities. "Do you know what the African American population might have been?"

Vinnie scratched his head. "Oh, I don't know. There were never many colored...I mean black. I honestly don't know. To be truthful color never seemed much of an issue in Connellsville."

I was curious about Vinnie's statement, but I didn't continue the line of questioning. Instead, I asked something different. "Do you know where most of the African Americans came from?"

Vinnie relaxed as he lowered the book from his chest and thumbed through it. He stopped on a page and said, "If my family record is accurate, most of the colored migrated from Virginia, Maryland, and Pennsylvania."

I said, "I'm surprised. For some reason I was under the impression that most of the blacks migrated from the south, like the Carolinas or Alabama."

"They could have, but that's not the information I have. By any chance, have you visited Connellsville's National Historic Society? You might find better answers to your questions about the colored...Negroes...blacks?"

"Yes I did visit them, but I didn't find much."

"Well the reason might have been because most newspaper articles and historical information written about Connellsville's residents rarely mentioned whether the person was white or black."

Vinnie's wife changed the subject. "Do you go back to Connellsville often?"

"My parents still live there and we visit maybe once or twice a year. What about you all?"

"We go during the summer for about a month. Vinnie's brother lives there."

Vinnie clapped his hands and said, "I love Pechins. You know the discount grocery store. Have you ever had that dollar lunch? You do know what I'm talking about, don't you?"

His loud outburst of excitement caught Lamont and I off guard. After I answered him, I stood up. It was time to leave.

CHAPTER 8

Our visit had been pleasant, but something bothered me about the dialogue we had with Vinnie. Unlike our first discussion with him, his demeanor appeared different. On the one hand, he was open to our questions, but at other times he was slow, uncertain, and distracted. I just couldn't quite put my finger on it and I wanted Lamont's impression.

When we arrived home, I asked immediately, "Did you think Vinnie's behavior was odd...." My voice drifted off as I thought how to describe my feelings about Vinnie's mannerisms and awkwardness when we talked about Connellsville?

"I think his discomfort came from discussing and answering questions about slavery and African Americans. If you noticed he didn't even know what to call African Americans. At times he said colored while other times he said black, Negroes, or African American."

"Why should that be odd? I don't even know what to call myself." I threw up my hand. "Anyway, back to Vinnie. Do you really think that was the reason for his discomfort?"

"Uh…yes, I think he didn't want to talk about race. Come on, don't be so naïve. Most white people aren't comfortable talking about race and especially someone from his generation."

"I think you're wrong. I sensed it was something else."

"Like what?"

"I don't know. Did you notice his wife? At times, she seemed on edge, listening and watching Vinnie with care. She reminded me of a mother visiting a neighbor with a small child, afraid he or she might say or do something wrong."

Lamont exhaled. "If all of that was going on, I missed it."

Under my breath I commented. "Yeah, you missed a lot."

"What did you say?"

Quickly, I said, "I didn't say anything, Sweetie."

"Are you finished analyzing Vinnie's behavior?" Lamont didn't wait for an answer. "What do you think now, about writing the book?"

The question made me wonder as I thought about how pleased I was to meet Vinnie, especially to have the opportunity to discuss Connellsville, but that didn't explain why I should change my mind about the book.

In addition, I had difficulty understanding Lamont's passion for my small town that may or may not be unique. As far as I was concerned, nothing had changed except that I had met a relative of the town's founder.

"Honey, did you hear me? Are you convinced now that you should write the book?"

"Why, because of Vinnie?"

Lamont smiled. "Babe, you're missing it. I think you're being sent a message."

I smiled. "Exactly, who's sending me the message?"

"Who do you think? The Connellsville African Americans, the ones from the past, the present and future."

I started laughing, but stopped as I saw Lamont's solemn face.

His voice was soothing. "Listen sweetheart, I know this is out of your comfort zone, but this could be a wonderful legacy for your hometown. Besides, I thought you would jump at the chance especially since you enjoy genealogy."

"That's different."

"Tell me how so?"

"Genealogy is about me researching information about my family."

Lamont jumped in and said, "And, why can't this be viewed as your hometown's genealogy?"

"When I research genealogy, I make impressions and interpretations of the information. I also exclude people based on a lack of information. Besides, people aren't always pleased to have things written about them, even when it's positive."

I stopped as I thought about some of the negative comments I had received while researching information about Connellsville. Some of the strong opinions and remarks sounded a lot like warnings, especially when telling me not to turn Connellsville into a Peyton Place.

"Maybe, but I think people will understand more than you think, even the omissions. What's the worst that could happen if someone isn't included or your interpretations aren't what they think it should be?"

I shrugged.

Lamont was convinced. "I think people will be happy about the book's publication."

He raised his hands and continued. "Please don't take this the wrong way, but if someone doesn't like what you've written, then they can write another book. Dozens of books are on library shelves about the same historical event, but from different viewpoints."

"Yeah, but I'm concerned about lawsuits and maybe even worse."

CHAPTER 9

Lamont was encouraging and he made some convincing points, but the entire discussion was bothersome. I sat in silence, pondering over the question of what could be the worst thing that would happen if I excluded someone.

For one thing, the book is about my impressions, memories, and research. Perhaps people wouldn't be that concerned if their name was included or excluded. I chewed on the inside of my mouth. "What would be my answer to those who were left out?"

My head was throbbing. A headache was beginning as I considered the possible omissions. Could my response be as simple as "I didn't find out about some people's accomplishments until after the book was finished?" Should I let these concerns stop me from writing the book?

Lamont could be right. Maybe someone else would be inclined to write a more comprehensive book. As I thought about it I began to see the possibility and the excitement of it all. What if I could inspire someone to do an all-inclusive compilation of Connellsville's African

Americans? That would be more than I could ever expect.

Then there was the prospect that other people would examine and document information about their small towns. I started smiling. Maybe, a student in pursuit of a Master's Degree would study the correlation between small towns and race relations.

"Earth to Lorraine, earth to Lorraine what's going on?"

"I'm considering everything you've said about writing the book." I couldn't miss Lamont's silly smile.

"Don't get too excited, but I'm beginning to give the book some serious consideration."

"What is there to consider? I don't understand your reluctance."

I sighed heavily. "My lack of enthusiasm is because I'm not sure about the structure of putting it together and more importantly the story I'm trying to tell?"

"I don't understand why you're having difficulty getting it. I believe your town is unique." Lamont paused and added, "I might be wrong, but what if your town was part of an experiment?"

My eyes grew wide. "What? Are you talking about some sort of conspiracy theory?"

"Nothing that deep and I have no proof, but didn't William Penn, Pennsylvania's founder, have some sort of holy experiment regarding how people should be treated as equals, the government, and freedom and respect of all religions?"

"I know about William Penn, but I have no idea what you're talking about."

"Oh. Well, I'm thinking that maybe your hometown was part of William Penn's experiment. After all, the African Americans in your hometown were treated like human beings...as equals...you know... Americans first, skin color second."

"Okay, that may be true, but what makes you think that other African Americans have not experienced the same thing in other Pennsylvania towns?"

"I don't know and I'm not suggesting you should do additional research. I'm just saying that based on my observations coupled with what I learned about Connellsville its story seems exceptional and needs telling."

"That's where we disagree. I don't see the uniqueness. Let's take me out of it and talk about our daughters. I don't think they see my town as being special."

Lamont threw up his hands. "Please!"

"Let me change that. I don't think they would get what you're implying because I don't."

Lamont exhaled nosily. In a soothing voice he tried again. "There are probably other towns similar in size and makeup much like Connellsville where blacks were treated as equals. However, did black students excel similar to the ones you went to school with? I don't have that answer and neither do you, but I'm not concerned about that and that's not what I'm asking you to write about."

He paused and looked at me. I remained quiet. "As for the girls, they went to a school where blacks excelled, but the makeup was very diverse with white, black, Asian, and Latino. Your school's diversity was white and black. Am I right or am I wrong?"

"You're right but…" I stopped, crossed my arms and with a sarcastic tone I said, "I have an idea. Since you have so much passion for the subject, why don't you write the book?"

Lamont equaled my tone. "Because you're the published author and it's your town."

In a huff, I stomped off to the den. Lamont was quick on my heels. "Why are you resisting this? If nothing else you should want to share the sports statistics about your town. You have to agree, they're unusual."

I rolled my eyes. My voice was firm. "Please don't repeat those stats to me. People aren't that interested when it comes to blacks who made it in the sports arena."

CHAPTER 10

That night, sleep did not come easy. Flashbacks of my deceased grandparents, neighbors, and people from church invaded my mind. The images reminded me of the movie where the little boy repeats over and over, *"I see dead people."*

Tired of tossing and turning, I eased out of bed, hoping not to wake Lamont. I filled the tea kettle with water, placed it on the stove, walked into the den and pulled out the three ring binders containing my research.

The tea kettle whistled and I headed to the kitchen to make a cup of green tea. On my way back to the den, I saw Lamont coming out of the bedroom.

"I'm sorry. I hope I didn't wake you. I couldn't sleep." I teased and added, "Thanks to you."

He ruffled his hair. "I couldn't sleep either. I was trying to think of a title for the book."

I sighed and watched as Lamont turned around and went into the kitchen. When he entered the den, he was carrying a cup of coffee. He sat down and asked, "What are you doing?"

"I'm going through some of the research. If I'm going to write a book, I'm trying to figure out how I would organize the information. Mostly, there's nothing but facts and how boring would that be?"

"Well, let's do what you usually do first and that's to find a title to get started."

For almost an hour, we tossed titles back and forth. "What do you think about, "Did Connellsville Look beyond Color?"

Lamont considered it, but shook his head. He suggested, "Beyond the Barriers"?

"No because we're sure to find some barriers." I formed a fist and pumped it. "I want a title that grabs you and gives the reader a hint of what the book might be about, similar to my other books."

A confused look covered Lamont's face.

"You know, like Sunday Golf. The book title suggests that the book might be about golf. After you read it you discover the story is about eight men who meet while taking golf lessons. The title ties into the story. The reader gets it."

"Okay, I understand what you're getting at, but this is a little different since your other books are fiction. That makes this book title more difficult."

Regardless of what Lamont said about understanding, I could see it in his face, he didn't get it. As weird as it might sound a working title was necessary for me. If not,

I'm similar to someone with writer's block, sitting in front of the computer, looking at a blank screen, hoping and waiting for inspiration.

We sat, neither of us saying anything. I sat up and blurted out, "Wait, what about, "Pennsylvania's Best-Kept Secret or The Best-Kept Secret." I waited for Lamont's reaction.

He repeated the title several times and said, "I like both of the titles. Both are catchy, but do they capture the book's essence?"

I thought about it and he had a point, but that was the best I could come up with. We spent another thirty minutes tossing around titles. Despite my need for a working title it seemed as if we were beating a rug that no longer had dust coming out of it.

Lamont glanced at the clock. "It's getting late, why don't we shower and eat breakfast. Until another title comes to us, we'll work with the last one you suggested."

I didn't respond and smiled as I thought how "we" were writing the book. I couldn't help but wonder how much Lamont was going to write.

CHAPTER 11

After breakfast, we went through the research material. Lamont had the first idea. "Why not start with something that will capture the reader's attention. A good beginning would be the sports facts. People are always interested and impressed with sports trivia."

"That's not going to happen." My decision was unyielding. "If anything, the first chapter will be about the church and from there we can move forward. After all, isn't church usually the foundation of any town?"

I paused and added, "And of all people, you should appreciate starting with religion since your father was a minister."

Lamont opened his mouth, but no words came out. Instead, he lowered his head and said nothing.

Not really talking to Lamont, I said, "Let's see what information I gathered about the coke and coal mines." As I thumbed through the papers I shook my head. The organization of the research was not in any logical order. The information about coke and coal mines was in all three binders and several envelopes.

"Wait a minute. What did you say? I thought the beginning chapter was churches?"

"It is, but I had a thought. According to Vinnie and my research, the major employer for whites and blacks was the coal and coke industry. To support that information, the genealogy I conducted regarding my mom's family, the Marillas, indicated that her dad, grandfather, and uncles worked in the coal and coke mines."

"Are coal and coke mines the same?"

I shook my head. "No. They're two separate operations. Coke was drawn from the furnaces while coal is mined underground, but we're getting off the subject."

Lamont was concerned. "I don't think so. I'm trying to understand what you're including about the African Americans who were coal and coke employees?"

"For one thing, African Americans have been omitted from many of the recent research projects written about coal and coke employees living in western Pennsylvania."

"Are you sure?"

"Well, at least the information I've read. Most of it excluded African American coal and coke employees. And, I have proof that says otherwise. The Marilla men worked for the H.C. Frick Coal and Coke Company."

"How did you find that out?"

"From the Census records and the World War I Draft Cards, but yet none of their names appeared in these projects. If nothing else, I should give honor to these men and mention their names."

"How will you include them?"

"I'm going to list their names?" I did not miss Lamont's expression. "What's wrong with that?"

"Type the list and then we can make a decision."

I sat at the computer and typed. Lamont watched as I copied their surnames.

Before I finished, Lamont exclaimed, "You don't even have the first names?"

"No, I only have their surnames."

Lamont shook his head. "I don't know. I don't like it."

"Fine, but do you have any other suggestions?"

"Not at the moment, but keep typing. We can make the decision later. The important thing is getting the information into the book's chapters."

I thought, but didn't say, "I hope our working together wouldn't be like some of our other projects we tried tackling together." A memory of us wallpapering was something I'll never forget. How we ever finished those walls are beyond me. I almost laughed out loud. I believe there are a few things husbands and wives should not attempt to do together.

COAL AND COKE COMPANY AFRICAN AMERICAN EMPLOYEES

BAKER—BONDS—DAVIS—FANT—GRAVES—HARDY—HARRISON—HENDERSON—HUNTER—KEITH—MARILLA—MCMILLIAN—MEADOWS—MILLS—MINOR—PARRISH—OVERTON—THOMPSON—TOLER—WALKER—WASHINGTON—WOODRUFF

Thinking out loud, I said, "After I list the surnames, I'll include this picture I obtained from the Connellsville National Historic Society."
Lamont held his hand out. "Let me see the picture." I handed it to him.

The photographer unknown, photograph courtesy of the Connellsville Area Historical Society.

Lamont examined the picture. "The photo certainly proves there were African Americans working in the coke ovens. Until I come up with something better, I guess typing the names of the workers is noteworthy enough to go in the book."

I gave him a defiant stare and bit my lower lip to prevent me from reacting.

"What's next?"

"Now I'm ready to discuss the churches."

"I still don't understand what's interesting or memorable enough that should be included about churches."

"As I stated earlier, I think religion plays a major role in most African Americans' lives and I want to start there."

"I think you're wrong. If you provide some quick eye catching facts about Connellsville's sports figures, you'll have your readers hooked and wanting to know what else happened in that small town."

"No-o-o. There's more to African Americans than playing sports."

Lamont must have sensed my irritation and our need for some individual space. He stood up and asked, "Babe, do you want me to make you a cup of tea?"

While Lamont was in the kitchen, the phone rang. I answered it. "Hello."

All I heard was heavy breathing, followed by a deep voice. "Is this Lorraine Harris?"

"Yes, it is. May I ask who is calling?"
No reply, then the voice said, "The book."
"Who is this?" No answer and then a click.

CHAPTER 12

Slowly, I put the phone into its cradle. The call had provoked all types of questions. Why would anyone be calling me and just say, "the book"? Which book was the caller referring to? Could the reference be about one of the books already published?

Or could it be one of the books I'm working on. Except for Lamont and the writing groups I attend, no one knows what I'm working on and even then, when I read from my works, I seldom give the book's title. I chewed on my finger nail and considered some of the critiques I've received.

Nothing came to mind as being strange. Although there have been times when someone would wait for me after a meeting to tell me that my work was provoking. Usually, they referred to the realism of some of the characters, actions, and storyline, but…I stopped and shook my head. The call didn't make sense.

Rather than wonder about a silly call, I turned my attention back to the material regarding Connellsville and its churches. By the time Lamont returned with my cup of hot tea, I had made a decision about what to include about religion.

"How's it going?"

"Okay."

"Who was on the phone?"

I thought about telling Lamont about the strange call, but decided against it. "It was a wrong number." I changed the subject as Lamont sipped his coffee.

"You're not going to believe this, but at the time of my research, there were approximately 32 churches in Connellsville's population of approximately 9,000."

Lamont started choking as I revealed this information to him. I jumped up from my chair and began patting his back. "Are you okay?"

Through coughs, he managed to utter, "Yes. Why are there so many churches in such a small town?"

I shrugged. "I have no idea."

Lamont grinned. "Maybe it gets back to the holy experiment. You know tolerance of religion. I believe that's one of William Penn's ideals." He shook his head. "Anyway, what are the denominations?"

"From what I can see, every major denomination is represented. The most common of course, but not limited are: Assembly of God, Baptist, Church of Christ, Catholic, Episcopal, Jehovah Witness, Methodist, and Presbyterian."

Lamont was bewildered. "I don't want to upset you, but what's important about this?"

I smiled and through clenched teeth I responded. "Please

be patient." Thinking of the mysterious phone call and Lamont's questions, my nerves were on edge.

I turned over several pieces of paper and shared. "I was double checking my facts from the National Historic Society and you won't believe this. In Connellsville unlike most of the United States, their churches were integrated as far back as 1790."

Lamont said, "Are you sure?"

"Yes. According to this National Historic Society document, in 1859, the town's African Americans met with town officials and asked their permission to hold separate Christian worship services."

"Does it say why?"

"Nope, there's no explanation."

"That's interesting and unusual, but what happened? Did blacks form their own churches?"

"Everyone I asked didn't seem to know what happened after the request was approved because it wasn't until 1875 before the first all-black church was founded. In fact, it's the church I attended while growing up and the church where my parents continue to worship."

"You mean Payne A.M.E (African Methodist Episcopal) Church?"

"Yes. It's known as Connellsville's first black and oldest church, often referred to as the **"Mother of Connellsville's Negro Churches."**

Lamont shook his head. "So, no one knows where the

blacks worshiped between 1859 and 1878?"

"Well, that's not exactly true. My mom said that after the town's approval, the A.M.E church did not begin having services until 1875 and met in a building on First Street on the West Side of town until 1878 when their church was built."

"What about the Baptists?"

I smiled as I thought about Lamont's endless questions. For someone who wasn't interested in Connellsville's churches, he sure had a lot of questions. "Mom didn't know where the Baptist congregation met. She indicated that it was possible they continued to worship with the white congregations.

"When was the A.M.E. church built again?"

"Uh…let's see. In 1878, the A.M.E. church was built and located between Sixth and Seventh Streets on the West Side of town. "The first church was a one-frame house." I handed Lamont a picture.

He looked at it and asked, "Who gave you this picture?"

The photographer unknown, photograph courtesy of Payne A.M.E. Secretary, Mrs. Elsie Webster Haley.

"Miss Elsie...Mrs. Elsie Webster Haley. She's the Payne A.M.E. Church Secretary.

"Was it always named, Payne A.M.E.?"

"No. The original name was Payne Chapel in memory of the late Bishop Daniel Alexander Payne."

"Why did they name it after him?"

"I don't know, maybe because he was the Bishop at the time. Did you know that he was the Bishop that purchased Wilberforce University, located in Ohio for educating black students at the higher level?"

Lamont grimaced. "No I didn't know that, but that doesn't explain why they named the church after him. I don't think that information adds anything. Therefore, I suggest you might want to eliminate it." He glanced at me, as if he was waiting for me to protest, but I kept quiet. "Do you plan on putting anything else in the book about African American churches?"

"Do you think I should mention anything about the Baptist church?"

"Like what?"

I was afraid to tell him. "I don't know. Maybe, mention the founder, Reverend J. C. Robinson. After all, he established the second black church in Connellsville and it was the first Baptist church—Mount Zion Baptist Church."

Lamont put his hand up. "Wait a minute. I don't think any church in Connellsville is totally black?"

"What do you mean?"

Lamont rifled through some of my papers, making them more disorganized.

"What are you looking for?"

"I thought I remembered reading something about the St. Rita's Catholic Church and the Jehovah Witness Church always having integrated congregations?"

"Yeah that's right, so what does that have to do with no church in Connellsville being totally black?"

Lamont scratched the side of his face and said, "If two of the churches are integrated then the statement has to say that some of the churches were segregated and if you look closer probably none of Connellsville's churches are truly segregated."

I was confused. "Why are you saying that?"

"Come on. When I visited the A.M.E. church there were quite a few interracial couples who attended the church. If there are other couples attending other churches then my conclusion is that most of the churches have been integrated despite the original request for separate churches." Lamont stopped and chewed his lower lip.

Before I could counter what he was saying he shook his head and said, "I don't know why I missed this. My observation is true about the integrated congregations, but the churches probably wanted separatism in order to have a black figure head that could preach, teach, and lead a congregation in a manner that best suited their needs."

I shrugged. What Lamont was stating was confusing to me. Since I had no thoughts on the subject I moved on. "Should I mention the names of the other African American churches?"

Lamont let out a heavy sigh. "Why?" From his crunched up nose I knew he didn't see the value in mentioning them." Before he could protest I said what he was probably thinking. "I guess there's no real significance about naming them except for giving them honor."

"Is that the only reason you're going to include them?" Lamont let out another noisy sigh.
I gestured. "I don't know."

"Where are these churches in Connellsville and have I ever been to them?"

As I answered him, I began typing the names of the churches. "Outside of the Baptist church on First Street, I don't think so."

My fingers ran across the keys as I said, "I can always take them out if it doesn't make sense." I continued typing, not waiting for any more of Lamont's objections.

Rocky Mount Baptist Church

Union Baptist/United Baptist Church

Highland Baptist Church

Bethlehem Temple Church

Lamont waited until I finished and asked in a low voice. "What's next, the sports chapter?"

I didn't even respond, afraid I would snap at him and possibly say something I would regret later.

CHAPTER 13

My gut feeling was that I had missed something important and felt the need to go back through the material marked church. I glanced up and watched Lamont sighing. I knew he was anxious and wanted to move on, but I knew I had missed something. My eyes widened as I glanced over several pieces of paper.

Loudly, I exclaimed, "I knew it. I almost forgot two important ministers, Reverends Henderson and Scott."

"Is that why you've been going through those binders and folders?"

"Yes and I'm glad I did. This information is too critical to omit and must be included."

Under Lamont's breath he remarked, "As important as the sports data?" I ignored the comment.

Lamont exhaled loudly. "Okay, let's take one minister at a time. What did Reverend Henderson do?"

"She was a community icon and everyone she came in contact with, loved her. When Reverend Henderson would visit hospitals, black and white patients, from all denominations would request that she stop in to see them."

Lamont raised his hand. "Please stop. What was her extraordinary accomplishment?"
Slowly, he emphasized each word. "What did she do besides be a minister? You know, what did she do other than carry out her ministerial duties?"

"You're being ugly and you know what they say how God doesn't like ugly!"

"I'm not being ugly. I'm being real. You forget I'm a preacher's kid and I know the duties and responsibilities of a minister. So, unless you have something significant, people don't want to read about the ordinary; they want the extraordinary."

"That is unusual! I don't think most people ask ministers other than their own, to visit them in the hospital, especially a black female minister."

"Okay, you're probably right, but what else is there?"

"In the 1960's, Reverend Marguerite S. Henderson was the first female assigned to Payne A. M.E. Church. No other black church in Connellsville had a woman assigned as a minister during that time."

"That's it?"

"No, that's not all. Connellsville honored Reverend Henderson by naming a street after her. She received this distinction because of her dedication to the ministry and community. The street—**Henderson Lane**—runs in front of Payne A. M. E. Church. She is the first African American and female minister in Connellsville to have a street named after her." I paused and added, "In fact, she's the only minister in Connellsville to receive such an honor."

"That is exceptional and the fact that the church is off of Main Street." Lamont grinned.

"What?"

"I was thinking how unusual it is that none of your black churches are located near each other and that they're in different parts of the town."

I said nothing as I saw nothing unusual about that.

"Okay, let's move on." He paused. "Do you have a picture of her?"

I showed him the picture I had taken off a church bulletin. He looked at it and said, "Good, include the picture and let's talk about this other minister. Who is she?"

Reverend Marguerite S. Henderson

The photographer unknown, photograph courtesy of the Payne A.M. E. Church bulletin.

"I'm not finished with Reverend Henderson."

"What else did she do?"

"Connellsville presented Reverend Henderson with the Distinguished Community Service Award. She was well-known throughout Connellsville for her ability to serve the community without regard to race, gender, or religion."

"That is noteworthy. Is there anything else?"

"Well, she was responsible for Payne A.M. E. receiving Connellsville's Beautification Award."

Lamont shook his head and said, "No-o-o. Don't even think about it."

"Why? Had it not been for Reverend Henderson, Payne A.M.E would not have had all the structural and beautification changes made to the interior and exterior of the church."

"Lorraine, that's not important."

"Wait, before you say, no. Look at the newspaper article."

"Okay, let me see it." Lamont examined the newspaper clippings.

The photographer unknown, photograph courtesy of the Payne A.M.E. Church 2000 Church Homecoming Program Booklet

"Don't include this. It might have been an award, but is there any value in including it?" He didn't let me defend my position. He continued, "Let's move on to the other minister. Who is she?"

I disagreed with Lamont, but I didn't pursue it. "Reverend Elizabeth Scott." Before Lamont could make a comment, I hurried on, reading only a portion of her bio.

"She served as an A.M.E. Minister for more than 30 years before being assigned as the second female minister at Connellsville's Payne A.M.E. Church."

Lamont was snippy. "How much background information are you going to include before you discuss her accomplishment?"

"I know you want me to get right to the achievement, but I think people want to know about her educational background."

"Maybe, what are you including?"

"She earned a Master's degree in systematic theology from Duquesne University in Pittsburgh. While serving as the minister at Payne, she was named the first female and African American Prison Chaplain at the State Correctional Institution."

I stuck my tongue out at Lamont. "That's it. I have nothing else regarding Reverend Scott."

"That was childish, but I'm going to ignore your behavior." He grinned. "Where's her picture?"

"It's not very clear because the picture came from a church program."

"Well, make sure you include the picture anyway."

I raised my hand to my forehead and saluted. "Yes sir."

Reverend Elizabeth Scott

The photographer unknown, photograph courtesy of the Payne A.M.E. Church 2000 Church Homecoming Program Booklet

"Are we finished?"

My response was a resounding, "yes," I smiled thinking how Lamont reminded me of a child, sitting in the back of a car who keeps asking their parents, "Are we there yet?"

CHAPTER 14

With the church chapter completed, my question was: "How to proceed next?" I pondered over whether to ask Lamont. When I voiced it out loud, I wanted to pull it back, but it was too late.

"You know what I think, make this the sports chapter. I mean you're killing your readers."

"I'm building up to it. I'm going to talk about sports when it's appropriate. This is not the time. Let's discuss the educational system."

Lamont's sorrowful expression spelled dejection, but he didn't object.

Batting my eyes, I said, "I love you."

Lamont smile and said, "I'm like Tina Turner, What's love got to do with it?"

"Absolutely nothing, but I still love you. Now, I bet I can make you happy. The next chapter will be about the educational system and sports are a part of it." I rushed on. "Remember, this is one reason why you thought Connellsville was so unique."

"I know, but depending on how you arrange the

information, this chapter could be a huge portion of the book."

"Why do you say that?"

Lamont leaned forward. "Have you forgotten how long it took us to go through every yearbook?"

"I haven't forgotten, but it's a necessary evil. I'm not looking forward to going over the data any more than you."

"We're wasting time." His voice was brisk. "Let's start, but I have to take a quick break."

As Lamont exited the room, the phone rang. I answered to nothingness. I was about to hang up when a deep voice said, "I strongly suggest, you forget about writing that book."

"Who is this?" Like all the other calls, there was no answer and then the click. I still couldn't make out whether the voice was male or female and unlike the other times, I considered this as a warning."

The phone calls were disturbing, but yet I couldn't make sense of them. I shrugged and went back to putting some order to the yearbook pages that had been copied. By the time Lamont returned, I was ready for the discussion.

Lamont didn't ask who had called and I didn't tell him about the call or any of the other calls. Instead, I asked, "Where did you go?"

"I went to the bathroom, Mother Nature called."

"Oh."

Lamont asked, "What are you going to include first?"

I hesitated before sharing. "Do you think I should discuss my thoughts about integration and segregation or go straight to the high school data?"

"Let's forgo your opinions..." Lamont saw the hurt look on my face and tried to clean it up. "Well, you forget I know your impressions about integration and segregation and I don't think sharing your thoughts will add much value."

I tried to hide my emotions. "Fine, what would you suggest?"

"Well, I think everyone knows that William Penn was a Quaker and he believed that everyone was entitled to an education, regardless of race, color, or nationality. From what I can tell, Connellsville practiced that philosophy. That might explain the reason for the school being integrated from the beginning."

Carefully, I listened to Lamont's explanation, but I didn't comment. His reasoning might be right about Pennsylvania's integration of schools, but how did that differ from other integrated northern schools? I wanted to pursue his line of thinking, but he hurried on, allowing no further discussion of the integration of schools.

"When was Connellsville's first school built?"
I held up and read from a National Historic Society document. "There was a school as early as 1804. However, no official records support the fact."

I stopped and glimpsed over the article. "This is weird. First, the article states 1804, but now it's saying the first school existed in 1829. No wonder we couldn't verify any early school information. In addition, it states that the school records were destroyed by fire."

Lamont was confused. "What's wrong with that?"

"If the records were destroyed I'm not sure how the article concludes that the first Connellsville High School graduating class was in 1838."

"I agree that is strange. What else does it say?"

"In 1895, Connellsville's first high school was built. Again, it says nothing else and we know the first yearbook we found at the National Historic Society and Connellsville's High School Library was dated 1911."

Lamont let out a sigh. "So, no documents are available supporting the fact that when the first school was built that it was integrated?"

I tried answering him, but a lump lodged in my throat and I felt defeated. The only proof that the schools were probably integrated from the beginning was my gut feeling.

Lamont picked up a photo. "Look at this picture from the National Historic Society." I leaned over as he pointed. "Is that a little black boy?"

The photographer unknown, photograph courtesy of Connellsville's National Historic Society.

"Hey, you're right. The young man is standing in the middle, about the third row up. I'm glad the inscription on the picture states, Connellsville Public Schools and the date, November 1899. I might not be able to say that the first school built was integrated, but at least I have proof from 1899."

CHAPTER 15

My eyes were blurry, my lower back ached and I no longer wanted to work. I stood up and rubbed the area that pained. The clock couldn't be right. Was it really 3 o'clock p.m.? Our breaks had been the bathroom and trips to the kitchen for drinks. My stomach growled, reminding me that breakfast had been my last meal.

Lamont must have read my mind. "Let's get something to eat. How about going to Cane Garden Country Club in The Villages?"

"That sounds good to me. Give me a minute."

At the restaurant we placed our food and drink orders at the same time. During our meal, our conversation focused on the best way to arrange the high school data.

Lamont suggested. "Rather than mention every student, why not look at each individual class accomplishments and discuss only those outstanding achievements. If not, the book could be too long and not to mention, boring."

"You're right. Not only that, I think the outstanding achievements would be overlooked."

When we returned home, we started what could be the most difficult part of the book, the yearbook data. If nothing else it would be tedious. Since we could not buy the yearbooks, we had photocopied of all the pages containing an African American student.

As we began, Lamont pointed out that he had a page from the 1911 yearbook. This was the earliest yearbook on record of graduating students.

"Who was the first African American graduate?"

"You mean the first and only black graduate." Lamont stopped and made a face. "Before we discuss the first graduate, maybe a discussion should be included regarding the number of African American students that were in each graduating class."

"I'm not following you, Lamont."

"Let's look at why the African American students' achievements are noteworthy." I said nothing, waiting for clarification

"What's most evident to me is that the African American student population was probably less than *"one"* percent of each graduating class."

"What? Where did you get that information from?"

"That's my point. To prove what I'm saying, a sampling of several graduating classes is needed. I'm not suggesting hard core statistics. Maybe you can make a table or something with the year, the total number in the class, and the total number of graduating African Americans."

"Please don't tell me we're going to count the

number in each graduating class?"

"No, an estimate is fine. The only necessary count is that of the African American students for each year. That should be easy because the number is so small."

I sighed. "I'm still not following you, but I'll do it."

"Wait a minute. Don't do it because I'm telling you to. It's not that difficult. I'm trying to prove that the achievements were not a fluke considering the number of African American students in relation to the white student population. For example, how many were in your graduating class?"

"I don't know the exact number, but I know it was over 300."

"And, how many black students were in it?"
I started counting off the names and finally said, "Twelve in total."

"What about your sister, Patty's class?"

I knew the answer because I had just had a discussion with her about it and I had written the numbers down. I picked up a binder and flipped through the pages until I found what I was looking for. "Let's see, she had 340 in her class and there were twelve black graduating students."

Lamont started chuckling. I was frowning, trying to understand what he was saying. He cleared his throat. "What's with the dozens? The school had a quota and would only allow twelve black students per graduating class."

"Very funny."

He wiped his eyes. "I'm sorry, but I find that hilarious." He raised his hand and said, "I'm sorry. Why don't you call your sister, Janice, and find out how many were in her graduating class."

I dialed her number and after the discussion, I wished I hadn't made the call.

"Well, what did she say?"

"She graduated in the class of 1978 and there were 750 and…it was the first year that other schools in the surrounding areas were combined into one high school." I was stalling, not wanting to give him the number of black graduating seniors. I bent my head and muttered, "Twelve black students."

I watched Lamont as his body shook, followed by an eruption of snorting and snickering. The fact that only twelve black students appeared in a number of graduating classes did seem odd, but I didn't think it was hysterical.

I waited for Lamont to compose himself. When he did, he asked, "Do you want to find a class that might have more than…" He paused, covered his mouth, sat straight in the chair and said, "Are you aware of any graduating class that might have had a larger number than twelve black graduating students?"

I shook my head. "Not really. When we were doing the research I don't recall any class having more than a dozen." I stopped, wanting to kick myself.

Lamont coughed hard, preventing another outburst of laughter.

I ignored him wanting to make sure I understood what he wanted me to do. "Okay, would a table something like this do?"

Year	Total Number of Graduating Students	Estimated Number of Black Students
1930	260	7
1940	165	8
1950	220	5
1961	340	12
1978	750	12

"This looks good." He paused and said, "Yes. I definitely like it. Can you do the same thing for Connellsville's population?"

I almost screamed, "Why is that necessary? What's the purpose?" Instead, I bit my lower lip.

"Well, can you put together a similar table for Connellsville's population?"

"I guess I can." As I typed the table, I found myself hitting the keyboard harder than I should, causing me to make mistakes.

Year	Estimated Population	Estimated Black Population
1930	12,000	360
1940	10,000	300
1950	10,000	300
1961	11,000	330
1978	10,000	300

CHAPTER 16

Since Lamont was educated in Washington, D.C., he seemed to have a better idea of what made integration in Connellsville unique in comparison to where integration had been legally forced. Therefore, I was following his lead.

I asked, "Now, do I include the information regarding the first graduate of Connellsville's High School?"

"I think so. We can always come back and add other information."

Lamont handed me the picture. The first documented graduate was Roy McNeal, the only African American student in the 1911 yearbook.

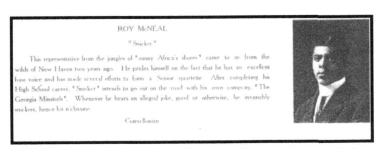

The photographer unknown, photograph courtesy of the 1911 Connellsville High School Yearbook.

While I typed, Lamont busied himself reading. "What are you going to do with the information Mrs. Elsie Haley gave you?"

"I don't know, but it should be included. After all, genealogy and family records have been used throughout the world documenting information as well as creating history."

Lamont asked again. "Are you positive you want to include it even though you can't validate the information?"

"Yes, I have no problem including it. After all, the Webster Family passed this story on from generation to generation and I'm accepting it as truth."

Lamont stated firmly. "Okay, then Pauline Johnson was the first African American female Valedictorian of Connellsville's High School. The graduating class is unknown."

With that decision made, we moved on. "What's the next year?"

Lamont thumbed through several documents before answering. "It's the class of 1929."

Proudly, I stated, "I know something about this particular class. This is the year that Connellsville organized a National Honor Society (NHS) chapter."

"You're right." He handed me a picture of the first NHS members.

THE FIRST NATIONAL HONOR SOCIETY MEMBERS

The photographer unknown, photograph courtesy of the 1929 Connellsville High School Yearbook.

"Who's the young black student?"
"She's Isabella Fletcher."

Isabella Fletcher

The photographer unknown, photograph courtesy of the 1929 Connellsville High School Yearbook.

I noticed Lamont's screwed up face. Before I could ask what was wrong, I heard a statement full of vehement as he snorted. "Clubs like that should be banned from schools."

I was surprised at Lamont's reaction. "Why do you say that?"

"Because I believe it's the club for the elite and bright. Not to mention it's a way for teachers to reward their favorite students."

This was the first time I heard Lamont demonstrate such venom toward a school activity. I should have kept quiet as I said, "Lamont, a student's grade point average was a critical part of being inducted into the National Honor Society."

"That might have been true in your school, but I experienced things that you did not in high school."

"Lamont, I don't agree with everything you're saying. You may have good reason…" I stopped when I saw the intensity in Lamont's eyes.

"Excuse me, if I'm not a component of this elitist organization. You have to understand this was the beginning of integration in Washington, D.C. schools. Believe me when I say not all children were treated as equals."

From Lamont's strong and passionate statements, this was not the time to continue a conversation about the National Honor Society. Lamont and I had many conversations about what he had gone through regarding the integration of schools.

Time after time, he explained how difficult it was to enter a school while parents stood outside with picket signs, protesting black children's attendance. He was right I didn't understand the environment of hatred and resentment of going to school based on the color of one's skin. Furthermore, I couldn't begin to understand the impact this could have on children being treated differently by teachers.

I could only imagine what it must have been like. I blinked back the tears as I considered how complicated the integration of schools must have been for white and black children.

On my way to the kitchen, the phone started ringing. "I'll answer it."

With hesitation, I picked it up. When I heard the heavy breathing, I sensed what was next, that mysterious voice giving me a warning. The calls were becoming more frequent and all too clear that this person did not want me to write a book, but there were no clues as to which book.

When I returned to the den, I had two wishes. I didn't want Lamont to ask about the phone call and I didn't want to resume our conversation about the merits of the National Honor Society. Both wishes were granted, sort of.

Before I sat down, Lamont asked, "Did you know that your two sisters, Nancy and Janice, were National

Honor Society members?"

I laughed. "Of course I did." He had to laugh too.

"I guess I put my foot into my mouth...." He hunched his shoulders and said, "....concerning my dislike for the National Honor Society and it being a class for the favored."

"Not really. You're entitled to your opinion. Let's move on. Isabelle Fletcher was a junior when she became the first African American and female inducted into Connellsville's National Honor Society.

Lamont's expression told me that he wanted to leave this area as he asked, "Is that it regarding the National Honor Society?"

CHAPTER 17

Despite Lamont's misgivings and strong opinions, I couldn't allow his influence to dictate how much or what I should include in this chapter. We were not finished with the National Honor Society and I had to take a firm stand.

As I was about to state my feelings, Lamont suggested, "You'll need to make a list of the African American students that were inducted into the National Honor Society."

My reaction to his statement was silence. I listened as he continued.

"I mean it's necessary to show that blacks were selected as early as 1929 and it didn't end there." He paused and asked, "Is there anything significant about the students that were inducted?"

I thought about it and didn't know how to answer him. If all of Lamont's conclusions are correct then the significance was that black students were inducted without prejudice. "Two facts I can mention is that some students were inducted as early as their junior year, and more than one African American student was inducted in one year."

"How are you going to do that?"

"From each year book, I'll list the year and their name, unless you have another suggestion."

"No, no. That will work."

Year	Name
1929—1930	Isabelle Fletcher
1941	Leroy Williams
1951	Helyn Clement
1959	Charles Hart
1959	Vivian Hart
1959	Marian Smith
1959	Les Wormack
1962—1963	Donna Little
1965	Roszella Canty
1965	Nancy Mockabee
1966	Janet Scott
1970	Carlyle Carter
1976	Robert Baker

Year	Name
1976	Kayan Johnson
1976	Cynthia Keith
1977—1978	Janice Mockabee
1978	Elizabeth Bonds
1982	Bernadette Grinko

Lamont glanced over the list. "Is this it?"

"We can mention the officers that the society members elected each year."

Making a face, he said, "Wait, why does the list end with 1982?"

"Remember, you suggested we end there because we weren't finding any new patterns." How soon he had forgotten. The decision had been made when we were at the high school in the library, researching data.

Timidly, he muttered, "Oh yeah, I forgot that was my idea wasn't it, but now, I'm thinking maybe we should have given this more thought."

"Why?"

"People might think that Connellsville's High School no longer exists."

"Well, the school is still standing and black students are still achieving as well as they were in 1929."

"Okay, but what are you typing?" Lamont glanced over my shoulder and made a face. "I know what I said, but we really need to rethink these lists."

"We just decided that there was no other way…." I stopped. "Fine, but until you come up with something better, it is what it is." I kept typing.

Year	**Name**	**Position**
1929	Isabelle Fletcher	Vice President
1958	Robert Harrison	Vice President
1959	Charles Hart	Vice President
1978	Janice Mockabee	Vice President
1982	Bernadette Grinko	Vice President

"Are we finished with this or is there something else? I mean when are you going to talk about school sports?"

"I think we should be systematic about this, rather than randomly start talking about sports."

"When will you include the sports data?"

I pursed my lips and counted to ten. Rather than answer him I say, "You can take a break any time you get ready. I think I can handle this now."

"I don't think so." Lamont teased. "You need my leadership to keep this book from turning into nothing but lists."

"Whatever."

CHAPTER 18

Rapidly, I flipped through one binder's pages and then picked up another binder. Not finding what I was looking for I started going through some of the other folders.

"What's wrong?"

I was going to discuss the Senior Council, but realized that the Student Council should go first and I can't find it.

Lamont's head was cocked to the side. "What's the difference between the two?"

"The Student Council is made up of the entire student body. Each class has a person who serves on the council. They make decisions regarding school activities."

"And the Senior Council does what?" I could tell Lamont did not understand why the two different councils, but I tried explaining it, the best of my ability.

I inhaled and exhaled. "Okay, the Senior Council is comprised of two seniors from each homeroom. Homeroom students elect the senior representatives to serve on the Senior Council. They are responsible for organizing senior activities such as the election of senior officers, class flower and colors." I paused and added, "And, I guess anything else that involves senior activities."

"Okay, what do you want to do?"

"I have to look through the binders and see what I can find. I know I had the information."

"Then, let's see if we can't find it." Lamont watched me as I combed through the binders. As I was about to turn another page, I felt Lamont's hand, stopping me.

"If you can't find the material, what affect will it have on the book's completion?"

I chewed on my lower lip giving his question some thought before answering. Sadly, I said, "None."

"Then, let it go. I suggest this be included in your items to research at a later date."

Reluctantly, I agreed, but it seemed to me that every school had a Student Council, but not necessarily a Senior Council. I ventured into territory I should have left alone. "Did your high school, Anacostia, have a Student Council?"

"Of course it did." Before he continued, his voice had taken on a harsher tone, but I knew his anger wasn't directed at me. "Please don't ask whether we had any black on the council."

I waited and hoped he would explain why.

"The high school was integrated, but the black students were included in school activities only as an afterthought or as a quota. Although it was 1965, everything was a battle for the black students. In my senior year, if it were not for the white students' insistence, a black student would not have been on the Student Council." I saw pride in Lamont's face as he said, "That was the first time I saw the white and black students unite."

Rather than discuss it any further, he asked, "When was the first African American student elected to the Student Council?"

"You mean the Senior Council. His name was Perry Wright. He graduated in the Class of 1948."

Perry Wright

The photographer unknown, photograph courtesy of 1948 Connellsville High School Yearbook.

Lamont stated, but I said nothing. "Don't wait for me, go ahead and type the list of names."
"I'm sorry, but until you come up with a better way to include this information, we have no other choice."

To make my point, I said, "Do you want to exclude the fact that from 1948 to 1983, the senior class continued to vote African American students to serve on the Senior Council?"

Lamont didn't respond right away. "No, that information is too important. If you don't list the year and student, then someone will conclude that it was a coincidence or a token, and we know that was not the case. Go ahead and type the list. In the meantime, I'm going to think of something more appealing."

Year	Name
1948	Perry Wright
1949	Leroy Rollin
1955	Raymond Hart
1956	Carole Pendleton
1959	Vivian Hart
1959	Marian Smith
1965	Roszella Canty
1965	Nancy Mockabee
1970	Kathy Haley
1970	Dennis Washington
1978	Janice Mockabee
1979	Bruce Meadows
1981	Tammy Meadows
1983	James Evans

"Don't get upset, but the Senior Council elected officers and you know what that means…"

Lamont groaned. "Yeah, you're going to make another list."

"Actually, the only information I gathered was the first elected Senior Council Officer and that was LeRoy Rollins, Class of 1949. He was the Senior Council Treasurer."

"Do you think he was the only black student elected as an officer?"

"No, I probably have the information, but misplaced it. Anyway, I've made a note to look at it again."

The photographer unknown, photograph courtesy of 1948 Connellsville High School Yearbook.

Lamont shouted, "Hey, is this your sister, Janice."

"Let me see. The picture isn't very clear, but yes, that's my sister Janice. Why?"

SENIOR CLASS OFFICERS: Pres. J. Mockabee, V.P. J. Kimmel, Sec. B. Welling, Treas. C. Salatino.

The photographer unknown, photograph courtesy of 1978 Connellsville High School Yearbook.

"According to this yearbook article, Janice was the first African American and female voted as the Senior Class President. In addition, it states that another first occurrence was that her entire cabinet was all female."

"And guess what?" The question didn't require an answer. I was proud of my sister. "It hasn't happened since 1978."

Inspecting the picture, I asked, "Do you think I should include a different picture? You can barely see Janice."

"I don't know. The picture came from the yearbook. You may not like the picture, but I'm not sure you can include something else because you don't like it."

"It's not that I don't like it. It's not clear and...." I threw up my hands. "Forget it!" I pursed my lips and didn't continue the debate. If I have my way, I will include a clearer picture.

CHAPTER 19

My stomach churned as I thought about making another list. These lists were becoming boring, but we had not yet to come up with a single idea of how else to convey the information. As much as I dislike saying it, Lamont was right.

The ringing phone interrupted my thoughts. Lamont answered it. I listened to the one-sided conversation and from what was being said, it wasn't my mystery caller.

When Lamont hung up the phone, I announced, "I'm going to take a break. You look at the information regarding Homeroom Officers."

"You think you're slick."

I chuckled. "What are you talking about?"

"You don't want to tell me that another list is needed."

"Really." I tried to play it off. "Remember, you suggested a list, not me."

"Right, like there's a choice."

"I'll be right back."

Lamont looked over the Homeroom Officers. The

graduating class was 1948 and the homeroom students elected Mercedes Mason. She was the first African American elected as a Homeroom Officer, Homeroom Secretary.

Mercedes Mason

The photographer unknown, photograph courtesy of the 1948 Connellsville High School Yearbook.

"Hey, Sweetie, how's it going?"

"Okay, but I was thinking how ironic it is that the Brown versus the Board of Education case occurred in 1954, but yet in Connellsville, Delnor (Duddy) Gales was the first African American student elected as the first Homeroom President."

Delnor (Duddy) Gales

The photographer unknown, photograph courtesy of the 1954 Connellsville High School 1954 Yearbook.

I shrugged as I contemplated what Lamont had said.

He continued, "How many times have I've tried explaining to you how monumental it was that in your hometown as far back as 1929 black students were being recognized, being voted as officers, playing on sports' team and participating in school activities? Instead of you admitting that your town was not the norm, you dismissed my observations and conclusions."

Lamont's voice was razor-sharp when he said, "You do understand the significance of the 1954 Brown versus the Board of Education decision, don't you?"

Before I could answer, the phone rang. I answered it. "Hello."

"Are you still writing that book?"

"Who is this?" My voice was louder than I realized. My question was met with the sound of a click.

Lamont asked, "What's going on?"

Nervously, I told him. "I've been getting telephone calls. The voice doesn't say much, but the warning is that

I shouldn't be writing a book. Until recently, I didn't know which book, but I'm beginning to think it's this book."

Lamont raised his hand. "Stop! What are you talking about? Are you saying that you've been receiving threatening telephone calls about you writing a book?"

"I don't know where to begin." I let out a heavy sigh. "I think the calls began when we started working on this book."

"Are you sure or could it just be a coincidence?"
I shook my head. "I don't know."

"Well, tell me everything about the calls."

"Well, there isn't much to tell." I shrugged. "At first the message was just two words, "the book." As the calls continued, the message was similar to a warning. Nothing threatening, just the same message—*"Don't write the book."* Since there's no mention of the book's title I concluded without any evidence that it's this book."

"That's a big leap to assume that you shouldn't write this book. You're always working on several books at a time. Not to mention that you read excerpts of your books at those writing groups you belong to."

"That's true, but my intuition tells me that it's this book."

"I don't know what to say except that you should have told me sooner about the calls."

"I'm sorry, but I didn't see any reason to. The calls

are more annoying than anything."

I heard the worry in Lamont's tone. "Maybe, but I don't like it."

"It's not a big deal. I just wish the person would talk to me. If the concern is about Connellsville and what I might write, I could assure them that the book contains nothing embarrassing."

"I agree, but maybe there's something that someone doesn't want told."

I shrugged. "Like what?"

"How should I know? Like families, everyone has secrets and they don't want them being told. That could be the case in your home town."

My voice was sharp. "Maybe, but I'm telling stories that can be found in reliable sources such as newspapers, high school yearbooks, and church records. I don't know any secrets or even if any exist."

Lamont threw his hands up in defense. "Don't get mad at me. I was just stating the facts." He paused and firmly said, Okay, but as of today, write down when you get a call and include the date and time."

"That's a good idea. Please hand me that tablet." I wrote down the information. When I finished, I said, "Let's move on. Where are we?"

"Before the phone rang, I was asking whether you understood the significance of Brown versus the Board of Education."

"Oh course I do. However as naïve as it might sound

I didn't see the necessity of integration. I thought everyone was receiving the same quality of education. I mean why would you want to ride a bus when you could walk to school?"

Lamont's eyes were sad as he said, "I can understand how you could arrive at that reasoning because of the education you were receiving. After all, why would you think that it was different for other children of color?"

"I guess my town must not have been the norm."

Lamont threw his hands up in the air and shouted, "At last, you've admitted it. Your town may not have been the norm."

I said nothing and typed.

Year	Name	Position
1948	Mercedes Mason	Secretary
1951	Helyn Ruth Clement	Secretary/Treasurer
1952	Clauzette Hill	Vice President
1954	Evelyn Washington	Secretary
1954	James (JR) Baker	Vice President
1956	Carole Pendleton	President
1957	John Johnston	President
1957	Wilbert Scott	President

Year	Name	Position
1958	Robert Harrison	President
1958	Madolyn Smith	Secretary
1959	Charles Hart	President
1959	Vivian Hart	Treasurer
1959	Marian Smith	Secretary
1959	Fred Thompson	President
1960	Ronald Washington	Secretary
1963	Donna Little	Secretary/Treasurer
1964	Cynthia Cole	Vice President
1965	Beverly Lockette	Secretary/Treasurer
1969	Dennis Washington	President
1970	Kathy Haley	Secretary/Treasurer
1976	Karyn Johnson	President
1977	Janice Mockabee	Treasurer
1978	Janice Mockabee	President
1979	Bruce Meadows	President
1981	Tammy Meadows	President

Year	Name	Position
1982	Michael Code	Vice President
1982	Bonnye Mason	Treasurer
1983	Derek French	Treasurer
1983	Charles Mills	Secretary
1983	Fred Reynolds	Treasurer

After typing the last name on the list, silence entered the room similar to an unexpected breeze of air on a warm summer evening. I stared at Lamont, waiting for him to give me direction about the next chapter.

From the deep lines running across Lamont's forehead, I could tell something was bothering him. Rather than ask, I waited for him to share.

CHAPTER 20

When Lamont began speaking, his comment was unexpected. His voice was slow and deliberate. "Unlike my high school, it seems like black students were accepted on all levels regarding school activities."

"What are you talking about?"

"From what I'm reading, black students were involved in extra curriculum activities, and white students had no problem electing someone of color as a club officer."

I didn't say anything. I mean the extra curriculum activities were encouraged, but not required. Clubs were established based on teacher support and student interest. Of course black students belonged to various clubs such as, but not limited to art, bridge, travel, drama, and the debate team. As far as blacks being elected as club officers, maybe that wasn't the norm."

"What year was the first club officer elected?"

"It's the Class of 1954. Don't say anything—it's my cousin, Burnack (Burnie) Scott. She was a member of the Tri-Hi-Y Club and was elected Vice President."

Burnack Scott

The photographer unknown, photograph courtesy of the 1954 Connellsville High School Yearbook.

Lamont's words were forceful "I could care less that this is your cousin. Again, it's the year, that period of time that's causing me so much emotion. You have taken all of this for granted while others were struggling for equality in the school system. Your town had already achieved it. This was 1954. If you can't appreciate its significance, something is wrong with you."

"I said that I got it, but I don't know what else you want me to say?"

"I know you admitted that your town was not the norm, but do you really understand?"

"Don't bully me. I'm beginning to grasp the significance of it all, but I bet there are other small towns with similar occurrences, especially in Pennsylvania if your theory is correct about William Penn."

Lamont made a face. "Don't start talking about other towns. You might be right, but right now we're concentrating on Connellsville and its unique circumstances." He fell quiet.

I wanted to move on and off of this subject. I was glad when I heard him say, "Now, let's see what's next?"

He glanced at me as his voice quivered with laughter. "Please tell me we are not going to make another list?"

I had to laugh too. "I'm sorry. I wish we could come up with something better?"

"I'm trying. Believe me, I'm trying."

Year	Name	Club/Position
1954	Burnack Scott	Tri-Hi-Y/Vice President
1955	Raymond Hart	Hi-Y/Treasurer
1955	Raymond Hart	Band/Vice President
1956	Carole Pendleton	Future Nurses of America/Vice President
1957	John Johnston	Sports Club/ Secretary/Treasurer
1959	Charles Hart	Camera Club/ President
1962	Mary Ann French	Girls Athletic Club/ President
1962	Donna Little	Tri-Hi-Y/Treasurer
1963	Donna Little	Tri-Hi-Y/President
Year	**Name**	**Club/Position**

1964	Cynthia Cole	Future Nurses of America/Vice President
1970	Dennis Washington	Varsity Club, President
1970	Dennis Washington	Spanish Honorary Society/President
1974	Patricia Washington	Girls Athletic Club/President
1976	Patricia Washington	Girls Athletic Club/President
1978	Virginia Braxton	Girls Athletic Club/President
1983	Derek French	Art Club/President

CHAPTER 21

A wide grin covered Lamont's face. Something told me not to ask, but I did anyway. "Why the big smile?"

"I think we're getting closer to sports. I can smell it."

Sarcastically I replied."Sure we are." I shook my head and continued, "I hate to disappoint you, but this chapter is about cheerleading."

Lamont was giddy. "I know and cheerleaders do what?"

"You mean the definition?"

"Yeah." I thought, why am I engaging in this conversation?

He pushed. "Well, what do cheerleaders do?"

"Basically, they generate school spirit and rally the student body in support of various sports' teams."

"See, "sports' teams," that means football and basketball. Need I say more?" He crossed his arms as if he had said something impressive.

I laughed.

Lamont's expression turned serious. "Besides being pretty, having long hair, and a nice shape, what was the requirement for becoming a cheerleader in your high school?"

I wasn't sure why the question, but my intuition told me that I wasn't going to like the direction of this dialogue. I threw my head back and said indignantly. "Connellsville High School cheerleaders were chosen on the basis of school requirements and they were followed to the letter."

Under Lamont's breath, he snorted, "I bet they did, no different than other schools." He cleared his throat and said, "You didn't answer my question."

I glared at him. "Fine, the students had to maintain a "C" grade in each class, not an overall grade point average. In addition to grades, students trying out had to demonstrate cheering skills and meet the physical requirements. The final selections were made by the current cheerleading squad and endorsed by the sponsoring teacher."

"If you say so…."

I interrupted him. "Why are you so cynical about the selection process for cheerleaders?"

Lamont shot back. "Let's get real. Back in the day and maybe even today, most schools chose cheerleaders based on looks and popularity." He grunted, "Everything else such as grades and cheerleading skills seemed secondary."

"I will agree with much of what you're saying, but that wasn't how it was in Connellsville. If that was the case...." I paused and showed him a picture.

**Varsity Cheerleader
Carole (Penny) Pendleton**
The photographer unknown, photograph courtesy of the 1956 Connellsville High School Yearbook.

Lamont held the picture and beamed. "I must admit I'm impressed. When was this?"

"She graduated in 1956." His mouth flew open as if he wanted to say something, but no words came out.

I waited and finally he asked, "Were there other African American cheerleaders?"

"Sure. Let's start with Marian Smith. She was the first Varsity Cheerleading Co-Captain. Her sister, Madolyn Smith (Class of 1958), was on the squad the same time as Marian. I think they were the only two African American sisters on the cheerleading squad at the same time."

The photographer unknown, photograph courtesy of the 1958 Connellsville High School Yearbook.

I glanced at Lamont, but he wasn't listening to me, even though he asked the question about other African American cheerleaders. What was he staring at? I leaned over the table to get a better look at the picture.

CHAPTER 22

Lamont peeped up at me. He smiled as I sat with my head cocked to the side. I broke the silence. "What's wrong?"

"Your sister, Patty, was a Cheerleader?"

"Yes and what's so fascinating about that?"

"I guess I didn't realize your sisters were that active in high school."

I threw my hand in the air and said, "Whatever."

"Why are you being so nonchalant about your sisters' achievements?"

I shrugged. "I never gave it much thought.

Lamont let the subject drop. "What are you typing?"

"What do you think?" I laughed and so did he as my fingers flew across the keyboard typing the names of the African American cheerleaders.

Year		Name
1956		Carole (Penny) Pendleton
1957		Beverly Burrell
1958	1959	Madolyn Smith
1958	1959	Marian Smith
1961		Patty Mockabee

The photographer unknown, photograph courtesy of Connellsville's High School 1958 Yearbook.

I took a deep breath before continuing. I wanted to tell Lamont something, but decided he could discover it on his own.

I chewed my lower lip. "I probably should have started with the Junior Varsity (JV) squad."

Lamont shrugged. "I don't think it matters. After all, don't the JV Cheerleaders automatically become Varsity Cheerleaders?"

"Not always. The JV Cheerleaders still have to meet the same requirements and tryout along with everyone else. The only advantage is that they would already know the cheers."

Lamont let out a loud yawn. I glanced over at him. From his drooping eyelids, he appeared tired and he was probably hungry. I frowned as I remembered I had not taken anything out for dinner. Our choices were either leftovers or a restaurant.

"Do you want to quit after this and get something to eat?"

Lamont agreed. "I need a break, but let's finish the JV Cheerleading Squad first?"

"Okay. Marian Smith who graduated in 1959 was the first African American JV Cheerleading Captain."

"Was there anyone else?"

"Yes, my sister, Patty. She was the second JV Cheerleading Captain.

Cheerleaders

The photographer unknown, photograph courtesy of the 1960 Connellsville's High School Yearbook.

I was waiting for Lamont, but he was busy looking at another picture. "Why didn't you tell me?"

"Tell you what?"

CHAPTER 23

Lamont stared intently at me before asking. "Why didn't you tell me you were a JV Cheerleader?"

"It wasn't a big deal."

I braced myself for the next question. "Why didn't you go out for the Varsity squad?"

"I did."

His eyes widened. "And, you didn't make it? That's hard to believe."

"I probably would have made it, but I had a "D" in my Algebra II class at the time of try outs. Remember a "C" was required in each class, not an overall grade point average."

"What about the next year?"

"What about it?"

"I mean, you never tried out again for the Varsity Squad?"

My answer was a shake of the head.

Lamont's jaw line was tight, showing tension. His facial expression said what he wasn't verbalizing. I had asked myself that same question. The next year, I had the grades, but I didn't try out. Maybe I was afraid of not making it, but I'll never know.

Finally, Lamont said, "I'm sorry, Babe."
I shrugged. "You have no reason to apologize. That was a long time ago."

"Before we go out to eat…" Lamont was chewing his lower lip and asked, "Do you see anything?"

He handed me the various cheerleading pictures. I inspected the photos, not sure what I was supposed to see. He must have read my perplexed expression.

"The cheerleaders aren't light skinned. You know the old saying about being light, bright, and damn near white."

"Yeah, but what's your point?"

"Back in the day, my experience with early integration was that girls that made the cheerleading squad would have been light skinned with long hair. Therefore, do you really believe any of these girls, including yourself, would have made the cheerleading squad?"

His inference staggered me. I started to argue the point, when the phone rang. Lamont answered. "Hello."

"May I speak to Mrs. Harris?"

"May I ask who is calling?" The phone went dead.

"Was that my mystery caller?"

"I'm not sure, but probably."

Before he could ask, I handed him the tablet that we were using to track the mysterious incoming calls. I waited until Lamont finished writing and then asked,

"What were you saying about color and cheerleaders?"

"As much as I don't want to talk about color I have to say that back in the day, a black girl's chances of becoming a cheerleader would have been based on how much her appearance resembled a white girl. You know like a Lena Horne."

"I never gave it a second thought. As you pointed out earlier, the girls that were cheerleaders at my school certainly didn't meet that requirement."

If what Lamont said was true, and I had no reason to doubt what he was saying, then my school deserved a gold star for giving every girl the opportunity to make the cheerleading squad.

CHAPTER 24

After dinner, I was rejuvenated and ready to work through the night, but I knew it wasn't going to happen. A glimpse at Lamont's gaunt face said he was fading.

"If you want to quit, I understand, but I'm on a roll and would like to continue for a little bit longer."

Lamont looked at the clock. "It's getting late, but I'm willing to work until ten o'clock."

My writing style would have been to continue until I was bleary eyed. When my creative juices are flowing, I try to take advantage of it, but to keep my husband happy I would stop at his suggested time. I couldn't complain because we accomplished a lot.

Lamont skimmed through the next set of pictures. He started rubbing his hands together and let out a "Whoopee!"

"What's that all about?"

His eyes sparkled. "At last, the topic of sports is next."

"What gave you that idea?"

"I've been watching you gather the pictures and

articles regarding the girls' basketball team?"

"That's not what I'm doing."

"I know a basketball when I see one."

"Let me stop you right now before you get too excited. This information is not about the girls' basketball team."

Lamont had a perplexed look on his face. "What? Why are you trying to confuse me?"

"You're confusing yourself. You're so anxious to talk sports that you didn't look close enough at the pictures."

"What do you mean?" He picked up the picture and pointed, "See—basketball."

"Sweetie, this information is about the girls' basketball cheerleading squad."

Lamont exhaled. "Wait a minute, you mean to tell me that the school didn't use the JV or Varsity cheering squad to cheer for the girls' basketball team?"

"No. Girls that were not on the JV or Varsity had the opportunity to cheer for the basketball team. There were two separate teams and two separate cheerleading squads."

"I'm amazed at your school. The opportunities were endless when it came to giving every student a chance at belonging...." Lamont stopped. "I'm not sure I can express what I'm trying to say. I guess the point I'm trying to make is that popularity didn't prevent students from certain activities."

"I'm not sure I'm following you."

"For example, any girl that didn't make the JV or Varsity cheerleading squads had yet another opportunity to tryout and the possibility of being a cheerleader."

"Oh, you're right because that's exactly what I did."

"Were you the only black basketball cheerleader?"

"No. Vivian Hart was one."

Lamont started laughing.

He reacted as if I had told him a joke. "What's so funny?" Rather than answer my question, he kept laughing.

"Lamont, Lamont." I asked again. "What's so funny?"

He wiped his eyes and finally uttered, "You and your family."

"What do you mean?"

"Come on Lorraine. I recognize the name Vivian Hart."

"Okay, but what about her?"

"Well, isn't Vivian your cousin?"

"Technically, yes."

What does that mean?"

"In high school she wasn't my cousin. Besides, she's my cousin-in-law. She married my first cousin."

CHAPTER 25

Before the clock reached ten o'clock, Lamont suggested, "We should clean up and get ready for bed."

I didn't want to stop. My artistic juices were flowing like water in a river, but because of my promise, I would have to wait. I shut down the computer and started helping to clean up.

In bed, I couldn't settle my mind. All types of ideas were leaping in and out of my thoughts. As much as I tried, the pictures and words of the book overpowered the counting of sheep. Questions kept creeping in and out about how to include information without making lists and about who didn't want me to write the book. I tossed and turned until at last, I fell asleep.

In the morning, I was fresh and ready to tackle the more of the data. Lamont had a tee time.
Lamont's words surprised me. "Why don't you work while I'm gone and when I return, we can go over what you've accomplished?"

"Are you sure? The next item is the girls' basketball team?"

"Whoa! In that case, please wait until I come back?"

"Okay. I'll work on my other book." We kissed and he left.

Unfortunately and not surprisingly, my attempts at writing on a different book were overshadowed by my preoccupation about my home town. Since I couldn't concentrate on the novel, I turned on the television and watched Family Feud and The View. The noon news was on when I decided to prepare lunch. I heard the garage door open. Lamont was back.

He entered the kitchen, gave me a kiss, and announced, "I'm going to take a shower." As he walked out of the kitchen, he added, "And, would you please make me a sandwich?"

After he showered, we ate lunch and discussed his round of golf. I talked about what I did and Lamont seemed surprised when I shared, "I didn't work on my other novel. All I thought about was the Connellsville book. As soon as we finish lunch I would like to start working on it again."

"Okay, but I need to relax for a few minutes."

We finished lunch and walked to the great room where I watched Lamont grab his blanket, sit down and push back the recliner. When he put the blanket over him and closed his eyes, I knew he was going to nap for at least 30 minutes to an hour.

While Lamont rested, I examine the remaining data and my notes. I had more material than I realized. The organization of it all was overwhelming.

After an hour, Lamont wandered in and announced, "I'm ready and anxious to begin." He paused, eyes narrowed. "You did say we're going to discuss the girls' basketball team?"

I smiled. "Yes, I did."

"Are you going to list the names of the African American girls who played on the girls' basketball team?"

"No. The list would be too long. You would not believe how many African American girls played on the basketball team. I thought that the information would have more meaning if I provided only significant information, such as the first black girl who made the team and anything else that might be out of the ordinary."

"Who was the first?"

"Isabelle Fletcher, the Class of 1930. She was on the team during her junior and senior years of school."

"Wait a minute. Are you just talking about the girls in this section?"

"Yes. Why, is there a problem?"

"I should say so. If you're talking about sports then all sports should be discussed and not just one aspect."

"Well, I'm mentioning the girls' basketball team because I just finished with the girls' cheerleading squad."

"There's no logic to your thinking. Why aren't you going to include the girls' basketball team with the other sports? I mean does that make sense to you?"

"Well, kind of. Since I discussed the girls' cheerleading squad, why not mention the basketball team?"

Lamont shook his head. "What are you saying? Listen, basketball is basketball, whether girls or boys are playing the game. This does not belong here."

"I think it does."

Firmly, Lamont said, "Lorraine, this information should be included with the other sports stuff. If you don't, then that means you don't see girls' basketball as being equal to other sports."

I frowned at Lamont's implication. "That was a cheap shot. I resent you indicating that somehow I don't think girls and boys sports are equal. You forget our daughter played basketball and you coached the girls' basketball team."

"That's my point. Now, are you going to move this material to the sports section?"

I pouted as if I had been scolded. Did I want to continue arguing about this? I sighed and didn't know what to do. Instead of relenting, I tried again. "There are only three points to share about the girls' basketball team."

"What are they?"

"Isabelle Fletcher, the Class of 1930, was the first African American girl to play on the girls' basketball team and she was on the team as a junior and senior."

Isabelle Fletcher

The photographer unknown, photograph courtesy of the 1929 Connellsville's High School Yearbook.

    I disliked repeating myself, but I had to make my point. "Secondly, there were too many African American girls on the basketball team to list them all and thirdly, there were two black basketball team captains. They were: Barbara Burrell (Class of 1959) and Bernadette Grinko (Class of 1981).

Captain: Barb Burrell

The photographer unknown, photograph courtesy of the 1958 Connellsville High School Yearbook.

Lamont persisted. "Explain to me again why this information should not be in the sports chapter?"

"I don't have an explanation. I only know we aren't seeing eye to eye on this. Can we drop it? If necessary, this can be moved later."

Lamont couldn't, or he wouldn't, let it go. "One last point, do you agree that basketball is a sport?" Before I could answer he hurried on. "If you agree and I know you will, then this information belongs where?" He smiled and waited.

Through gritted teeth I said, "Girls' basketball is a sport." I had said enough without admitting I was wrong.

CHAPTER 26

Lamont seemed pre-occupied and had no desire to work on the book. Perhaps, a day away from it would give us an opportunity to clear our heads and rethink some of the material we had already organized. Furthermore, we still didn't have a title.

"Do you want to go to Lake Sumter Landing? We probably need a break from the book."
Lamont did not hesitate. "Let's go."

I told myself that today would be a fun day. I would not permit myself to think about the book. However, I knew it was easier said than done.

As we backed out of the driveway and drove down the street, we saw Vinnie and slowed the golf cart. When it came to a complete stop, we got out. In unison, we said, "Hi Vinnie."

"Hi. How are you doing?"

I took the lead. "I want you to know that I'm making progress on putting my research together regarding the Connellsville book."

"Oh yeah, how's that coming?" Before I could answer, Vinnie asked, "Where do you live on this street?"

Lamont and I glanced at each other with puzzlement. Despite Vinnie's question, I pointed, "Across the street."

Before anything else was said, Vinnie's wife rushed toward us. "Hi, Lamont and Lorraine."
Vinnie turned toward his wife. "Do you know these people?"

Dot didn't answer Vinnie. Her face strained as she tugged at his arm. They turned and walked toward the house. As they walked away, Lamont and I looked at each other. I was sure Lamont had as many questions as I did about what just happened.

We climbed back into the golf cart, both of us waiting before we said anything. I spoke up first. "What do you think that was about?"

"I don't know. When we first talked to Vinnie he seemed fine, but then within minutes he was clueless as to who we were. Maybe, he suffers from dementia."

"I don't know, but it was strange."

When we arrived on the square, we began window shopping and commented on the mild weather. Before the nightly entertainment began, we decided to have dinner at the Whiskey Creek Restaurant.

After dinner, we ventured over to the square. The band that was playing was a favorite of ours because they played rock and roll from the late 60's into the 70's. We watched the dancers and talked to people we knew while introducing ourselves to Villagers and visitors we didn't know.

Hours later, we returned home. To my surprise, Lamont wanted to discuss some of the book's data and maybe put together one or two chapters before calling it a night.

We began with the high school band. Lamont wanted to know. "How were band members selected?"

"Like other school offered electives, band was for a select few who would play in Connellsville's marching 100. Students had to try out and the band sponsor, the music teacher, chose band members based on grades and their talent."

Before Lamont asked, I already knew what he wanted to know. "Were there any African American students in the band?"

"Are you kidding? In 1943, three of the Betters—James, Edgar, and Harold—were in the school Band."

"When you went through the yearbooks, did you remember seeing more than one black student in the band?"

"Uh...I don't remember. Why?"

"Because I think the Betters Brothers were the only

African American brothers in the band at the same time."

Lamont sat up straight in the chair. He was looking at a picture from a church program. "Who's this?"

"James Betters. When he tried out for the high school marching band, he became the first African American Drum Major."

"When was that?"

"He was in the Class of 1943."

Lamont sat looking at the picture. "He must have been good."

JAMES BETTERS

The photographer unknown, photograph courtesy of a Payne A.M.E. Church Program Bulletin.

"Everyone said he had more talent, skill, and expertise than any previous drum major."

Lamont shook his head. "In 1943, I bet he might have been the first African American student to twirl a baton in front of other high schools."

"You might be right. One thing people admired about

him was his desire to make sure that baton twirling was passed on. He shared his talent with as many young people as possible, black and white, male and female. In addition, he competed and won national competitions all over the Eastern Region in places such as Buffalo, New York, Perryopolis, Pennsylvania, and Washington, D.C.

"Was he the only African American Drum Major at Connellsville?"

"No, in 1950, his brother, Jerome Betters was a Drum Major, as well as Robert Lewis in 1983."

CHAPTER 27

"Was there anything else notable about African American students and the band?"

"The band, like other school sponsored activities, elected officers. Raymond S. Hart (Class of 1955) was the first elected African American Band Officer, Vice President.

Charles Hart

The photographer unknown, photograph courtesy of the 1955 Connellsville High School Yearbook.

"Is Charles Hart, Vivian's brother?"

"No, I believe he's her cousin."

Lamont blinked his eyes hard. "Is that Vivian?"

The photographer unknown, photograph courtesy of the 1958Connellsville's High School Yearbook.

"It sure is. She graduated in the Class of 1959 and was the first African American female selected as Head Majorette for the Connellsville High School Marching Band."

"Was she the only African American head majorette?"

"Yes, but her sister, Stephanie Hart (Class of 1970), was a majorette."

The photographer unknown, photograph courtesy of the 1970 Connellsville's High School Yearbook.

"Is that it for the band?"

"No, Connellsville's Band started having flag carriers in the 1970's. In 1972, Sharon Dooley was the first African American Flag Carrier."

Sharon Dooley

The photographer unknown, photograph courtesy of the 1972 Connellsville High School Yearbook.

Lamont was rubbing his eyes as he inquired, "Are we finished with the band?"
"Why, do you want to quit and pick it up tomorrow?"
"It all depends on what's next."
I grinned and in a low tone, I said, "Sports."
"Finally!" Lamont blinked his eyes several times and said, "I'm ready. Let me get something to drink and we'll go to bed after we complete the sports chapter."

CHAPTER 28

A newspaper article from the Connellsville Courier Newspaper caught Lamont's attention. Once or twice, I glanced at him, trying to see what he was reading.

Lamont's voice was laced with either concern or disbelief. I couldn't tell as he asked a question. "Is this information correct?"

"What is it?"

"This newspaper article states that in 1941, the United States was on the brink of World War II. Despite the chaotic time, the Connellsville High School Football Team won the state tournament."

"That's correct. That was one of Connellsville's shining moments in sports history."

Lamont seemed lost in his thoughts. I wanted to know what was bothering him.

"What's wrong?"

Sadness filled Lamont's voice as he said, "I'm trying to imagine how these four African American players felt about serving in the United States Armed Forces."

1941 Connellsville Cokers

In the summer and fall of 1941, the United States was on the cusp of entering World War II. It was a turbulent time, but through that darkness, Connellsville fans had a ray of light in their local high school football team.

The Cokers featured some of the finest athletes Connellsville has ever been associated with, including the likes of 1947 Heisman Trophy winner John Lujack, former Pittsburgh Steeler Garry Feniello and former University of Pittsburgh head coach Dave Hart.

Although many of the players on the 33-man team went on to great careers in a variety of different fields, their first taste of success came during that 1941 season in which the team fin-

The photographer unknown, photograph courtesy of Elsie Haley's private collection.

"I'm not following you. Other than fighting in the war and staying alive what else would they be worrying about?"

"Be for real. These black guys attended an integrated school and played football on an integrated team that just won the state tournament, but yet they would be serving their country where the troops were segregated."

I squirmed and wanted to pull back my words, but it was too late. "I never gave it much thought."

"You wouldn't." Immediately, Lamont apologized. "What I mean is that you take racial issues far too lightly, not always understanding the impact. It had to have been hurtful as well as shocking to these guys."

I didn't know what to say and breathed a sigh of relief when Lamont changed the subject.

"This has nothing to do with football, but if you think it makes sense to put the girls' basketball team with cheerleading, then I can mention this fact about a graduating Veteran."

"What are you talking about?"

"In the Class of 1947, an African American male did not have his graduation picture taken."

Definitely, Lamont was getting tired. "That's not unusual. There are many graduating seniors who don't have their picture taken."

"If you'll give me a chance, I'll explain." I sat quietly as he continued.

"It states here that his picture, along with other white males, were not taken and put in the yearbook because these young men were serving in the armed forces. What's unusual is that the school allowed them to graduate with their class even though they were already fighting in the Armed Services."

"What was the name of the student?"

"Leon Straughters. Why does that last name seem familiar? Straughters…Straughters."

I tensed and hoped Lamont wouldn't remember why he knew the name.

The telephone ringing interrupted Lamont's attempt at trying to recall why he knew the Straughters' name. As much as I welcomed the intrusion my hope was that it wasn't another hang-up, but Lamont's expression told me it was. After he hung up, I should have, but didn't share with him that the more I heard the voice, the more familiar it sounded to me.

CHAPTER 29

Our work stalled with Lamont's constant repeating of the surname Straughters. Then, I watched Lamont's expression go from dull to bright, similar to a fresh lit candle that grows more brilliant as it burns.

"I know why I know that name. When you finalized your mom's family genealogy, I think there were some Straughters." Lamont waited for my answer.

I sighed. "Technically, you might be right."

"Here we go again. Why can't you ever give me a straight answer when it comes to your relatives?"

"Well, he married my first cousin, but not until they were out of high school."

A smirk crossed Lamont's face. I could see the wheels going round and round. His expression was a give-a-way; I waited for his sarcastic remark.

"Are you related to everyone in Connellsville?"

"No-o-o."

"It seems that way to me."

I tried to explain. "You have to remember, Connellsville is a small town and as we discussed earlier the population declined after the 1920's." As a reminder I stated, "When the town's population stabilized to around 8,000, the African American population remained constant at an estimated 350."

"In other words, the probability is that most of the African Americans in town could be related?"

I threw up my hands. "That's not what I'm saying. In a town with a limited black population, you can expect some of them will be related."

A laugh escaped Lamont. "That's what I said."

I ended the conversation. "Can we stay focused and finish the football facts?"

"No problem, but please tell me you're not going to make a list of all the football players?"

"I'm not unless you want me to." I laughed. "Seriously, there are too many African American students that played and there is nothing noteworthy about that."

"Are you kidding me? What about John Lujack? He received the Heisman Trophy in 1947?"

I snickered. "You're forgetting two things. One, he's not African American and secondly, he won that honor when he was in college."

"Okay, a small technicality. What about your cousin, Bo Scott? He played on the state football team with Joe Namath."

"And that's noteworthy because?"

"Joe Namath is in the Football Hall of Fame."

"Yeah, but you're mixing apples and oranges. I mean Joe Namath was inducted into the Football Hall of Fame for being a NFL player, not because of high school achievements. You'll do anything to get the sports trivia written into this book and it's not going to happen." He made a wry face at me.

I turned my attention back to the papers I had and thumbed through them, trying to find something significant to write about. "In the Class of 1958, Robert (Bob) Harrison was the first black selected as the high school Football Captain. The only other black Football Captain was Donald Graves, Class of 1978. William (Peter) Bradley was the only black Football Co-captain, Class of 1959."

"I think you need to review the basketball teams for each school year one more time."

"Why?"

Lamont shook his head. "I can't believe you didn't have any African American males that were captains or co-captains." Lamont tried to suppress a smile. "With everything that I know about Connellsville's sports and with the girls' basketball team having black captains, there's a good likelihood that there was a black male captain or co-captain."

I stuck my tongue out at him. I didn't miss the jab.

Without saying it, he was reminding me that the girls' basketball information belonged in this chapter. He was right and when I begin to finalize everything then I would make the change.

"Let's stay focused."

"Now this is what I call unusual."

"What?"

"The yearbook states that all season the Connellsville High School mile relay team was unbeaten, including the Western Pennsylvania Interscholastic Athletic League (WPIAL) competition."

With pride I said, "I don't want to brag, but Connellsville usually had a good track team."

"Maybe, but what's **notable** to me is that the entire 1957 track team was black."

"Why, who was on the team?"

Instead of answering my question, he stated with a smile. "I should have seen this coming."

"What?"

"You had a cousin on the track team, Wilbert Scott, the one married to Vivian Hart."

I ignored him and asked, "Who else was on the team?"

"There was Bob Baker, Ralph Tennessee, and Mike Johnston. Someone by the name of Jim Hart replaced Bob Baker in this event."

I thought Lamont was finished, but he was thumbing through some old newspaper clippings as if he had forgotten something.

"What are you looking for?"

"Nothing except I can't believe the school yearbook article and none of the newspaper accounts of the event mentioned that the team was *"all"* colored or Negro."

BOB BAKER—WILBERT SCOTT—RALPH TENNESSEE—MIKE JOHNSON---JIM HART

The photographer unknown, photograph courtesy of the 1957 Connellsville High School Yearbook.

I had to agree with Lamont that no mention of color was exceptional.

Lamont's arms were moving back and forth and his face bright as a candle lit Jack-O-Lantern. "Listen. In that same year, John (Mike) Johnston, a black male, set school records in the 100-yard dash and the 440. He anchored the mile relay team. Mike set a new Fayette County 100-yard dash record of 9.8 and broke the state 440-yard record with a time of 48.6."

John (Mike) Johnston

The photographer unknown, photograph courtesy of the 1957 Connellsville High School Yearbook.

Lamont asked the same question again, "Did the yearbook or the newspaper mention color?"
With care, I inspected the yearbook copied pages and the newspaper clippings. "Not one color reference."

"Again, I find that amazing."

"Me too."

Lamont inquired, "Is there anything else regarding the track team?"

"Not really." I took a closer look, making sure I didn't miss anything.

"You must be tired," Lamont said. "Maybe we need to call it a wrap."

"Why are you saying I'm tired?"

"You are because you missed the African American students who were Track Captains. In 1981,

Tammy Meadows and in 1983, Bruce Meadows and Charles Mills were Track Captains."

Just when I was about to argue about my sleepiness, I yawned. "I guess you're right. Let's go to bed."

CHAPTER 30

The next day, we reviewed our calendar and it was full of commitments. Lamont was shooting pool and I had a luncheon with the Plum Red Social Butterflies, a chapter of the National Red Hat Society.

Despite our scheduled activities, I had other things on my mind. I shared my intentions with Lamont. "I think I'm going to skip the luncheon today."

"Why?"

Under my breath I said, "I want to work on the book."

Lamont gathered me in his arms and whispered. "I don't think so. You need a break and that means getting out of the house. We can work on the book later. Today calls for recreation." Reluctantly, I agreed.

As I was going out the door to the garage, the ringing phone caused me to stop. I thought about letting it ring, but decided it might be important. When I picked up the phone and heard the heavy breathing, I immediately regretted my decision.

"Hello! Who is this?"

No response. I rolled my eyes and was about to hang up the phone when I heard the raspy voice say, "You know why I'm calling."

"No, I don't." Annoyed, my voice grew loud. "Tell me what you want?"

Instead of the caller giving me an answer, the phone went dead. I blew air out noisily and returned the phone into the cradle. These calls had gone from annoying to disturbing.

I glanced at the clock. I needed to leave if I was going to make the luncheon on time.

Although Lamont had to push me into keeping my lunch date, I was glad that he had. The Butterflies were full of laughter and the conversation was lively.

When I pulled into the garage and climbed out of the car, I realized Lamont had not arrived home yet. The phone was ringing. Instead of rushing to answer it, I let the answering machine pick up. I turned on the machine to listen to the messages, there was only one and it was from my caller. This time the meaning was clear—"Do not write a book about Connellsville."

At least one part of the mystery had been solved. However, I still didn't know who didn't want the book written and why.

I changed from my purple outfit into something more casual and tried to put the call out of my mind. I wandered into the den and began scanning pictures that might be included in the book. By the time Lamont arrived home, I had scanned all the pictures and had begun typing notations under them.

Lamont entered the house and yelled, "Where are you?"

"I'm in the den." He walked in, gave me a kiss. "How was your luncheon?"

"Fun was had by all. Thanks for making me go." I stopped and asked, "What about you? Did your pool team win?"

"No. We were outmatched, but I had a good time with the fellows. I'm hungry. What's for dinner?"

"I had a big lunch so I'm not eating dinner. Why don't I warm up some leftovers and make you a salad." From Lamont's frown, I could tell he wasn't happy with my suggestion, but he didn't protest.

During dinner, we discussed the book and the progress we made last night. When dinner was over, we went into the den; I picked up and flipped through one of the binders and I commented, "I think we've included all the information regarding the educational successes. What do you suggest we do next?"

Lamont asked, "Did you say we're finished with the high school entries?"

"Yes and we're ready to move on." Rather than answering me, Lamont was staring off in. I asked again. "Where do we go from here?"

Lamont smiled. "I know, but I'm not going to

mention the word…" He stopped and then spelled, "S-p-o-r-t-s."

I crumbled up a piece of paper and threw it at him.

"On a serious note, I'm curious about something and this doesn't have to be included, but I want to talk about it."

"What is it?"

"How were the social aspects of high school? You know, were the dances and proms integrated? Were black students invited to attend them?"

"Of course, why wouldn't they be? The dances and the prom were school-sponsored."

Lamont scoffed, "What does that mean? At my high school, the prom was all inclusive, but when it came to other school dances, black students were not invited. Usually, we didn't find out about the dances until they were over."

A rueful expression covered my face. "Oh, Lamont, that's really sad."

"Not really, it was the times and that's just the way it was. What about outside of high school?"

"You mean were black students invited to parties and dances outside of high school?"

"That's exactly what I mean."

I thought about the question and didn't know how to respond. I mean you invite whomever you want to your birthday or slumber parties. I never gave it much thought. I could only speak from my experience. Growing up, black and white kids played together, went to each other's houses, and even ate at each other's homes. I can't remember if color was an issue.

"Well, are you going to answer the question?"

"Give me a minute. It's just that my answer isn't that easy. If you're referring to dances outside of high school, yes, blacks attended them. My sister, Nancy, and I attend the Saturday afternoon dances that were held at the South Connellsville Community Center."

Lamont kept pushing. "What about other dances?"

"Let's see. If I remember correctly, my sister, Patty, and her friends went to the South Connellsville Firehouse dances. So, if the question is whether the dances outside of school were integrated, then the answer is yes."

Lamont made a face and said, "That's definitely not the norm."

"I'm not sure why you would say...." I didn't finish my sentence and hurried on. "To be honest, most black teens from Connellsville preferred going to the Uniontown dances that were held at the Ivory Ballroom, Club 36, and Uniontown Layette School. Not to mention...."

Lamont interrupted me. "Are you saying that Uniontown had all black dances?"

"No. Uniontown's dances were integrated, but the black teen population was greater and it was a chance to see black singing groups, hear black artists' music and learn the latest dances."

CHAPTER 31

A strange expression covered Lamont's face, frown lines creasing his forehead.

"What's wrong?"

"I don't know about you, but the question remains, why did Connellsville's black students excel?"

"I'm not sure they excelled any more than other black students in similar situations."

Lamont threw up his hands. "Please! Your town had such a small minority of black students, but yet they did extremely well academically and blended in socially without regard to color."

"But, I still contend that this may have been the norm in most small towns with a small number of minorities. Since we started looking at my hometown, I've asked myself the same question and I posed it to other blacks who were part of the Connellsville experience and no one seemed to have a viable answer."

Lamont pushed the issue. "Would you and other blacks agree that their school accomplishments probably had more to do with intelligence, skill, and talent, rather than color?"

"I think most of us took for granted that we were no different than anyone else attending school. I can only speak for myself, but it's only been since we started to review and discuss all of the researched information that I'm beginning to understand how color wasn't a factor and that my town probably wasn't the norm." I paused and added. "If color was an issue, it was subtle."

Lamont reiterated. "Maybe someone might write a thesis on Connellsville and other small cities where there were small percentages of African Americans and explain the impact, if any."

I shrugged. "Do you really think anyone would be interested in writing about such a subject? Better yet, who would want to read about it?"

Lamont let out a heavy sigh. His voice laced with irritation, "Most definitely! Since the late 1800's, the schools were integrated, the majority attending the school were white, most of the teachers were white, and the black student population was not significant enough to make an influence on any decisions affecting school activities."

"What's your point?"

"My point is that Connellsville's school system demonstrated what can happen when all students are given the same opportunities. The city certainly dispels the myths and misconceptions about integration. Children can exceed in any environment if they are not systematically excluded."

I exhaled nosily. "Whoa." I raised my feet off the floor and said, "It's getting deep in here."

Before Lamont could respond, the phone rang. I picked it up. "Hello."

"There will be no book written about Connellsville. Do you understand?"

Like the other phone calls, I attempted to ask who was calling, but my question was answered with a click. Since I knew which book the caller didn't want written I now wanted to know why.

When I hung up the phone, Lamont said, "The caller again?"

"Yes."

Lamont hedged. "I...I don't...don't get mad, but I stopped by the police station."

"Why?"

"I can't be with you twenty-four-seven and I'm concerned. Besides, I wanted to know our rights."

"And, what did you find out?"

"Unfortunately, there is nothing the police can do because the calls haven't been threatening. **The suggestion was that we change our telephone number, but that's about it.**"

"I'm not mad, but the police visit was a waste of time. Regardless of what the police suggested, we aren't getting a new telephone number."

"I agree, but I did call the phone company to add the caller ID feature. Maybe, we'll get lucky and find out **the** person's name and telephone number.

"Okay, but let's get back to what you were saying."

"I was saying that children can exceed in any environment if they're not systematically excluded."

"Oh yeah. You were getting philosophical on me."

"Not really. It's just that I had to make a profound statement before you would listen to me."

I shook my head. "That's not true. It's just that I don't have any answers. Now that you've explained your logic, maybe someone might be interested in writing about the topic, but don't look at me. This is way beyond my ability."

Lamont slapped his head. "Why didn't I think about it before?"

"What?"

"Maybe your town represents another facet of the western Pennsylvania mystic." Lamont was animated. "I'm surprised no one has written about the reason for the large number of successful athletes coming out of western Pennsylvania."

I chuckled. Why didn't I see it coming? Before I could comment, Lamont rushed on.

"Before you start with me, let me defend my point. You would be surprised at the number of outstanding athletes from western Pennsylvania."

"I should have known you'd work in the sports statistics."

"No, no. This is serious. Let's start with Arnold Palmer, the famous, world-wide golfer. He's from Latrobe and what about Joe Namath, he's from Beaver Falls." Lamont stopped, but hurried on. "And there's Joe Montana, he's from..."

"Don't look at me. I have no idea where he's from."

"I know, but at the moment I can't remember where in western Pennsylvania."

I raised my eyebrow and snickered. "I'm surprised that you have forgotten such an important sports fact."

He threw up his hands. "It doesn't matter. The point I'm making is that someone should research, study, and document the various peculiarities of western Pennsylvania."

CHAPTER 32

With the high school chapter completed regarding what might be included, I was mentally and physically exhausted. Every inch of my body felt fatigued. With my energy level low, I had no desire to continue. In addition to my tiredness, my creative juices had stopped flowing.

Lamont must have sensed I was worn-out. He had stood up and was behind me, massaging my neck and shoulders. "Your muscles are tight," he said. His fingers were like magic and I gladly accepted the kneading action and began to relax.

The ooohs and aaahs I was uttering was my way of telling him how appreciative I was of him giving me a much needed massage. As I slumped backwards in the chair, Lamont took advantage of my relaxed state. His hands made circular movements, all the while wandering down my arms and easing into forbidden territory.

I slapped his right hand and started giggling. "What are you doing?"

"You're distracting me."

My voice was husky. "No I'm not. You're the one

creating the distraction."

Lamont stopped and moved away from me. I turned and gazed into his eyes and said sweetly, "What about getting into the hot tub?"

Lamont needed no bribery. "What are we waiting for?"

The temperature of the water was calming and gradually it reduced the tension in my body. After we got out of the hot tub, we decided to watch a television program. Since neither one of us were interested in the program, we turned off the television and went to bed.

The next day, I stated, "Let's go to the movies."

"That's fine with me, but...I thought you wanted to finish putting everything together for the book?"

My voice was snippy. "I do, but you know I'm not that disciplined and I want to get away. I need...no we both need a break."

"What movie do you want to see?"

"Something that's not too heavy."

"What about the Bucket List?"

I groaned. "Isn't that a tear jerker?"

Lamont shook his head. "I don't think so."

How did I explain that I wanted to see something that would lift my spirits, not bring them down? I had reservations, but Lamont began quoting the critic reviews and how much I would enjoy it, so I relented.

During the movie, I had shed tears, but yet my emotions were filled with a happy sadness.

Hand in hand, we walked out of the theater. When we reached the sidewalk Lamont could no longer wait. "What did you think?"

"I liked it. What about you?"

"I enjoyed it." I paused and added, "If you think about it, we've always had a bucket list, but didn't know it." We laughed.

Lamont was right. Our list included specific goals as well as places we wanted to visit.

For the next several weeks, we didn't work on the book, not because Lamont didn't want to—it was me. I wasn't in the mood. Not to mention the telephone calls were beginning to make me question all over again whether or not the book should be written. I knew my reasons, but I had no idea why this other person didn't want the book written.

Lamont didn't pressure me, but I could tell he was anxious to continue. Rather than ask me, he tip-toped around the subject. My reaction was to ignore his hints.

Although Lamont never voiced it, I think he was wondering how I ever produced any books. Days turned into weeks and the only reason I turned on the computer was to retrieve, read, respond, forward, or delete my email messages.

What Lamont didn't understand was that writing had to come naturally. Creativity could not be forced.

One morning, rather than skate around the issue, he asked, "Do you have writer's block?"

"No." I know he wanted me to say more, but it was difficult to put into words my reasons for not wanting to write. My lack of interest had nothing to do with the book, but more about my style. Poor Lamont, all he wanted was an explanation and all I gave him was a blank stare.

"What are we doing today?" Patiently, he sat, waiting for my answer.

Taking my time to respond, I took a deep breath and dug deep to muster up the sweetest voice possible.

"I think I'm going to vegetate, maybe read a book, do a few cross word puzzles, or watch television." My tone was not very pleasant when I added, "Why don't you shoot pool, go to the golf range or maybe do one of those projects you've been putting off?"

Lamont opened his mouth, but closed it. With disappointment and saddened eyes, he left me alone.

CHAPTER 33

I was lounging on the sofa when Lamont walked into the den and handed me the mail. I reached for the envelopes and a magazine. One envelope was an advertisement for a credit card application. After tearing it up I looked at the other envelope. I thought it was strange that there was no return address.

Opening it, I took out the folded letter. It resembled the type of ransom note you see in movies or on television. Magazine and newspaper clippings had been pasted on a single sheet of paper revealing a message. The awkwardly arranged sentences were clear—"Why do you want to write a book about Connellsville? If you do, you may regret it."

Before saying anything to Lamont, I re-read the message. I tried to remain calm. "Lamont, take a look at this." I handed him the letter.

I watched him as he read it. He shook his head. "This is getting out of hand and now you've been threatened."

Without warning, Lamont jumped up and left the room. When he returned, he had placed the letter inside a plastic freezer bag.

My lips were turned inward, trying hard to hold back the laughter. Lamont's solemn face let me know that he was not amused.

"This may seem a little dramatic, but I've watched enough CSI TV programs to know that this may preserve any fingerprints that might be on it."

With hesitation I asked, "So, you're thinking about taking this to the police?"

Lamont didn't hesitate with his response. "Yes! This is the type of evidence we need to show that someone is threatening you."

"Uh...let's rethink this before we go to the police."

Lamont was adamant. "No. Let's go."

We drove to the Sumter County police station. When we entered the station, Lamont walked with a purpose as he approached the police officer sitting at the desk near the entrance.

"Hello. My name is Lamont Harris and this is my wife, Lorraine. She's been receiving telephone calls, warning her not to write a book about her home town and today she received this."

Lamont handed the officer the plastic bag. The officer reached for the bag and looked at it. From the officer's turned up lips, I could tell he was close to letting out a chuckle.

With narrowed eyes, Lamont said, "I thought if there were any fingerprints on the letter...."

The officer interrupted Lamont. "Mr. Harris I'm sure the telephone calls are annoying, but...."

He looked from Lamont to me and continued. "What I'm trying to say is that there's nothing we can do. If there are any fingerprints on the letter, you might have already comprised them. Furthermore, if this person has never committed a crime, the finger prints would not be in our database. To be honest, I think this person is harmless. You and your wife don't have anything to fear."

Lamont talked through gritted teeth. "You might be right, but what can we do to make sure nothing happens?"

"Do you have caller ID?"

"Yes, but the caller is using a blocking device, preventing us from obtaining the name and telephone number. I also hit star 69 after the caller hung up and nothing happened."

"Well, outside of that there isn't much more you can do."

Disappointed, Lamont continued to pursue the issue. He grabbed my hand and we left. I didn't voice my opinion, but I wasn't surprised at the officer's response. The bottom line was that no crime had been committed. At least the complaint was on record in the event something should happen to one of us.

When we were in the car, Lamont exploded. "What's wrong with the police? The letter is a threat. Maybe it's time to buy a gun."

"Wait a minute. Our complaint is formally on record along with one piece of evidence. Before we do anything hasty, we need to build our case."

"I disagree." Lamont was angry. "Since the police won't take this matter seriously I'll take matters into my own hands."

"Lamont, please calm down. I understand the officer's position. They have more pressing matters requiring their attention. Our complaint doesn't begin to compare to murder, theft, and assault."

Lamont ran his hand over his face. "I hear what you're saying, but I'm going to take steps to protect you, especially if the threats continue to escalate. My actions would be justified and within the Florida law."

CHAPTER 34

The room was dim. The Florida morning sunshine was not peeping through the bedroom blinds. Heavy raindrops were beating against the window. The left side of the bed was empty indicating that Lamont was already up. I climbed out of bed, put on my robe and strolled to the kitchen. Lamont was sitting at the table, drinking a cup of coffee, reading the newspaper.

He glanced up. "Good morning. How do you feel?"

"Good morning to you. I feel fine. Florida's liquid gold woke me up. Is it supposed to rain all day?"

"That's what the weather channel is predicting, but we know how much we can rely on that." Lamont raised an eyebrow. "Why? Is the rain going to spoil your plans for today?"

I thought, but didn't say, "A perfect day to stay inside and vegetate by reading or watching movies or talk shows." Instead I said what I thought he wanted to hear. "This might be the perfect day to work on the book."

Lamont's response was a gaped mouth with no words coming out. I could understand his surprise, after all, it had been weeks and this had been the first time I had mentioned anything about working on the book.

After we showered together and I was dressed, I asked before going to the kitchen, "What do you want for breakfast?"

"Since it's raining, I have an idea. Why don't we go to Katie Belle's for the breakfast buffet? It probably won't be crowded and I understand there is a large food selection and the price is under six dollars."

I shook my head. "Why don't I make you pancakes? That way I can stay on my gluten/wheat free diet and not worry about eating food that will make me sick for several days."

Lamont offered, "You can always order an omelet or eat fruit."

"You're right, but I don't trust their griddle being wheat free and I want more than fruit." I emphasized. "You know better than anyone that a mere teaspoon of flour or gluten will upset my stomach followed by diarrhea."

To end the conversation, I began pulling out the bacon rack and the two griddles to cook breakfast while Lamont pouted like a small child who couldn't have his or her way. After we finished eating, Lamont left the kitchen as I cleaned up. After putting the dishes away, I joined him in the den. He was busy skimming through the research binders and other folders.

I stood in the doorway, watching. I sat down and turned on the computer. While I waited for it to boot up, I watched Lamont rifle through the binder, removing several pages and placing them on the table. Once or twice, I glanced at him, thinking he was going to give me the papers, but instead he ignored me, continuing whatever he was doing. Rather than hurry him, I busied myself, inserting the scanned pictures in their appropriate chapters.

My back was throbbing; I had been sitting too long. I stood up and bent over, holding that position for a few minutes, hoping to alleviate some of the soreness. I went to the bathroom and then to the kitchen.

The phone rang. I picked it up. "Hello."

"I hope you're not writing that book. If you do...."

Before the voice continued, Lamont was on the extension. His voice was loud. "Who is this? Don't call here again." The hang up didn't come until Lamont finished his outburst. "Believe me you don't want to deal with me."

Carrying two glasses of iced tea, I returned to the den. I handed one to Lamont. "I'm sorry."

"Why are you sorry? The person who's calling should just tell you why he or she doesn't want you to write the book."

Why should we spend time and energy on a person who won't identify themselves? As I sat down and placed the glass on a coaster, I asked with reservation. "Have you decided how to continue?"

Lamont handed me a stack of papers. "I think so. Since the last chapter was about the educational system why not continue by discussing the African Americans that worked for the school."

"That just might work." I took the papers from him and flipped through them. "Let's see who we have."

Lamont asked, "Why not begin with the first African American hired to work in the school?"

"Ummm...I'm not sure I know who that was." Lamont chewed his lower lip before suggesting. "If that's the case then put the jobs in alphabetical order."

"That a good idea." I paused. "Wait a minute, now that I think about it, I bet the Athletic Trainer was the first black hired by the school."

"He was black?"

I tried not to sound annoyed. "Yes."

"That's pretty unusual."

"If I remember correctly, he began working for the school after he gave up his boxing career. So, he might have become the Athletic Trainer as far back as the late 1930's."

"Who was this man?"

"His name was Billy Carter. I don't think Connellsville has had another black Athletic Trainer since he retired."

"Wow that is impressive. Okay, what's the next job?"

"I guess the cafeteria staff."

Lamont snickered. "Don't tell me!" He raised his hand and said, "Let me guess. The cafeteria workers were all black."

"Why would you say that and why is it funny?"

"I'm sorry. It's just that from my experience is was common to have blacks working in the cafeteria."

"Well, that wasn't the case at my high school. When I was in school we had one black cafeteria worker"

"Okay, who was this person?"

Before answering Lamont, I made sure I had her picture. "Her name is Gladys Cole. She was probably the first African American hired as the high school cafeteria cook. Her career started in the early 1950's until she retired."

Gladys Cole

The photographer unknown, photograph courtesy of the 1955 Connellsville High School Yearbook.

"I can't believe there weren't other black cafeteria workers."

I challenged him. "How many black people worked in your school cafeteria?"

"That's not the issue. I'm just surprised there weren't more."

"Well, in the 1970's, there were other blacks

working in various cafeteria positions."

Lamont asked, "Do you know who they were?"

"I'm not sure who gave me this information, but I have a paper titled, Connellsville High School Cafeteria Staff. The employees were: Ida Alsop, Betty Gales, and one other person, L. Taylor. I don't have a first name for L. Taylor."

Lamont suggested, "You should find out who L. Taylor is?"

"I'll make a note of it."

"Is there anyone else on that paper?"

I combed over the paper carefully. "There aren't any more cafeteria workers, but George Furman worked on the high school custodian staff."

"Okay, if that's it, let's move on." Lamont tilted his head and asked, "Is a Crossing Guard a part of the school staff?"

"I don't know, but it won't hurt to include it in this chapter." Lamont handed me a picture with the name of Sally (Henderson) Overton.

Sally (Henderson) Overton

The photographer unknown, photograph courtesy of the 1945 Connellsville High School Yearbook.

Lamont added, "I noticed she graduated in the Class of 1945. Were there other black crossing guards?"

"I don't know, but I think she was the first black and female school crossing guard. When I was in elementary school, I think her assignment was on the West Side of town. That means she was a Crossing Guard in the 50's."

Lamont was ignoring me as he blurted out, "Uh…In 1998, Maxine Wormack was the first African American who worked as a secretary for the Connellsville School Board."

My voice was unyielding. "If we're doing this by alphabetical order, then this is out of order."

Lamont was huffy. "Fine." He rubbed his chin thoughtfully and blurted out. "Teachers, did you have any African American teachers?"

"Yes, but it's a matter of who was the first documented African American teacher."

Lamont's mouth flew opened. Before he could make a comment I cut him off. "I'm giving you a straight answer. Miss Elsie told me that in the early 1900's Pauline Johnson was a Connellsville teacher."

"So, she was the first?"

"Yes, but unofficially. I couldn't find any documentation to support the Webster genealogy."

CHAPTER 35

Lamont shrugged. Before he could ask me again about the black teachers, I handed him a picture.

"She's really pretty. Who is she?"

Jane McPherson

The photographer unknown, photograph courtesy from Jane McPherson's Obituary provided by Roy Taylor.

"Jane McPherson. She graduated from Connellsville's High School and was the first official African American teacher hired by Connellsville and Fayette County." I stopped and read over her bio. By

Lamont's standards, it was too long and I would have to cut it down.

"What are you doing?"

"I'm reviewing her bio, trying to shorten it, but making sure I retain the important highlights of her life. She graduated from West Virginia State College with a Bachelor of Science in Education and a Masters' Degree in Education from West Virginia University. She taught English in Logan, West Virginia, Leakesville, North Carolina, Fairmont and Farmington, West Virginia. In 1976, she retired from the Connellsville High School."

"You didn't say when she taught at Connellsville's High School."

"The obituary doesn't say, but it had to have been in the 1960's."

"Is there anything else significant about her that should be mentioned?"

Pulling in my lower lip, I pondered over something that might be worth mentioning. "Uh…this isn't about Mrs. McPherson, but it may be something people would find interesting."

"What is it?"

"Well, Connellsville's NAACP might have been responsible for her being hired."

"Wait a minute! You mean Connellsville had a National Association for the Advancement of Colored People (NAACP). You've got my attention. Why was it needed?"

"Everything wasn't as equal as you might think. It's

my understanding that Charles Payton organized Connellsville's first chapter and the primary concern was equal employment opportunities."

Lamont shook his head. "This is certainly a shock. He stopped and then proceeded. "I bet if I had asked you whether segregation or racism existed in your town, you would have said, there was none."

"You're probably right. When talking to my parents and other older blacks about racism, they stated that the racial divide was subtle. Knowing what I know now, I believe racism did probably rear its ugly head from time to time. For example, do you remember a man named, Leon Hunter?"

"I don't remember him."

I tried jogging his memory. "We were in the Uniontown Kmart. Leon stopped us and shared the story about my dad and uncle."

"I think I might remember, but tell me the story again."

"The story went something like this,

Leon was a Boy Scout. The Scout Leaders were my dad and Uncle, James Scott. The Boy Scout Troop wanted to swim in Connellsville's YMCA indoor pool. However, the boys were not allowed in the pool because they were colored. Not to disappoint them, my dad and uncle drove the troop thirty-five miles where they could swim in an indoor pool.

Leon said he would always be grateful to my dad and uncle for that memory and experience."

"Oh, I remember now."

"As you can see, there were some instances of prejudice in my town. As I think about it, this isn't the only example of discrimination."

"I would like to hear about these stories you're referring to." Lamont threw up his hands in defense. "Before you get bent out of shape I'm saying that if you're going to tell the story, tell the good, the bad, and the ugly. That way, people will get a true sense of the town."

"You're probably right, Sweetie, but I can only speak about the stories I know about or can remember."

CHAPTER 36

"Please hand me that folder marked Payne A.M.E." Reverend Aquanette Osborne gave me a picture I was trying to find. After going through the binder, I found what I was looking for and gave it to Lamont, but said nothing.

"Is this what I think it is?"

FIRST BLACK GIRL SCOUT TROOP
The photographer unknown, photograph courtesy of Payne A.M.E. Minister, Acqanette Osborne.

"Yes, an all-black Girl Scout Troop. The difference

between the Boys and Girls Scout Troops was that the girls' black and white troops used the same facility for their meetings. The scout meeting place was held in what was known as the Little White House."

I picked up a picture labeled The Little White House. I made a face when I looked at the old meeting place. I gave it to Lamont and said, "Here's a picture you took of the Little White House."

WHITE HOUSE

The photographer Lamont C. Harris, photograph courtesy of Lorraine M. Harris private collection.

"What do you mean? Let me see that picture?" Lamont turned his nose up. "This doesn't look like something I would have taken. This seems more like your handy work."

Although I didn't say it I was sure he had taken the picture. Rather than argue about it, I said, "Let's stay focused."

"I suggest you take another picture of this house." Lamont hesitated, "Does the house still exist?"

I thought but didn't say, "This time I will take the picture."

"To answer your question, yes, the house is still standing, but the Girl Scout Troops no longer use it for their meetings."

Lamont had gone back to looking closely at the Girl Scout picture and asked, "Are you in this picture?"

"No." I pointed. "There's my sister Patty in the front row, my cousin, Roberta Scott Thomas is in the second row and my sister Doris is in the third row."

Lamont asked, "Since the troop met in the White House, does that mean the leaders were white?"

"Oh no. We had black leaders. Naomi (Taylor) Wright and Anna Harrison started the first black Girl Scout Troop. Other Scout Leaders were: Josephine Carpenter, Kathleen Walker, Shanana Gales, Bertha Payton, and Bertha Woods.

"I find this odd. Your hometown seemed like an ideal place where differences did not matter, but yet...." Lamont's voice trailed off.

"I agree especially since all the troops, black and white, had their annual awards ceremony for receiving badges together." I paused and continued, "The other odd thing was that when my sisters Patty and Nancy and my cousin Roberta and I went to Girl Scout Camp, it was integrated."

"You're right, that doesn't make sense. Are the troops still separate?"

"No."

"Are there other examples like this that you want to talk about?"

"Listen, there are probably many situations, but I'm not aware of them all because I never gave it much thought until now."

"You're being defensive. All I want is for you to talk about what most towns faced regarding segregation and integration. I know the subject is sensitive, but you need to talk about it."

"It's not the sensitivity of the subject, but I feel as if you're trying to make me remember things that may or may not have happened."

"No, I'm not. I just want you to reveal everything." Lamont threw his hands up. "That's all I'm trying to do."

"Fine." I took a deep breath. "Do you remember John

Regis Taylor? He graduated with me." I didn't wait for Lamont to acknowledge me. "Anyway, he told me a story about the Crawford Tea Room."

"Is this a restaurant and is it still there today?"

"It was a restaurant, but it went out of business. Now, can I tell the story?"

Lamont waved me on.

"This may not be completely accurate, but it's close.

The Crawford Tea Room was located near the Library. John used to shine shoes nearby. He said one of the local African American ministers went into the tea room and ordered lunch, but was refused service. He was told that the only way he could eat was to go to the back door. John thought this was strange because the cook was black.

That's it."

Lamont started laughing.

"What's so funny?"

"I was thinking about what John Regis said. Back in the day, it wasn't unusual to have blacks cooking for establishments that didn't allow us to each in them. What struck me funny was when I cooked for Marriott and if my people weren't allowed to sit down to eat, well...." Without Lamont finishing his statement I could imagine what was going through his mind.

"Okay, this is the last example I'm aware of and then let's get back to the primary purpose of the book. My dad, Cornelius Mockabee, tells a story about the local cemetery."

"Is it the only cemetery in town?"

"To be honest this cemetery really isn't located in Connellsville. Ummm…now that I think about it, most of Connellsville's cemeteries are church owned. All other cemeteries are on the outskirts of town. Why do you ask?"

"I wanted to know, if there was a black cemetery?

"Not that I'm aware of. Blacks and whites were buried in the same cemeteries and they were not put in separate sections."

"I didn't mean to interrupt you, but I wanted a clarification. Because in D.C., there were all black cemeteries. I'm sorry, go ahead and tell your dad's story.

"Okay, this is about the Green Ridge Memorial Park Cemetery.

My dad was upset that blacks could not be buried in the beautiful Green Ridge Memorial Park Cemetery. What makes it so special is the picturesque, hilly, flowing greenery and there are no above ground headstones. Anyway, one day dad stopped by the cemetery office and discussed his concern with the owner."

"Good for your dad."

"If you keep interrupting me, I'll never finish the story?" Before, I could continue the phone started ringing. I watched as Lamont answered. The mystery calls had increased to at least one call a day.

Since Lamont wasn't talking and he was not giving me the phone, I knew it was our *"mystery caller."*

Lamont put the phone in the cradle and didn't say anything. "Go ahead and continue."

"Let's see. Where was I? Oh yeah.

Daddy asked the owner if there was a reason why no one colored was buried in the cemetery. The owner's answer was a shrug. My dad asked if he could buy two cemetery plots. The owner said, "Of course," and Daddy did.

That ended the segregation of the Green Ridge Memorial Park Cemetery."

Lamont shook his head. "I don't call that an example of segregation. It seems to me that the blacks assumed the owner wouldn't sell plots to them. The truth was no one ever asked."

In an offended voice, I responded. "You know what? We're finished with this discussion. You were surprised to hear that segregation existed in Connellsville and I shared what I knew, but yet…" I stopped. A memory flashed before me.

"What's wrong?"

CHAPTER 37

Until Lamont brought up the questions about Connellsville's segregation, I never thought about it. But now that Lamont jogged my memory, I was recalling specific situations to talk about. Perhaps I didn't remember because they didn't seem relevant or they had no effect on my overall life. As Lamont pointed out, it is important to tell all facets of the town.

However, I didn't want to write another book filled with stories of struggle, bitterness, or hatred. If I write the book, the focus would be one of hope, telling how people with differences were able to live, work, and socialize together.

Lamont stood up and put his arms around me. "Come on, give me a kiss. I didn't mean to stir up bad memories or to upset you."

Gently, I pulled away. "I'm not upset and these aren't bad memories. It's just that this is the first time I've talked about segregation or racism in Connellsville. Maybe, the subtly wasn't worth addressing, similar to a painful family problem—you ignore it, hoping it will go away or that it doesn't interfere with your life.

Lamont tried to comfort me. "Listen, the few instances you've shared may have had an impact on some, but in my opinion I would say many African Americans in other cities would have gladly traded what you all experienced. I can only speak for me, but I know how skin color played an important role in denying people jobs, housing, education, and Lord knows what else."

Hearing what Lamont said was probably true, but it still remains that my hometown *did* have elements of segregation and racism. Why was I reluctant to talk about it? It wasn't a secret. Perhaps, it wasn't something that was present every day and, therefore, I chose only to discuss the good qualities about Connellsville. But, the subject had staggered me and now I was mulling over it.

"Lorraine, Lorraine. Are you okay?"
I glanced up. I took a deep breath and swiped at a falling tear. "If you're looking for an example of real segregation and racism, well I have one."

Lamont sat up in his chair, leaning forward, as if he didn't want to miss a single word I was about to utter.

"As you know, no city, small or large, is immune from having men and women serve in the armed forces. Connellsville was no different...." I paused and cleared my throat. "When the African American Veterans returned home, they met the same segregation and racism they had experienced while serving their country."

"I'm not following you."

"First of all, Connellsville had an African American

male who fought for this country as far back as the Civil War." I threw my hand up to stop Lamont from disrupting me.

"His name was John (Wash) Johnson, a slave. Along with other slaves, he was captured by Company H, 5th Calvary, Massachusetts Volunteers. Wash was made an orderly to the Colonel of that unit."

Lamont raised his right eyebrow and inquired, "Is there a point regarding the information you're sharing?"

I threw him a hard look. "If you'll be patient I'm getting there."

Under his breath, I heard him say, "I hope she's not going around the barn just to tell a story that has nothing to do with segregation."

CHAPTER 38

Instead of defending what I was leading up to, I continued as if I had not heard what Lamont said. "I mention John (Wash) Johnson so I can talk about some of the significant men and women who served in the military. Then, you'll appreciate why I was appalled at my discovery."

"Okay, I'm listening." He waved his hand in front of him. "The floor is yours."

I rolled my eyes, knowing it would be difficult for him to remain quiet. Then, instead of him paying attention to me, I noticed he was reading something.

Instead of continuing, I stopped and asked, "What are you so engrossed in?"

"I think maybe this goes along with what you might be talking about." His eyes sparkled. "You have to include this."

As I looked at it, I screamed. "I don't remember obtaining this information. I can't believe it, a Tuskegee Airman."

Lamont said, "It is pretty amazing knowing that a Tuskegee Airman came from your hometown."

I corrected him. "Actually, he was born and raised in Trotter and now it's considered Connellsville."

"I don't know the difference and neither will anyone else." Annoyed, Lamont scoffed, "What's the big deal?"

Irritation filled my voice when I responded. "It's important because I want as much accuracy as possible, besides you have no clue how sensitive people can be about something that simple."

"You're probably right. I'm not from a small town and couldn't possibly understand." He lifted his eyebrows and his face lit up. "However, everyone will take pride in knowing there was a Tuskegee Airmen from the Connellsville area."

"You're right."

"Now that we've cleared that up, don't write anything else about this man until a brief background is given about the Tuskegee Airmen."

My voice had a southern twang as I placed my hand to my chest. "You want little old me to include background information, but keep it brief."

"Don't be a smarty pants. Everyone should know about the Tuskegee Airmen, but you shouldn't assume that everyone does."

I quit typing, clicked the mouse on the Internet icon and waited. Using Google, I brought up the Tuskegee

Airmen Website. Lamont stood up and began reading over my shoulder.

"The Tuskegee Airmen were America's first black military airmen. They came from all parts of the country with large numbers coming from New York City, Washington, Los Angeles, Chicago, Philadelphia and Detroit. Most of the men were college graduates or undergraduates trained as single-engine pilots and later twin-engine pilots, navigators, or bombardiers. Enlisted men trained as aircraft and engine mechanics, armament specialists, radio repairmen, parachute riggers, control tower operators, policemen, administrative clerks and all of the other skills necessary to function as an Army Air Corps flying squadron or ground support."

"Is that what you want me to include or is it too much?"

"Nah, that's good. Not too much, but yet enough. Make sure you mention there's a website and anyone wanting more information can do additional research."

I highlighted the portion, hit the print screen button, returned to Microsoft Word, and included the paragraph.

"Here's the Tuskegee Airman that needs scanning." Lamont added, "And, don't forget to put his name under the picture."

Sylvester Parris

The photographer unknown, photograph courtesy of the Parris family private collection.

"Thanks for reminding me." As I typed in Sylvester Parris's name, I thought about when I worked for the Department of Transportation, Federal Aviation Administration (FAA).

"Lamont, do you remember when I worked for the FAA, Office of Civil Rights?"

"Of course, why?"

"Do you remember how the office sponsored Black History Month Programs, celebrating and honoring outstanding blacks?"

Lamont's eyes were narrow as he grimaced at me, his

voice weary and forceful. "Lorraine, let's not do this. Just make your point." After shouting at me, he softened his voice and added, "Please."

My lower lip quivered as I continued, "Okay. One year, the program featured the Tuskegee Airmen and we tried locating men to share their stories and experiences while serving in World War II. During our search I wished I had known that there had been two Tuskegee Airmen from Trotter."

"There were two? Who was the other man?"

"Connell Reed and he served as an Airman."

Lamont added, "I'm glad you said that. Make sure you include the fact that Mr. Parris served in the Gunnery Division."

"Are there any other military men or women we should discuss before moving on?"

"I talked to Ted Davis who provided me with a list of all the black veterans, but there wasn't anything significant." I made a face. "And, I don't want another list of names. However, there are two women who served in the Air Force during World War II, Thelma Ward, an Air Force Pilot and Ida Bell Sledge."

Ida Bell Sledge

The photographer unknown, photograph courtesy of the Webster family private collection.

"If that's it, can I ask one question without you getting upset?" I listened as he asked his question. "Where is the example regarding segregation?"

I blew out a loud sigh before answering him. "I was getting to it when we got side tracked. Then when I was explaining information about the military and segregation...."

Lamont interrupted me. "Yes, everyone knows that during World War II, the military was segregated, but what does this have to do with Connellsville?"

"That's what I've been trying to tell you. Haven't you been following me?"

Lamont made a wry face at me and threw up his hands. He opened his mouth, but closed it and motioned me to continue.

"When my dad and other black veterans returned home, they could not join or even go into the VFW."

Lamont cocked his head to the side. "I've always

seen the VFW sign, but what does it stand for?"

"VFW is the Veterans of Foreign Wars. Blacks couldn't join the American Legion either."

"Lorraine, let's stick with the VFW."

"I am, but the point is both of these organizations were started to honor the dead and to help living Veterans."

"Okay, so what happened? And, did the Connellsville NAACP do anything?"

"I guess before the NAACP could address the issue, the black Veterans formed their own VFW and American Legion. What's sad is that both organizations are still separate today."

I waited for Lamont's reaction, but instead he stood up and pulled me up from the chair and gathered me in his arms. After he released me, he gazed into my misty eyes.

"Are you okay?"

"I'm fine. Let's continue." I sat back down. Lamont inquired. "Are you going to include this in the book?"

"Yes, I'll work it in some kind of way. To the naked eye, no one would know that the organizations are separate because the black and white VFWs perform certain rituals together, like parades and funerals."

"That's odd."

I agreed and asked, not expecting an answer. "Do you

think the national VFW was segregated at the time and therefore, it trickled down to the local level?"

Lamont pursed his lips and answered. "At the beginning that may have been true, but if that was the case why has Connellsville maintained the two separate VFW's?"

"That's a point and I don't have an answer."

"I wonder what explanation Vinnie might have regarding the whole idea of segregation and racism in Connellsville."

CHAPTER 39

With no answers to the VFW issue, I saw no reason to continue the conversation. I changed subjects. "Have you ever heard of the CCC Camps?"

"Not until your dad told me about them."

"Well, the CCC stood for the Civilian Conservation Corp. From 1933 to 1942, about 200,000 blacks served in the Pennsylvania unit. Although I'm talking about daddy's experience I'm sure there were other blacks from Connellsville that served in the corp."

"Sweetie, before you continue, was the CCC Camps, part of the military?"

"No."

"Then, why are we talking about it?"

"I'm not sure, but it wouldn't hurt."

Lamont shook his head and mouthed the words, "This should not be included in the book."

Instinctively, I started to argue, but changed my mind. Instead I began explaining, "The CCC Camps were segregated...."

"Okay, but where is this leading? Lorraine, you need to...."

I butted in. "Let me finish."

"Fine, please continue."

"My dad's troop was the Northern District with three camps located in Pennsylvania and Western Maryland."

Lamont let out a heavy sigh and gave me a long searching look. From his expression, he wasn't happy however, he let me ramble.

"Although the camp's primary jobs were in the state and national forests, the men were supposed to receive training for employment opportunities. When my dad graduated from the program, he joined the United States Army."

I handed Lamont a tattered book.

"This is my dad's graduating class book." From Lamont's close review, I could tell who he was looking for.

I pointed and said, "Daddy's in the last row, fifth man in from the left."

NORTHERN DISTRICT CIVILIAN CONSERVATION CORP

GRADUATING CLASS

The photographer unknown, the photograph was taken from the CCC Camp Graduating Book.

"I'm still not following your thinking regarding the CCC Camps."

"Although the camps weren't military my dad should have been prepared for serving in a segregated Army. From what I understand the camps were similar to serving in the military that were also segregated."

Quickly Lamont said, "I'm not seeing the relevance...." He didn't finish his sentence. He paused and continued in a soothing voice. "Honey, you have taken me on a long trip and back again and I'm still not sure of the point you're trying to make. I don' think you want to put information in the book that doesn't relate to your home town. I mean what is the message...."

He stopped and proceeded. "Never mind, can we move on?"

I glared at him and my voice was loud. "I understand what you're saying, but my point is that although the town was integrated, many of the men who served in a segregated Army, Navy, Marine, or Air Force might have experienced situations that were segregated before serving their country, such as the CCC Camps and therefore the military segregation wasn't that much of a shock to them."

Lamont's mouth fell open, but did not comment on what I had said. Instead he asked a totally unrelated question. "When we came out of the public library I noticed across the street, a building with the Masonic symbol on it. Is that where the black Masons met?"

"No. My dad, a Mason, and my mother, an Eastern Star, held their meetings in Uniontown. This is another example of the town's segregation."

"Well, that's not necessarily true. Masonic Orders have been segregated from the beginning because of issues too complicated to discuss right now. However, it's changing and many of the Masonic Orders are integrated.

CHAPTER 40

With the military chapter completed, I raised my hands toward the ceiling and stretched. Soreness had wormed its way into my shoulders. I rolled them forward and backwards, releasing the tension. As I relaxed, I licked my lips. Without warning, I had a strong sensation of wanting something sweet or salty to eat.

"I don't know about you, but I'm hungry. I think we deserve something that's not diet-restricted."

Lamont shot me a questioning look. "Certainly, you're not talking about eating something that isn't on your gluten/wheat free restriction."

"No. I just want something that would satisfy my craving, like popcorn or potato chips."

We walked to the kitchen. I washed my hands and opened the refrigerator. "What do you feel like eating?"

"Whatever you feel like cooking?"

"What about a grilled hamburger with homemade French fries?"

Instead of Lamont answering my question, he blurted out. "What about dessert? Do we have any cookies or ice cream?"

"I think so." I sighed. "I wish I could eat cookies. Oh well, I'll settle for the grease."

As I busied myself making lunch, we tossed around some ideas about what to include next. My mind drifted, thinking that for the most part, working with Lamont has gone smoothly and the book's organization was developing much better than I had expected. Without Lamont's love, support and encouragement, my notes would still be on the shelf, collecting dust.

Lamont interrupted my thoughts. "Is lunch ready yet?"

"Give me about ten more minutes."

"Do you want to eat on the lanai?"

"That's fine."

Lamont gathered the napkins and silverware while I put the finishing touches on the salad. By the time he had set the table and finished fixing our drinks, I was putting the food on a tray.

With the lanai enclosed in glass-like material, I thought how enjoyable it was eating outside especially when the weather was cool or rainy.

Taking a sip of cola, Lamont placed the glass on the table and turned towards me. "Well, what do you think about...." He stopped and didn't complete his sentence.

"I think we're making lots of progress. The work so far has given me a lot to consider when making the decision as to whether or not I'll write the book."

Lamont let my statement hang in the air for a few minutes. "Whatever you do, don't let the phone calls enter into your decision."

CHAPTER 41

The palm trees swayed as the rain pounded against the window. I took a minute to watch the downpour. The rain pellets were coming down fast and hard. What central Florida needed was a slow all-day rain to alleviate the brown grass and drooping flowers. As quickly as the rain had filled the sky, now the liquid gold was beginning to slow and soon the sun would shine.

Lunch was over and I returned to the den. I was unsure where Lamont had gone when suddenly he walked in the den.

"What's in the napkin?"

"I have a couple of oatmeal cookies. Do you want a piece of fruit or would you rather have some chips, or nuts?"

I shook my head. My craving was still nagging me. I blinked and prayed I would not snatch that cookie from Lamont's hand. I inhaled and exhaled. That was a mistake as the aroma of the oatmeal cookie filled my nostrils. *Concentrate Lorraine, the cookie is forbidden and besides it's only empty calories.*

With all the strength I could muster I said, "This may be a good time to talk about Connellsville's employment."

I should have known Lamont had something else on his mind. "What about housing?"

"What about it?"

"Could blacks live anywhere in town?"

"Why wouldn't they? If you're asking, did we all live in the same area? The answer is no. We did not live on one side of the tracks and whites on the other side."

I paused and shared with Lamont my discovery. "You remember my friend, Judith? Well, my eyes were opened when she told me that many Pennsylvania small towns did not always rent or sell to blacks. Judith used to work for the State and investigated claims of housing discrimination."

I took a sip of iced tea before continuing. "I was stunned to learn that a town twelve miles from Connellsville had housing discrimination cases. What stunned me was that this town, Uniontown, had been the pathway to the freedom of slaves." I passed Lamont a picture showing a plague that stands in Uniontown regarding the Underground Railroad.

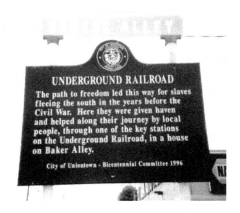

Lamont Harris was the photographer. The photo was taken from the Harris private collection.

Lamont wanted to know. "Did she say anything about Connellsville?"

"No."

"Then why are we having this conversation?"

I was aggravated and made no attempt to mask it. "You must be tired. Maybe we should quit. Besides, it's near dinner time and I should start cooking."

"That's fine with me. What are you cooking?"

"I thought I'd grill the fish I took out."

"I want mine fried."

I thought, but didn't say, "Didn't you have enough fried foods for one day?" Lamont didn't have my weight and cholesterol issues. Despite his snacking habits and eating ice cream almost every night, he was in excellent health for a man his age. I envied him. Over the years, his six feet tall, slender build and weight had basically remained constant.

I thought Lamont had followed me into the kitchen, but he had stayed behind in the den. I guess he was organizing the mess of papers scattered throughout or maybe he wanted some distance between us.

Before I could call Lamont for dinner I smelled the fragrance of his cologne as he stood behind me. Embracing me tightly, he snuggled my neck, followed by a kiss. In a low and husky voice, he spoke. "What's cooking, good looking?"

I giggled. He turned me around and kissed me deeply. After his release, we sat down at the table. Dinner conversation was about the weather, upcoming commitments, and our daughters. We avoided any talk about the book.

I suggested, "Why don't we quit for the day?"

Lamont agreed. "Let me remind you that if we stop now, we'll be putting it on the back burner for several days because we both have tee times, luncheons, and dinner invitations."

CHAPTER 42

Two days of not working on the book had turned into a week. Retirement life in The Villages can consume every waking moment of your time if you make too many commitments.

The entire week was crazy! Monday morning, we bowled; in the afternoon, I had Bible study, followed by playing cards. Tuesday, both of us had morning tee times and that evening I played cards again. Wednesday morning we rested. Later that evening we attended the weekly church dinner and Bible study. Somehow we had overbooked on Thursday and because of it, we would attend two parties. The week ended with dinner on Friday with friends; Saturday morning we bowled with the African American Club, had lunch, and attended church.

In reality, we were overloaded with social activities, but the interruptions were probably needed. When I thought about the last time we worked on the book, I recalled how often I had sunken my teeth into my tongue, keeping hurtful words from spilling out. The real indicator for a much needed break was when I had bitten down too hard and tasted blood in my mouth. From time to time, I tried reminding myself how working on projects with your spouse wasn't always such a good idea.

While watching The View, Lamont sauntered into the den and asked, "Are you ready...." He stopped when I raised my finger to my lips, attempting to silence him. I had not succeeded. "You made me miss what Barbara Walters was saying."

"I'm sorry. I was curious about...." Lamont let his words drift off and tried again. "I wondered if we were going to continue our work."

"Not now." I snapped. "I'm watching The View. Maybe after it goes off and we have lunch. Better yet, we should do some yard work."

"What?"

"Don't be surprised. The weeds need pulling. Have you noticed them lately? If we're not careful, one of our neighbors might report us."

Sarcastically, Lamont said, "Yeah, that's what happens when you let blacks move into the neighborhood."

"That's real funny."

"I wasn't joking. There are some people who still think like that. You forget many of these white folks, your neighbors and church friends, have never lived, worked, or socialized with blacks. In many cases, this is a new experience for them."

I shrugged. "Thanks for the explanation, but that has nothing to do with the weeds taking over the yard."

"Fine, we'll pull weeds. If I didn't know better, I would think you had given up working on the book."

"You forget I'm the one who takes care of the yard. If you want my full attention on writing, then I can't have yard work on my mind."

Defensively, Lamont raised his hands. "Okay, I give up. Let's go."

"You mean, now! It's the middle of the day. We'll have a heat stroke?"

He left the room, shaking his head. After lunch, Lamont took a nap and I finished reading the book I started several days ago.

Later that evening when the sun was no longer bright and a slight breeze filled the air, we pulled weeds.

"We have three full bags. Didn't I tell you the weeds needed pulling?"

Stepping back with my hands on my hips, I admired the yard. I didn't know about Lamont, but after three hours of bending, kneeling, stretching, and pulling, all my body muscles and joints ached. Three times a week I exercised, but yet the yard work made me question my routine of lifting weights and walking three miles.

Lamont was quiet and hadn't answered me. I watched as he put the last bag near the curb for pickup.

I whined. "Can we hire someone to pull weeds?"

"We can, but why? We did a good job pulling the weeds."

Inwardly, I screamed, "Yeah, but only after nagging and he seemed not to notice the overgrown weeds that needed pulling."

After we showered, we welcomed the hot tub. Our conversation focused on the weather, our trip up North, and the latest Villages' news. From Lamont's startup and stopping sentences, I knew he wanted to resume our work. The problem was I wasn't in the mood and my only thoughts were on watching, the TV show, "Deal or No Deal."

Although Lamont had been staying up beyond his usual nine o'clock bedtime to work on the book, I knew tonight he would not make it beyond eight-thirty. The manual labor had worn him out. As he handed me the remote control, he pushed the chair back in the reclining position. Within minutes, I watched his head bob downward to the side and backward.

As I watched television, I turned up the volume. Lamont's snoring was drowning out the sound. I shook his arm. "Lamont, Lamont!"

He seemed dazed. His eyes were unfocused as he looked at me. Annoyed, he asked, "What?"

"Why don't you go to bed?"

"I'm not sleeping. I'm watching television."

"Sure you are."

With a loud slam, the recliner returned to its down position, Lamont stood up and sulked off to the bedroom.

CHAPTER 43

When the program ended, I turned off the television and walked to the den. When I put my finger on the computer's turn-on button, the telephone rang. As much as I had begun hating to answer the phone, I picked it up before the second ring, not wanting to disturb Lamont.

Cautiously, I answered. "Hello."

"Hi." My breathing eased. It was Nicole, our eldest daughter who lives in the Washington, D.C. area.

"Hey. Are you okay?"

We had not mentioned the calls to the girls, not wanting to worry them. "I'm fine."

"What are you doing?"

"I was in the process of turning the computer on, why? What's up?"

"Nothing much, but I was thinking about you while watching Deal or No Deal." She paused and chuckled. "Did you see that last contestant? Why didn't the woman take the $425,000?" Nicole answered her own question. "Because she knew the million dollars was in her case. And what did she get? What she deserved--$75."

We both laughed. "I don't know why I keep watching that show. All it does is raise my blood pressure. I scream at the TV as if the person can hear me."

"Mom, I know what you mean."

"Have you talked to Baby Girl today?" Baby Girl is our younger daughter, Natalie, who lives in Chicago.

"We talked earlier in the day. She's fine. You said you were about to turn on the computer. What are you working on?"

I hesitated. "I'm working on the Connellsville book."

"Not that again."

"This time, your dad is helping me."

Nicole laughed. "How long have you been working on that book?"

"I don't know, five, six...." I stopped. I didn't want to have this conversation. I paused and let silence invade the phone.

"Mom, are you there? What's wrong?"

"Nothing, it's just that I'll be glad when we finish putting the book together."

"I bet you will be, but...." Nicole stopped. "When did you decide to write it?"

I emphasized each word. "I haven't decided. When I refer to the book I'm talking about organizing the research." I paused and added, "At least your dad has been encouraging. I must admit, he's been extremely helpful with arranging the material. He's had some good ideas and I can see the project ending."

"That's good. I'm glad you're telling the story. Connellsville is different. As a kid, it reminded me of Mayberry, U.S.A." She laughed.

"I'm not going there."

"You wouldn't because daddy, Natalie, and I know there's Connellsville and then the rest of the world. It's very similar to you and dad living in The Villages."

"Please."

"Come on mom. Sometimes you're naïve when it comes to…." She stopped and added, "Things like people and reality, especially when it comes to African Americans. Sometimes you don't get it."

"That's not true."

Nicole grunted. "I'm not going to argue the point. Overall, you have difficulty admitting and recognizing that you grew up in a town where you were privileged in comparison to other African Americans and their experiences."

Silence filled the telephone line. Then she added, "You had an equal playing field and that's all you know. You have little patience when it comes to the possibility of people having prejudices that might have caused another person's failure."

I wanted to protest loudly. Instead I heard myself say, "I'll agree that every African American has a different story. Each of us faced different life experiences, as well as prejudices."

"Mom, you may not know it, but sometimes you forget and I guess that's what I'm trying to say."

"You're right. I'm a product of my environment. I must admit that organizing the material for a possible Connellsville book has given me a different perspective regarding one's environment and exposure. Both factors can certainly impact education, housing, and one's overall life."

Loudly, I yawned. "It's getting late and I'm going to bed."

"Okay. Goodnight mom. I love you."

"I love you, too. I'll talk to you soon."

When I hung up the phone, I pushed the start-up button and turned on the computer. Waiting for the screen to come alive, I glanced at the clock and decided the hour was late. The conversation with Nicole had taken a toll on me. I was tired. When the computer was fully booted, I turned it off and went to bed.

Before my head reached the pillow, I was asleep. The warmth from the sun made me realize morning had arrived and it was probably time to get up. Before I could reach over in the bed to feel if Lamont was there, he was crawling under the covers. I cuddled up next to him.

"You're cold."

"I went for a morning walk and it's chilly out."

"What time is it?"

"It's a little after seven o'clock."

I groaned and turned my back to him. He nudged up behind me and whispered, "You need to get up. You have an eight-thirty doctor's appointment for lab work."

I groaned, "I forgot. I wish I could stay in bed."

Lamont's hand massaged my leg in a circular motion. "Why? Do you have something else in mind?" I put my hand on his, stopping the movement.

Lamont's voice was husky. "We have time before you get up." In reality we didn't, but his strokes and kisses delayed us from getting up.

A quick glance at the clock told me that the shower would be short if I was to make my appointment on time. While we were dressing, Lamont decided he would go with me.

After my blood had been drawn, I walked back to the reception area. I paused for a moment as I watched Lamont talking to Vinnie and Dot.

Before I reached them, Vinnie spotted me and in a loud voice asked, "How's that book coming along?"

"Hi Vinnie." Vinnie stood up and asked, "How far along are you with the book?"

"I'm not at the writing stage. I'm just organizing the material."

Vinnie's facial expression seemed confused by my answer. Before Vinnie could say anything else, the nurse called out his name. Dot was standing close beside Vinnie and nudged him toward the nurse and didn't bother to say good-bye.

In a way I was glad the conversation had ended because my stomach was growling. I had not eaten since midnight. Lamont and I left the doctor's office and stopped for breakfast at the Glenview Country Club.

CHAPTER 44

When we returned home, I went into the den. I had to step over the papers that cluttered the floor. As I glanced around, it appeared messier than I had remembered. Besides the floor, papers were everywhere—on the desk, sofa, printer, and in the chair where I was about to sit down. I picked them up and turned on the computer.

"I don't remember leaving this room like this last night."

Guilt filled Lamont's face as he heard what I said when he walked into the den. "While waiting for daybreak this morning, I was sorting through some of the employment information, putting it into some sort of order." He shrugged. "I thought it would help speed up our discussions."

I surveyed the room, allowing my face to adopt an encouraging expression, but in reality thought, "If this is organized what is disorganized?"

"Did you say everything was ready for discussion?"

"Yes and no. I browsed through the notes marked employment and we need to discuss a few things before going forward."

My curiosity was piqued. "What did you find interesting that requires clarification?"

"There's an article about the Lions Club." He raised an eyebrow. "This could be another example of segregation and racism."

I frowned. "Okay, let me hear it."

Lamont continued. "According to this article...." Lamont stopped. "First of all, do you know anything about the Lions Club?"

"Not really. Since I don't know about it, I'm sure there are others who won't either. Let's include a brief description."

"Uh…that's probably a good idea." Lamont paused. "I've already been on the Internet and printed off a short description." He read it aloud.

"The Lions Club is an international organization and the world's largest service club with approximately 1.3 million members with a...." He glimpsed at me before continuing. *"I guess you don't want all the statistics, but this organization is huge and they do a lot for the blind and visually impaired."*

"I didn't know you were so passionate about the Lions Club."

"You forget my dad was blind. They have been around since the 1900's."

"Okay, but what does this have to do with Connellsville?"

"In Connellsville, I think the Lions Club might have been segregated."

I was annoyed. "Didn't you say the club started in the 1900's?"

Lamont exhaled. "Yes, but what's your point?"

"I'm not defending Connellsville, but during that time the national headquarters was probably segregated."

"That may be true, but I know that the Lions Club isn't segregated now. I believe this could be in the same category as the VFW and the American Legion being segregated even today."

"You're right, but I don't know that the Lions Club is still segregated."

"I suggest you checked it out."

"I will. Are any of the members listed? If so, who are they?"

"Uh...Let me see." Lamont skimmed over a paper he picked up. "Here they are: Irene DiNaci, Elsie Haley, Dorothy Jones, Evelyn Ridgely, Roxanne Ridgley, Ted Davis, Charles Wright, and Otis West."

"I'll call my mom later and ask what she knows about it. Now, let's start the employment chapter?"

From Lamont's expression, he wasn't finished. "Ted Davis was given the Melvin Fellow Award."

"What is that?"

"It's a Lion's Club award usually awarded in recognition of a commitment to humanitarian work."

I watched Lamont skim over the paper he was holding. He continued, "The fellowship award is the highest honor and represents humanitarian qualities for generosity, compassion, and concern for the less fortunate. In addition, the recipients receive a lapel pin and a personalized wall plaque in honor of their commitment of helping others."

"Wow. What an honor. Is that it?"

"Well, Charles Wright was the Lion's Club District Governor."

I responded and commented. "Maybe Connellsville's Lion's Club wasn't segregated."

Lamont shrugged. "Make sure you check it out." He rubbed his hands together and said, "Before we proceed, I think we should discuss the reasons blacks left Connellsville after high school graduation or even why those who left to attend college didn't return."

CHAPTER 45

The answer to Lamont's question was probably the same as for most small towns and it surprised me that he even voiced the question. The reasons were obvious, but maybe the reasons weren't that clear.

Lamont was tapping his fingers on the arm of the couch. "Why did they leave?"

Before I answered, I asked, "Why do you think?"

He gave it some thought and came up with no answer.

"If you'll remember the coke and coal companies were the major employers for white and black. With the big bust and Connellsville having limited employment, regardless if you were white or black, people left because there were no jobs."

"So, there were no other companies in town?"

"Uh...not really. Well, there was Anchor Hocking, a glassware factory and manufacturer. The business started back in 1918 and it didn't employ that many people and blacks did not work in the factory until the mid-1960's."

Lamont was holding a paper and raised his hand. "Wait a minute. You're right about blacks not working in the factory. However, two black men around 1920, Raymond Keith and Frank Robinson worked as chauffeurs for Anchor Hocking."

Lamont stopped and continued to read. "You're right that in the mid-1960's, the company hired blacks to work in other factory positions."

"Isn't that what I said?" I shook my head and continued, "The men who couldn't find work in Connellsville worked in other towns, like my dad."

"That's right, your dad worked for the United States Steel Company. How far was that from Connellsville?"

"He worked in Clairton while others worked at the Homestead Steel Mill near Pittsburgh. He drove approximately 100 miles round trip. Many of the men rode together." I laughed. "My dad and his co-workers were carpooling before it was popular. But, I remember my dad saying they did it for two reasons: to save money and to help those who didn't own a car."

"That must have been hard."

"Why do you say that?"

"The steel mill was no different than me working for the transit authority. You know, it operated on a day, afternoon, and evening shift schedule."

"Oh, I never thought about it."

"Your dad told me about the unsafe conditions and long hours. Not to mention the difficulty blacks had when trying to attain better positions. When easier, higher paid positions became available it was an unspoken understanding that these positions held by whites would pass them on to other whites, such as father to son or relative to relative or friend to friend."

"He never told me that."

"We had quite a discussion about it. I bet you didn't know that many blacks couldn't get hired without a notable worker vouched for them."

"Wow! I had no idea."

Lamont was curious. "Were there many black men from your hometown working in the steel mills?"

"Like the coal miners I know some of the surnames, but that's about it." My eyes widened in disbelief. "You want their names listed in the book? Why?"

"Well, for consistency sake. You acknowledged the coke and coal miners why not the steel workers."

I shrugged. I tried taking the list from Lamont, but he wouldn't give it up as he read the surnames while I typed.

STEEL MILL WORKERS

BETTERS—BOND—BURTON—DAVIS—EVANS—
FURMAN—GRAVES—HARDY—HARVEY—
HAYNES—HICKMAN—KENNEDY—LOCKETTE—
MOCKABEE—MOON—REID—SHELTON—
WALKER—WALLACE—WRIGHT—WOODS

CHAPTER 46

Friday, Lamont would golf eighteen holes. That meant I could work alone for at least five hours and possibly longer if he decided to eat lunch before coming home. I wasn't going to tell him. He knew I had a meeting at Barnes and Noble with my small writing group and would assume that I would spend the remainder of the day perhaps doing some domestic work around the house such as washing clothes.

After my meeting, I had lunch, exercised, and glanced over the papers marked employment. I exhaled and started talking to myself. "This is more difficult than I expected. I know we agreed on this chapter, but I don't see what's so interesting."

I picked up a picture from Reverend Osborne's collection marked Baltimore and Ohio Railroad. I read the back of the photo. "Garfield Taylor was the first African American hired by Connellsville's railroad yard located on Water Street. Garfield is the man identified in the photo with a circle around his head."

The photographer unknown, photograph courtesy of Reverend Osborne's private collection.

"I guess that's important." I wish someone would have provided names for the other men in the photo. Maybe the other men were not from Connellsville. A notation was made that Enos Fox and Ernest (Ernie) Haley also worked for the railroad.

I looked at a list of employees who worked for the Bell Telephone Company. I was surprised. "I had no idea that the telephone company hired African Americans. They held various positions. The black employees were: Elmer Cole (Custodian); Leon Hunter (Custodian/Lineman) and Nate Milton (Lineman).

I jumped up. "Where had the time gone? Lamont would be home soon and I had not taken anything out for dinner."

I opened the freezer and took out fish. Before I could return to the den, I heard the garage door going up. Lamont walked into the den and kissed me.

"How was golf?"

"It was great."

I knew what was coming next. In great detail, Lamont would describe each golf shot, especially the long drives, the birdies and pars he missed or made. In addition, he would tell me how the other guys golfed.

I smiled with pride. "And to think, five years ago, he didn't even golf."

CHAPTER 47

During dinner and when Lamont finished his account of his golf round, he asked, "What did you do today?"

"I met with my writing group and…." I stood up and said, "I didn't do much of anything."

"You can't fool me. You worked on the book, didn't you?"

"I did, but just a little. To be truthful, I'm stuck. As I went through the employment material, I kept asking myself who would be interested in whether or not African Americans were employed."

Lamont shook his head. "Did you mention that the police force had an African American and what about the Post Office?"

"I didn't get that far."

"Honey, trust me. These jobs held by blacks were not the typical. In Connellsville, blacks were holding jobs that were usually reserved for whites before integration was an issue."

"Okay. Let's finish dinner and we can look over the items you're referring to."

After I finished cleaning the kitchen, I joined Lamont in the den. He was flipping through a stack of papers. He peeped over them when he noticed me standing in the doorway.

"Are you ready?"

"I guess, but aren't you tired?"

"I'm okay."

I sat down at the computer and Lamont had already turned it on. "Did you find the material you were talking about?"

"Yes and I have the information."

"Who's first?"

"Eva Brown. She worked as an elevator operator in Connellsville's tallest building."

I had no idea what structure he was referring to. "What building is that?"

Lamont's voice sounded less than confident as he said, "It's the Brimstone Building. Do you know the building I'm talking about?"

"Yeah, I know the building, but I didn't know it was called Connellsville's tallest building."

"That's what your notes say." He teased, "Don't shoot the messenger. Anyway, the building housed a variety of businesses, such as, but not limited to, doctors, dentists, and insurance companies."

I made a face. "So an elevator operator is important?"

"No, but with everyone vying for the limited employment opportunities in your town, I'm surprised that blacks were employed by town businesses."

My voice was snippy as I commented. "If that's the case then I should mention every African American in town. Like my granddad, Daniel Marilla. He worked as a janitor for Duggan's Bakery, located on the West Side of town on Main Street. They had the best donuts I ever ate."

"You're getting distracted and missing the point."

I closed my eyes and licked my lips. "I wish you could have tasted them. They were the best."

"Lorraine, I get the picture. Now, can you refocus?"

"I'm sorry. I guess all food products that I can no longer and will never eat again make me vividly remember their taste. It's like a person who is sighted and loses his or her sight. They never forget what they once saw."

"Can we continue?"

"Sure, but I hope you have something different because I believe people were hired as elevator operators in other towns."

Lamont's nostrils flared. "Maybe in your eyesight this information is nothing. I can assure you others will find difficulty believing that some of the things you mention actually happened."

"Fine, let's continue. Who's next?"

Lamont raised an eyebrow and smiled. "You'll agree that this is impressive. Connellsville's original hospital was called the Cottage State Hospital and was erected in 1891. Today, it's the Connellsville Highland Hospital."

Irritated, I stated, "Now who's not focusing?"

"No, no. I think the background information is needed."

My voice softened. "Okay when was the first African American hired by the hospital?"

"I don't know."

Lamont handed me a picture from Reverend Osborne's collection. "According to the notes, Dr. Clifford McPherson was the first African American Pharmacist in Fayette County and he worked at the Connellsville Highland Hospital."

Dr. Clifford McPherson

The photographer unknown, photograph courtesy of Roy Taylor's private collection.

"He's distinguished looking and that is notable, but the rest of the employment information should be omitted."

"Before you make that decision, please review all the information you have regarding the jobs held by blacks?"

Whew. "Lamont, can we stop?"

"Why?"

"I'm right back to where I was when you first suggested that I write this book. No one wants to read page after page about people working in a bank or a bakery."

Lamont's voice was saddened. "You really don't understand. During the 1910's through the 1950's and maybe even later, blacks struggled to hold positions that were reserved for whites only. Your hometown might have had some segregation and racism issues, but blacks were employed by the local businesses in a variety of positions."

CHAPTER 48

Nothing Lamont said convinced me that a book should be written. As much as I wanted to quit, Lamont was more determined than ever to continue. According to him, the chapter on employment was necessary.

With little or no enthusiasm, I relented. "Fine, let's go on."

Lamont's face glowed like a beaming light was shining on him. "Thank you for hanging in there with me. Now, the National Bank was one to the largest banks in town. They hired Bertha Baker, Mary Bonds, and Edith Smith as Elevator Operators."

I typed as Lamont provided the information. So far there had been nothing to make me say, *"wow."* Maybe, this was above my head or I was too close to it. I figured I would go along rather than slow down our progress.

"I know you think I'm wasting time, but again I'll emphasize, this is crucial."

"Who's next?"

"It's your uncle, James Scott, better known by friends and relatives as Scottie."

I was glad Lamont didn't make a smart remark about me being related to him. "I agree his story is unusual. The trash company he worked for is out of business, but I believe he was the first black hired by the trash company. He started out on the trash truck and was promoted to Bill Collector."

Lamont did not hide his surprise. "You mean Connellsville had a black man in the 1950's going door-to-door, collecting monies owed for the trash bill.

"That's correct and the customers were black and white."

"We should include his picture."

"You're right, but this is the only one I have."

Lamont took it from me. "It's not very clear. In fact, it's pretty grainy." "Maybe one of your cousins will give you a better one."

James Scott

The photographer unknown, photograph courtesy of Lorraine M. Harris' private collection.

"I'll try."

Lamont laughed. "I can't believe that at one time Connellsville had a department store."

"Troutman was located on Main Street and as far back as I can remember, it was the only department store in town. It was considered an upscale store with expensive merchandise."

"What happened to the store?"

"Economics—lack of money. Like most of the stores on Main Street, they went out of business. Before you ask, Troutman did hire African Americans as Elevator Operators."

"Do you know who they were?"

"Is it important to include their names or the fact that Troutman hired blacks?"

Lamont was firm. "I would say, both. If nothing else, the names can be deleted later." Lamont smiled. "Stay with me."

"Okay." I would have agreed to anything if it meant it would keep us on track. "Please tell me the names and I'll type them."

"The Elevator Operators were: Hattie Banks, Shanana Gales, Florence Griffin, Elsie Haley, and Geneva Robinson."

Lamont had a strange expression on his face. "Did you know there were other blacks working for Troutman?"

"If they did, I didn't know. Who were they?"

"Lawrence Gales worked in delivery and Elsie Haley worked in alterations."

I finished typing and asked, "Now, can we go to bed?"

"Not quite yet. Connellsville's West Penn Electric Company hired African Americans in a variety of positions. The employees were J.R. Baker, Sr., Evelyn French, Beverly Lockett, and Toni Walker."

I was about to shut the computer down when Lamont said, "We missed one company."

"What is it?"

"The South Connellsville Lumber Company, you even have a picture that was part of the information you obtained from the National Historic Society."

"Let me see the picture." Lamont handed it to me.

The photographer unknown, photograph courtesy of the National Historic Society.

I studied the fuzzy picture. "Although it's not clear, I see two black men sitting on the right side."

"Well, according to the information you obtained, the lumber company started in 1896 and built most of the houses and buildings in Connellsville."

"Are we finished?"

"We are. Let's go to bed."

CHAPTER 49

After finishing the employment chapter, it was as if a weight had been lifted off my shoulders. Progress had been made and, as much as I hated to admit it, there were some pertinent facts about African Americans working in Connellsville. After writing about the unbelievable high school achievements, everything else seemed dim in comparison.

Again, I was at a crossroads about writing the book. Beyond Connellsville's residents, would anyone else be interested in reading about these facts? It reminded me of when I completed my family's genealogy book. The family's reaction was mixed: some were overwhelmed with the information; some had little or no interest while others focused on the mistakes and wanted them corrected as soon as possible.

This was a contention Lamont and I had often. Once more, I shared my concerns with him. He didn't have to say anything. His brooding eyes and frowning face said it all. The discussion about the book being written was getting old for both of us.

His voice matched his melancholy expression. "You don't want to finish, do you?" He didn't wait for my answer.

He pouted. "We didn't even talk about the unusual sports facts. I strongly suggest we continue until everything is finished. The organization of the facts should make it easier in making your decision about whether the story is worth telling. Without reviewing everything, how can you decide?"

I shook my head. "I can't explain it. It's just a gut feeling."

"We should take a break. Let's go to the movies, play bocce golf, or go to the swimming pool. You've been sitting in front of the computer too long. A little fresh air and sunshine will make you feel better, about everything."

Maybe Lamont was right, but I wanted to quit. The employment facts were enough for me to know there wasn't a story.

"Come on, Sweetie." Lamont started tickling me. "Get up."

I tried to suppress my laughter, but as he tickled me I could no longer resist.

"Stop it!" I hit his hand. "I give in. Let's go out and play. Recreation might help me adjust my attitude."

In the car, Lamont wanted to know what changed. "Why don't you want to continue?"

"I think it was the employment information. With all of the details I began to worry about the story angle. I think it might get boring."

"Watch out!" I yelled. My heart was beating rapidly.

With a calm, professional move, Lamont steered the driving wheel, changed lanes and swore under his breath. If it wasn't for his quick reaction, he might have hit a golf cart that had swerved into our driving lane.

Although Lamont's posture was again relaxed, his words were angry. "I'll be glad when the snowbirds...."

Not wanting our outing spoiled, I tried to add some humor. "You mean seasonal or snow flake residents."

"Whatever! Did you see that idiot? I almost hit him."

"I know, and if it were not for your professional driving skills, it could have resulted in a bad accident. The birds have such a short period before going back up North that I think many of them forget about road rules and their manners."

Although Lamont's attention was on the traffic, he did not forget our topic of discussion. "Aren't most nonfiction books full of facts? If so, why are you concerned about the chapters being page-turners?"

"I have no idea what goes into a nonfiction book. I write fiction and my style is to keep the reader's interest in a fast-paced story where they are turning the pages and wanting to know more."

I paused and added, "If it were me reading this book, I would flip through the pages and ask, "Why was this book written?" I still say unless you have an interest in Connellsville, you probably could care less about the town."

"Well, I wasn't born and raised in Connellsville and I was, and still am, interested. In fact, the whole western Pennsylvania phenomenon is of interest to me. How is it that so many small towns produce such outstanding athletics?"

It took everything I had not to respond. I was constantly amazed at how he could turn most subjects into a sports topic.

"Maybe you're too close to the subject matter. You know, similar to a skunk that can't smell his or her own stink."

Lamont laughed until his eyes brimmed with tears. After recovering from what he thought was funny, he continued. "You've never thought the book's topic was worth writing about."

"You might be right."

"I know I'm right. For a slight moment, I had hopes that you were beginning to understand what I see. Oh well…" Lamont's voice drifted off as he turned onto Rolling Acres and entered the Tree Tops Driving Golf Range.

CHAPTER 50

"Funky" was the word to describe Lamont's mood. In addition, he had spoken about two words as we drove back to the house from driving golf range. I almost suggested we eat out, but after thirty some odd years of marriage I knew when I was treading on thin ice.

Involuntarily, a groan escaped from my mouth. Instead of Lamont asking me what was wrong, he met my eyes with a glare. In return, I responded as if he had acknowledged me.

"I'm okay. I was thinking...." My voice lost its sound. I cleared my throat and said, "I don't feel like cooking dinner, do you want to eat out?" Lamont's cool exterior was my answer.

When we entered the house, I entered the kitchen without hesitation, washed my hands, and started pulling out leftovers. As I warmed up a variety of food, Lamont walked in and sat down. The silence he brought with him caused my emotions to erupt.

I slammed my hand on the counter and shouted, "What do you want from me?"

With sad eyes, he looked at me. My anger slowed as tears brimmed my eyelashes.

Lamont started to stand, but sat back down. "Honey, I want nothing but happiness for you and I've been selfish. You should do what you want with the book. You're right, this is my idea. Although I've encouraged you, it probably has felt more like pressure to you."

His words stabbed at my heart followed by guilt. I walked over to Lamont and began speaking while holding my breath, trying not to cry. I picked up his hands while gazing into his eyes.

"Don't get me wrong, I really appreciate the patience and support you've shown me, but as we reviewed the material it's as if something is missing."

I dropped his hands and turned around to check on the food. What I didn't say was that the book facts were overwhelming. Maybe I was afraid of the feedback the book might generate.

Dinner was ready, but I had lost my appetite. The entire dinner conversation was reduced to, pass the salt and pepper. As I cleaned up the kitchen, the question kept creeping into my thoughts, "Why was I opposed to this book?" Uncovering the mysteries of the past had always been one of my passions. Instead of being excited and proud, I was uncomfortable and disheartened.

Our routine was for Lamont to keep me company while I cleaned the kitchen, but tonight he left me. When I finished, I was going to the den when I spotted Lamont on the lanai, reading over the book pages I had printed out.

I joined him, but I did not interrupt him. I watched the traffic and waved at the occasional walker and passing golf cart. The temperature had dropped and the breeze was chilly.

I watched as Lamont finished reading the last page.

I was curious. "Well, what do you think?"

"You're being too hard on yourself. I believe it's better than you think. Why don't we continue, finish it, and then decide."

I glanced at Lamont, trying not to gaze into his beautiful dark brown eyes. He held my hand, his voice was seductive as he cooed, "Come on, Baby, do it for me."

How could I resist? I pulled my hand away and said, "I've got an idea. We'll complete the book's organization and when we finish and if I feel it has no merit, then that's it."

A glint of triumph crept into Lamont's eyes. He smiled and said, "Thanks, but before I agree to your proposal, I think another person should read it and give us their opinion."

CHAPTER 51

The cool air drove me inside the house. Lamont leaped from the chair and followed me. As I was about to sit on the sofa to read a book, Lamont grabbed my hand and nudged me into the den.

"What are you doing?"

"Giving you the push you need." Lamont grinned.

Back in the den we took our familiar places—me at the computer, Lamont on the sofa.

"The next chapter I believe is about blacks owning and operating businesses in town. Were there many?"

"Well, I have no proof, but I believe most of the black businesses started during Connellsville's thriving 1920 industrial period and declined like others when the economy slowed."

"When the black businesses were operating, do you know whether the whites patronized them?"

I thought about it before answering him. "I would say yes. Businesses need everyone to shop or eat at their establishment if they are to survive."

Lamont recommended that we put the businesses in alphabetical order. "Who's first?"

"Um...Sylvester Parrish had an Accounting and Tax Firm."

"According to this article, he lived in Trotter, not Connellsville."

"Remember I told you Trotter is now a part of Connellsville."

"I forgot. What else do you know about his business?"

"Here's his picture." I passed it to Lamont.

Sylvester Parrish

The photographer unknown, photograph courtesy of the Parrish family's private collection.

"Is this the same Sylvester Parrish who was a Tuskegee Airman?"

"Yes. He graduated from the former Dunbar,

Pennsylvania High School. As I said, he lived in Trotter. He received an accounting degree from Pennsylvania's Waynesburg College."

"He had white clients?"

"As far as I know he did. The next business was Johnny Johnson's car dealership."

"Where was it located?"

"It was on the West side of town."

I flipped through a few pages and handed him the next entry, Elsie (Webster) Haley. She worked for a number of businesses where she became proficient in making alterations. With her work experience and reputation, she established an alteration business.

"Do you have a picture of her?"

"The only one I have is from the yearbook."

Elsie Haley

The photographer unknown, photograph courtesy of the 1945 Connellsville Year Book.

"If we are finished with the A's, I know what's next." He smiled. "All towns had at least one black barber shop."

"You're right. Benjamin Sledge was nicknamed, BJ. In fact, he cut men's and women's hair. He is the only person I can remember who had a disability."

Lamont lifted his head and gave me a puzzled look.

"I mentioned that because he had one eye and operated the only black barbershop in town." Before Lamont could ask, I added, "It was located on Water Street, near the railroad station."

"You said, the only barbershop in town. Were there other barbers?"

"There were two others. Charles Hart and Charles (Charlie) Payton were barbers. Their barbershop was located in Charleroi where there was a larger black population."

Raising my hand to stop his question, I said, "I have no idea where in Charleroi."

We were about to move on when I remembered something. "Charlie Payton did something you don't find today. He made house visits, cutting hair for the elderly and sick."

"Are any of these business owners still living?"

CHAPTER 52

After mentioning that most of the business owners were deceased, Lamont formed a tent with his hands.

"Something just occurred to me. If someone has passed away, it should probably be noted."

I shook my head. "Thanks for the suggestion, but unfortunately my research did not include the dates of death."

Frowning, Lamont chewed his lower lip and said, "Okay, but if you have the information, it won't hurt mentioning it."

My response was a nod. Exhaling loudly, I stood up and rolled my shoulders several times. A break was calling my name. When I returned to the den, I was carrying two bottles of water.

Just as I passed Lamont one of the bottles, the phone rang. It had been several weeks and there had been no hang-ups or threatening telephone calls, but for some reason I knew it was the call. Lamont answered and as I had thought, it was a hang-up.

I asked, not expecting an answer. "I wondered what happened. This is the first call in weeks."

"I hadn't said anything and wondered the same thing. Well, whatever had caused the calls to stop, they're back." Lamont didn't miss a beat. He acted as if the call never happened. "I was surprised that the only beauty shop was located in Trotter."

I took a long sip of water before I answered. "The owner's name was Dorothy Bonds and she operated out of her house."

Lamont was curious. "Did she ever do you and your sisters' hair?"

"My mom straightened our hair, but on occasion we had it done by Miss Bonds. She did ours as well as most of the women in town unless they went to a beautician in Uniontown."

A memory made me smile. "When Miss Bonds did my hair I remembered how much I liked listening to the Lone Ranger on the radio."

"You don't look old enough to remember radio programs."

"Thank you. That's a sweet compliment."

"Okay, getting back to Miss Bonds, does she still operate her shop?"

"No, she moved to Fort Wayne, Indiana. I think she left in the late 50's. Once when my family took a vacation to Fort Wayne, we visited with her."

"Were there any other beauticians?"

"In Connellsville, I think Elsie Wheeler Mills operated a beauty shop out of her home. Who's next?"

Instead of answering my question, Lamont had picked up some papers off the floor and table. Neatly, he began stacking them in several piles.

"What are you doing?"

"The day has been long and we've done enough for one day."

"Are you tired?"

"Let's say it's past my bedtime and I have a seven fifteen tee time. If I was playing one of the executive courses, I wouldn't mind staying up, but I'm playing eighteen holes. I'll need all the energy I can muster up if I'm going to win any money from my golf buddies."

Rather than argue or stay up working on my own, I relented. I turned off the computer and followed Lamont.

CHAPTER 53

As Lamont was about to leave for his tee time, I almost hinted at my intention to work on the book until I heard him say. "Why don't you wash clothes, scrub the floor, or do something domestic?"

With hands on my hips, my lips were formed to tell him what he could do with his suggestions when he burst into laughter.

He grabbed me tightly and said, "I love you. You know I was kidding."

We kissed. Easing his embrace, he gazed at me. "Seriously, what are you going to do today?"

Not answering right away, I said, "I might work on the book."

"Fine, but don't do too much."

"I hope you hit the golf ball straight and win some money."

"Please! I'll try to hit it straight and not too often." He chuckled and gave me a kiss before leaving.

Although Lamont joked, I did wash two loads of clothes. I was folding the last load when I heard the garage door going up.

Lamont climbed out of the van. When he approached me, we kissed and went into the house.

"Did you have lunch?"

"Unfortunately, no and I'm starved."

"You're always hungry."

We laughed and through chuckles, Lamont teased, "What can I say, I'm still growing. Will you warm me up the chicken wings from last night's dinner?"

While I prepared lunch, Lamont showered. He returned to the kitchen and sat at the table down. I placed the plate of wings in front of him and sat down.

"Did you work on the book?"

"No, Master. I had too much domestic work to do."

"That's funny."

"Are you going to nap or join me in the den?"

He grinned. "I'm going to take a much needed nap. That way my mind will be renewed, my body refreshed, and I'll be able to concentrate on the task at hand."

Lamont's eyes widened. "I have an idea. Since you've been the Domestic Goddess today, why don't we take a nap together?"

"You would like that wouldn't you?" I shook my head, smiled and left him sitting at the kitchen table.

He shouted, "I don't know how you can resist my offer."

The book was beginning to wear me down and Lamont had no idea how much I wished it was finished. Maybe while he's slept, I could tackle the rest of the business owners.

Making a mental note, I would thank Lamont for putting the businesses in alphabetical order. It made it easier to see where we had left off. So I wouldn't wake Lamont, I closed the den's door.

"Wow, there were two cleaners, the Coles and King Family. Imagine two black dry cleaners owned and operated in Connellsville."

Both, white and black, recognized the Betters Family as one of the wealthiest black families in town. They lived on Eighth Street on the West side and were the only black family I knew that had a maid.

I didn't hear the den door open, nor did I hear Lamont enter. I jumped.

"I'm sorry. I didn't mean to startle you. How far have you gotten?"

"Not far at all. I was reading about the Betters Family."

"Who are they?"

"They were the richest black family in town. From about 1910 or so there were a number of hotels in town and the Betters owned and operated one of them. Their upscale hotel was located across the street from the railroad station."

"When was it erected and is it still operating today?"

"I don't know when it opened, but like all of the other hotels that once had a flourishing business, it too closed. I don't have much information about it."

"What about a picture?"

I shook my head. "I don't have one."

Lamont suggested, "Maybe a Betters' family member could provide you with one."

A tint of frustration entered my tone. "I'll try, but I'm not encouraged when attempting to obtain information and pictures. Remember, most of the pictures I have are from yearbooks, someone's newspaper clippings, the church, and family members' photo collections. That's why some of the photos are blurry and not clear."

I must have been rambling because I saw Lamont's eyes glazing over. "Sweetie, it's okay." Lamont urged, "Let's not concentrate on what we don't have. Everything will be okay."

I blew out air. "That's fine. Uh...let's see what's next. The only black doctor was Dr. Robert A. McDaniel. He graduated in 1932 and after attending Howard University's medical school, he returned to Connellsville. Affectionately, everybody called him "Doctor Mac." His office was on Eighth Street on the West side."

"Did he live far from the Betters Family?"

"His house was maybe four or five houses down from them. The one thing I remembered about Dr. Mac was that his patients were white and black." I pointed to my chin. "My stitches were compliments of Dr. Mac."

CHAPTER 54

From Lamont's facial expression and the lowering of his eyes, I could tell that the last thing he wanted was to hear the story about my stitches."

"I promise it's a short story. I was in elementary school, maybe I was in the third grade."

I waved my hand. "That's not important. Anyway, my school project required cutting pictures from a magazine. My mother kept them in a small glass-faced cabinet. Rather than wait as I had been told, I sat on the floor with my legs under the cabinet and pulled hard on the doors. The cabinet tumbled over as the glass doors broke causing a cut to my chin."

Lamont laughed. "I bet that was one of those Kodak moments. Your mother was probably screaming that she could kill you while blood was everything."

"You know it." We laughed.

"Does he still live in Connellsville?"

"No. He's dead and of course, his office closed."

"What about a picture?"

"The only picture I have for Dr. McDaniel is from the yearbook." I handed it to Lamont.

Robert McDaniel
The photographer unknown, photograph courtesy of
Reverend Osborne's private collection.

"Is that it?"

"No, there are still a few more individuals to mention. A man named Jim Landers was the stepfather of Archie, Bob and Ed Taylor. Do you remember Patty Taylor?"

Lamont repeated, "Patty Taylor, Patty Taylor."

"You remember her. She lived in Washington, D.C. for a while."

"Oh yeah. She had a design business or something before moving to Hawaii. When her mother became ill she returned to Connellsville."

"That's her. Well, her dad and his brothers ran a successful plastering business. It operated from the around 1930's until they retired."

Lamont was curious. "I wonder how they managed to stay in business so long."

"Good question, but I have no idea except maybe they were good at their craft or they were the only ones in town doing that type of business.

CHAPTER 55

The more we organized the research data the more questions kept coming up. Even if I tried getting answers to the unsolved questions, I wouldn't know who would have the answers or if anyone would remember.

With my eyes closed, I didn't realize Lamont was waiting for me. "Let's see. The next person is Isabelle Fletcher."

"Is she the same woman from the class of 1930?"

"Yes. She passed away in 1998. She graduated from Hampton Institute in Hampton, Virginia." I was reading from her obituary.

"In 1934, she received her Bachelor of Science in Music. While in college, she was much sought after as an accompanist. In her senior year of college, she performed with the Hampton Institute Symphonic Orchestra. After college, she was a Music Teacher in Oxford, North Carolina and Conway, South Carolina."

"It sounds as if she had a successful career. Why did she return to Connellsville?"

"She was single and her ailing parents needed her. She continued her career in music by teaching private piano and voice lessons to everyone regardless of race, gender or age."

Lamont's expression was one of confusion. "She didn't think about being a music teacher at the high school?"

"I have no idea. She taught lessons out of her home on Eighth Street on the West side from the late 1900's until she retired."

"What is it about the West side and Eighth Street?"

"What do you mean?"

"You had the Betters Family, Dr. Mac and now Miss Fletcher."

"Maybe it was the luck of the draw." I shook my head. "How am I supposed to know? They were the only three black families on the street."

"There's no need to get testy." Then he teased, "Inquiring minds want to know."

I shook my head and moved on. "Black restaurant owners are next. There seems to have been quite a few black-owned restaurants, but I can't tell you when any of them started or how long they stayed in…."

Lamont interrupted me. "Do you have a picture of Isabelle Fletcher? I don't' want you to forget her."

"Here's a picture that my mom gave me of her. It was probably taken in her home at the piano she used when teaching lessons."

Isabelle Fletcher
The photographer unknown, photograph courtesy of Dorothy Mockabee's private collection.

Lamont emphasized. "I didn't mean to stop you, but pictures tell the story as much as the words."

"No, I'm glad you're reminding me to include the pictures." I rubbed my forehead.

"I wonder if Vinnie has any pictures."

"Why don't we ask him?"

My stomach was growling. "What time is it?"

Lamont glanced at this watch. "It's almost dinner time. Why don't we work for another hour and then go to dinner. Maybe on our way we can stop by Vinnie's house."

"Let's stop by Vinnie after we finish dinner."

Lamont agreed and beamed. "What about dinner at Arnold Palmer?"

"Nah, I have a taste for ribs. Why don't we go to Oakwood Grill?"

"Yeah, I could go for some ribs and pulled pork. Anyway, let's finish up so we can be there before four o'clock and beat the hour wait."

I patted Lamont's knee and said, "Let's get started. We don't have that much time if we're going to beat the Oakwood crowd. What's next?"

CHAPTER 56

Lamont turned over a paper he had been reading. "As you mentioned, black-owned restaurants are next, but your notes are vague. There is nothing here indicating when they began or ended. I'm not sure whether to include them without additional information."

"I told you the information wasn't always complete. Give me the names and the restaurant owners."

"Alsop Restaurant was owned and operated by Jim Alsop and the Rivera Bar was owned and operated by Tom Fant. Then your notes have some names of restaurant owners, but nothing else."

I was confused. "What do you mean?"

Lamont's voice was laced with irritation. "All you have written down are their names and nothing else."

Before I could comment further, Lamont called out the names. "Edna Keith, John and Fannie Wallace and Cornelius and Clara Washington."

"I see what you mean. That information might get eliminated." I paused and asked, "You forgot the Betters Bar and Grill."

"No, I didn't. I wanted to get that information out of the way and then tell you what you have about the Betters. Are you ready?"

I nodded my head.

"According to this, the bar and grill was located near the railroad station. The family owned and operated it around 1910 into the late 1950's." Lamont stopped reading and asked, "Was it part of the hotel?"

"It must have been. I don't remember the hotel, but I recall the bar and grill. It was a place where blacks dined and enjoyed live entertainment. The primary band consisted of the Betters' sons—Harold, Jerome, and James."

I handed Lamont a picture.

"My sister, Patty, gave me this picture. Two of the men in the picture are Betters, but she wasn't sure if these were the actual band members. Anyway, it's worth including."

Lamont glanced at the picture and agreed.

Left to right, Harold Betters, Man Unknown, Jerome Betters, Man Unknown
The photographer unknown, photograph courtesy of Patty White's private collection.

"Could anyone go to the bar and grill?"

"If I remember correctly, it was a popular black place, but whites frequented it too. It might have been one of the few places in town where people could hear good, jazz music." I sighed. "Is that it? I'm hungry."

"I have two more businesses, but we might have mentioned this one earlier. I can't remember."

"Who is it?"

"Clifford McPherson, the Pharmacist. He owned and operated a drug store in Uniontown."

I tried finding it, but without success. "I believe we included him being the first black Pharmacist hired by Fayette County, but I don't recall saying anything about him owning and operating a drug store."

Lamont suggested, "You might be right, but double check it. The last business is Carol Johns. She was born and raised in Connellsville. She left and had a successful career, retired, and returned to town. She owned and operated the Heath Cliff Bookstore, but it went out business."

"Please, say we're finished."

Lamont raised his arms and gave me a victory sign. "We're finished with black-owned and operated businesses. You can turn off the computer."

On our way to Oakwood, we drove pass Vinnie's house and saw a "For Sale" sign in front of the house.

CHAPTER 57

During dinner, Lamont and I speculated as to why Vinnie and Dot might be moving. We discussed how it wasn't uncommon for people in The Villages to buy more than one house. Usually, the sales resulted from residents wanting to have a smaller or larger house or a different model. To satisfy our curiosity, we would stop by Vinnie's house on our way home.

After dinner we went to Lake Sumter Landing and listened to the band before heading home. As Lamont slowed the car at the curb of Vinnie's house, we sat debating our unannounced visit.

I was having second thoughts. "Lamont, I think we should have called."

"Oh, come on. Since we're here let's go. I mean we won't stay long. We'll ask Vinnie our question about having any pictures and ask why they're moving."

"Okay, let's go."

We climbed out of the car and walked to the front door. Lamont rang the doorbell several times, but no one answered. As we turned to leave, the door opened. Dot stepped outside, closed the door and joined us on the porch.

In unison, we greeted her.

"Hi, Lamont and Lorraine."

When Dot spoke I heard something in her voice, but I wasn't sure how to describe it. Silence invaded the cool air as we stood, no one saying anything.

Dot broke the stillness. "I'm glad you stopped by, but this isn't a good time."

When Dot spoke I realized her eyes were puffing and red. She might have been crying. I knew we shouldn't have stopped without calling. With Dot pausing briefly, it brought more tension in the air with no one saying anything.

Finally I spoke up. "I'm sorry. We should have called, but we were on our way home from dinner and wanted to ask Vinnie a question."

Dot's eyes were misty. "Under normal circumstances, it would be okay to see him but…" She coughed, clearing her throat.

Before Dot spoke she pointed towards the sign. "You saw the for sale sign." She didn't wait for an answer.

"We're moving back to Maryland."

We responded with opened mouths. We were unable to hide our surprised expressions. I was about to ask why, but Dot answered without me having to inquire.

"Vinnie…" Again, she cleared her throat.

"As I was saying, I…we…the doctors thought Vinnie had dementia, but that day when we saw you at the doctor's office, I received the results from Vinnie's tests." Dot wiped a falling tear as she added, "He's in the early stages of Alzheimer."

I glanced at Lamont. Neither of us knew what to say. Finally, I uttered. "We're sorry."

"Thank you."

Lamont asked, "Is there anything we can do?"

"Oh, thank you, but I have everything under control. Besides, when it's time for the move, my son will come and help us. That's one reason why we're moving back to Maryland. I'll be near the kids and they can help me with their father as he...." She cleared her throat, fighting back the tears.

We talked for a few more minutes and left. Lamont repeated his offer to help.

"Thanks, Lamont. If I need you I'll let you know."

CHAPTER 58

Several days passed and Lamont and I had not resumed working on the book. I was getting antsy. With neither one of us having anything on the calendar, I knew what was on the top of my list.

After breakfast, I broached the subject. "What's on your schedule today?"

"I thought I would go to Lowes or Home Depot."

That would be punishment to me. "Are you looking for anything in particular?"

"No, I haven't been over there for a while and thought I would see what's new. After that, I was headed to a golf demo at Arnold Palmer."

I chewed the inside of my mouth until it hurt. I told myself, "Be calm and don't react." A plastered smile covered my face.

Sweetly, Lamont asked, "What do you have planned?"

Through gritted teeth, I responded, "I thought I'd write a little."

Quickly, maybe too quickly Lamont suggested, "Why don't you wait for me and when I return, we can work on it together?"

I shook my head. "Why don't you go by yourself and do what you want today. I can work on my own. After all, everything is pretty much…."
Lamont raised his hand. "No! That's not going to work."

His eyes were twinkling. "You require close supervision. You're like an employee who's been given a project, but haven't bought into the idea."

I laughed. "Okay, I remember when I was working and was given what I called *"failed projects"* and you're right that's how I'm treating this."

Lamont showed his triumph by giving me a wide toothy grin. "I also remember how you usually ended up with outstanding results."

I couldn't say anything because Lamont was right. By my standards this book was close to some of those God-awful assignments I had been given. The difference is that I'm not sure what the result will be.

"Look, I'll be back in a couple of hours. Why don't you get a pedicure? It will be my treat."

A lot of things came to mind as to what I could have said, but I decided it was better to let his comment go unsaid. Since it's his choice to do something different, why couldn't I put that time to good use?

I gave him a cheery good-bye and waited for the garage door to go down before I turned on the computer. As I began skimming over the next subject, a noise caught my attention. I listened. I heard nothing. It must have been my imagination.

I thought, "Maybe it was something or someone outside."

I stood up and peeped out the window. To the left and to the right, I didn't see anything or anyone. I turned around and screamed.

CHAPTER 59

My hand went to my chest. "Are you trying to give me a heart attack?"

"I'm sorry. I thought you heard me come back into the house."

"No, I didn't. Anyway, why did you come back? Did you forget something?"

"I came back because something told me you were going to go behind my back and work on the book."

Annoyed, I said, "I'm not doing anything behind your back. You can always review what I do."

"I have an idea. Why don't you come with me?"

My head began throbbing. "You know I hate Lowes and Home Depot." Aimlessly, Lamont could walk through the store browsing, going up and down all the aisles, with no intention of buying a single item.

Lamont waited. "Are you coming?"

"I don't know."

"Trust me. You need a change of scenery. If I don't keep an eye on you, you'll be content sitting at the computer, typing all day."

That wasn't true, but I wasn't going to argue.

"How long do you plan on being in Lowes and Home Depot?"

"Not long."

###

After an hour in Lowes, I wanted to scream. Now I could identify with our daughters when we made them go somewhere and they didn't want to go. I tried being polite, but it was difficult as we wandered up and down the same aisles for the second time.

"Are you looking for anything in particular?" I asked.

"Not really, but you never know what you might find."

I blew out air and prayed for patience. After all, Lamont never complains when he takes me shopping. But, the difference is that I know what I'm buying when I enter the store and I don't shop often.

He took my hand and gave it a gentle squeeze. "I love you."

I managed to smile and returned his affection, but with every passing moment, it became more difficult to remain calm and not to show my emotions.

"Can we leave now? My feet are tired, my back hurts, I have a headache, and I want to leave." My whining reminded me of a small child.

Finally, we walked toward the exit door. As I climbed into the van, I collapsed in the seat and placed my head back on the head rest.

With enthusiasm, Lamont chirped, "Let's go to Home Depot."

When he pulled into Home Depot's parking lot, I begged. "Can I stay in the car?"

"Are you crazy? It's nearly 100 degrees and with gas prices I can't leave the air on."

Before I could respond, he was around the car, opening the door. "Come on Babe, I promise I won't be long."

Under my breath, I muttered, "One minute is too long."

CHAPTER 60

True to his word, Lamont spent less than an hour in Home Depot. As we drove home, he glanced at me. My eyes were closed.

"I guess you're tired and probably don't want to see the golf demo at Arnold Palmer?"

To hide my true feelings, I merely shook my head. Silence filled the van for the rest of the ride home.

Relief filled my body when Lamont pulled into the driveway. The van came to a halt. In one motion, I opened the door and climbed out. Lamont called my name, but I was already in the house, answering the ringing phone.

"Hello."

"Hi, may I speak to Lorraine Harris."

"This is she."

"You probably don't know me, but I'm from Trotter." Before she continued my first thought was, could this be my mystery caller?

Rather than say anything, I listened. "I understand you're writing a book about Connellsville. Is that correct?"

Inhaling I took a deep breath and exhaled. I was curious as to how she found out about the book, but yet I couldn't form the question because I was in shock.

I heard myself utter, "Well..." I stopped, not wanting to commit. "At this point, I'm gathering information."

Her voice was laced with disappointment as she said, "I see. If you're including information about people who used to live there, I have some things I would like to share with you."

Searching for something to write with, I pulled out a kitchen drawer. No such luck. "I'll tell you what, send me an email with the information you want included."

The woman agreed to send me an email.

When Lamont entered the kitchen, he asked who was on the phone.

"You're not going to believe this. A woman called me about the Connellsville book."

He stared at me in disbelief. "What? How did she find out about it?"

"I don't know. I was so taken back that I didn't ask her."

Lamont's eyes were wide. "Well, what did she want?"

I exhaled in a heavy sigh. "Depending on what I put in the book she wanted to provide me with some information. She's going to email it to me."

"What's wrong?"

"I haven't even decided if I'm writing the book and all of a sudden I've got people calling me with facts I could possibly use."

Lamont smiled. "I hate to say it, but this could be another sign. You keep fighting it, but eventually you're going to notice the handwriting on the wall."

"What? That sounds like one of those old sayings people say, but no one understands the meaning. You know like, "If that don't take the rag off the bush I don't know what will." Anyway, I have to say I am curious as to how she found out about it."

CHAPTER 61

The side of my head was throbbing. A headache was developing and the source of its origin was obvious. After receiving the telephone call from the woman from Trotter I was feeling the pressure about the book from more than just Lamont.

Lamont came in holding two glasses. He gave one to me. "Aren't you hungry?"

"Not really."

"In case you change your mind, I'm broiling two hot dogs. After we eat lunch, we can continue."

I gave him a weak smile. "That sounds good."

After lunch, we began where we left off—local government.

Lamont handed me a picture. "Do you know where this picture was taken? Do you see the African American man in the back row?"

"This picture is from the church collection and it was taken in front of the old City Hall building."

I turned the photo over and read the notation. "The man in the back row is William Shaw. He worked for the Police Department as a janitor and later became a chauffeur."

The photographer unknown, photograph courtesy of Reverend Osborne's private collection.

Lamont was chewing on his lower lip and said, "Have you thought about putting names on each chapter? If you do, this one should be titled, City Government and not local government. People will understand the term better. What do you think?"

I shrugged. "I don't know if I'll use chapter titles. I did that in my notes to make it easier for reference purposes."

"Here's another African American who worked for the city. And I'm surprised. Look at this picture."

I examined the photo. On the back of the photo the name, James (Jimmy) Alsop had been written. Like Lamont, I was impressed that Connellsville had a police officer back in the late 1940's.

"Is that the best picture you have?"
"I'm afraid so.

JAMES ALSOP

1ST AFRICAN-AMERICAN
POLICE OFFICER
CONNELLSVILLE, PA

The photographer unknown, photograph courtesy of Reverend Osborne's private collection.

Lamont took the picture from me and uttered, not really talking to me. "So, this was Connellsville's first black Police Officer."

I had moved on and was looking to see if there were other black city workers. Since I didn't see any, I moved to State government employees.

CHAPTER 62

As we continued talking about the book, the doorbell rang. Lamont glanced at me and asked, "Were you expecting someone?"

"No."

Lamont answered the door. I heard him invite someone in. "Lorraine, Lorraine."

When I joined Lamont, he had invited Dot in. "Hi Dot. How's Vinnie?"

"He's doing okay. Today's a good day."

"Please have a seat."

"I can't say long. I only came over because one of our neighbors took Vinnie for a haircut." I could tell Dot was nervous as she bit on her thumb nail. We waited.

"I owe you and Lamont an apology." We glanced at each other. She went on to explain. "As I mentioned, Vinnie has the beginning stages of Alzheimer's disease. I don't know how much you know about it, but it's a complicated, ugly disease."

She looked at me and I nodded with sympathy. As Dot continued, I was shocked with what she asked, "By any chance have you received any hang-up phone calls?"

Our wide-eyed expressions answered Dot's question.

"I'm sorry. With Alzheimer's disease, everyone is different. Some people become aggressive and that's Vinnie's case."

"Dot, can I interrupt you for a minute. Are you saying that Vinnie might harm someone?"

"Well, I don't know. I just know that I overheard him calling someone...I mean you and Lamont, telling you not to write the Connellsville book."

"Oh my, gosh," escaped from my mouth before I realized it. I recovered and asked, "But, why?"

"Well, Vinnie was concerned that you might write something that was less than flattering about Connellsville. With him being a descendant of the town's founder, he has a lot of pride in Connellsville and wanted to protect its good name."

"Can you assure him that I'm not writing anything that should upset anyone or defame the town? I mean my folks still live there and I would never embarrass them."

"I understand, but Vinnie may not be able to understand. He has good and bad days."

"I have an idea. If it will help him and you, why don't I tell him that I'm not writing the book."

Dot's eyes began to tear. "You would do that?"

"Of course, but again I assure you I would never write anything embarrassing about the town or the people."

"I believe you." She glanced at her watch. "I really

need to go. Thanks again."

When Dot left, I didn't know what to say. Lamont said, "Do you believe it?"

"No, I would have never have guessed it was Vinnie. At least the mystery is solved. Let's get back to what we were doing."

CHAPTER 63

My words came out louder than I had intended. "Now, this is interesting."

Lamont glanced at me; waiting for me to share my discovery.

"John (Wash) Johnson may have been the first black from Connellsville to work for the Commonwealth of Pennsylvania. He was a messenger for Senator Mathew S. Quay, State Supreme Court and retired from the State government."

"Does it say when he worked for the State?"

"No, but it had to have been back in the 1930's."

"Why do you say that?"

"I don't know. I'll try to find out from Miss Elsie. He was her uncle."

"Was he the only State employee?"

"No. Do you remember Sylvester Parris, the Tuskegee Airman?" I asked the question, not waiting for a response.

"After 30 years, he retired as a senior field tax auditor, the first black tax auditor for the State."

"Wow. He was quite successful."

"He was. He died in July of 2004." I paused and expressed an idea. "If I title chapters, I could make just one heading, Government?"

"You could, but let's not get hung up on chapter titles. If we do, we'll have to go back and we've made too much progress to go back now."

I opened my mouth to say something, but didn't. I thought, "He just recommended a chapter title, but when I make a suggestion, it can wait." I told myself not to get distracted and to move forward.

"What's next?"

"The Federal…United States Government. This picture was taken on the steps of the Post Office."

Lamont snatched the picture from my hand. "Too bad you can't show the inside of the Post Office."

He chuckled. "When you step inside the Post Office, as well as the library, it's as if time has stood still."

With pride I replied. "That's why both buildings are on the historic register."

He shrugged. "Okay, it states here that…" Lamont took a closer look. "Can this be correct?" He handed the picture back to me.

"What's the question?"

"Connellsville has had black Post Office employees since 1938."

"Well, the newspaper article has the date of November 1938 and the two black men are Louis Keith and William Thompson."

"I'm surprised that they were rural carriers."

CONNELLSVILLE POST OFFICE EMPLOYEES   NOVEMBER, 1938

Row 1, Left to Right: Lee Hoover, Jessie Brooks, Laura Clark, Minerva Keffer, Frances Oglevee, Harriet Smith, Damon Critchfield, Ralph Kessler. ROW 2: Fred Joy, Walter Huey, Jack Craig, Robert Dunston, Jacob Miller, Charles Raymond, John Collins, Ben Robbins, Joseph Flanigan, Norman Harshman. ROW 3: John Kelley, Albert Seaman, Russell Filburn, Leslie Dunston, Lewis Wandel, Thomas Hunt, Frank Witt, Furney Lambert, William Thompson, ROW 4: Sam Putt, Edgar Collins, Danny Baker, Ray Lambert. ROW 5: Simon Snyder, Ralph Nicolson, Ralph Hyatt, William Gebhardt, Charles Yaw, John Thornton, Charles Cockrell, Stanley Phillips, James May, Louis Keith.

The photographer unknown, photograph courtesy of Reverend Osborne's private collection.

"I didn't know that and it is amazing. Let's continue."

Lamont wanted to quit. "Are we going to have dinner today?"

I thought, "It's always about the food." I shut off the computer and entered the kitchen to cook another meal.

CHAPTER 64

During dinner, Lamont and I talked excessively about some of the facts we found earlier. That made me happy because maybe after we finish eating, he might be interested in continuing. In fear that Lamont might change his mind, I tried not to show too much excitement.

With the kitchen cleaned, we walked to the postal station to pick-up our mail. I didn't want to rush Lamont, but why are we having a conversation with most of the neighbors? Once we retrieved our mail, we headed home. When we crossed the street, neighbors waved and stopped us.

The conversation went on longer than I had hoped. To help gear us toward home, I grabbed Lamont's hand several times; pulling on it, similar to a child anxious to go.

Since my focus was elsewhere, I wasn't paying a great deal of attention to the conversation, until I heard a question that needed answering.

"Do you all want to come over and perhaps play Mexican Train Dominoes?"

Instead of responding, I gave Lamont the lead. He glanced down at me and as hard as I could, I tried sending him a nonverbal message—I didn't want to play.

Instead, I heard Lamont utter, "That would be great. How about seven o'clock?"

With a plastered smile on my face, we turned, waved and Lamont said, "We'll see you later." While he was saying his good-byes, I had walked off. By the time he caught up with me, I was unlocking the lanai door.

"Why did you leave me? What's wrong?"

My voice was low. "I didn't want to play Dominoes."

"Then why didn't you say so?"

"Because I thought you could tell from my body language."

"I'm sorry, but I couldn't read your mind. Fine, I'll call and make an excuse."

I raised my hand. "No, no. It's okay. We'll go over and play Dominoes."

"Regardless of what you might want, you're in need of time away from the computer and the book. I love you and I don't want you getting sick."

Lamont was probably right, but I was disappointed. Instead of working on the book, we would be socializing. Before leaving for our neighbors, we watched the evening news.

Lamont was rummaging through the kitchen drawers.

"What are you looking for?"

"I'm looking for a bag to put this bottle of wine in. I

thought we should take something with us. You might want to take your own snack in case they don't have anything for you to eat."

As we walked next door, Lamont put his arm around my shoulder. "Are you okay?"

"I'm fine." I pouted. "I really wanted to work on the book."

"For someone who doesn't want to write the book, you spend a lot of time wanting to work on it."

Before I could respond, we were standing at our neighbors' front door. The evening was pleasant and I have to say I had a good time. In addition, not once did I think about the book.

When we arrived home, the hour was late and all I wanted was my bed. I hoped I would get a good night's sleep.

CHAPTER 65

The following morning I had difficulty getting out of bed. I staggered to the kitchen. Anyone watching me would have thought I had a hangover. My stomach was queasy and bloated. My head was light.

I ran a quick mental checklist to determine what I had eaten yesterday. Nothing seemed out of the norm, but something had made me sick.

"Lamont, Lamont." Where was he?

After making a cup of herbal tea, I went back to the bedroom. I sat the cup down, propped up two pillows, turned on the television and climbed back into bed.

My nausea had eased after I finished drinking the ginger tea, but I was wiped out. My symptoms were similar to the flu, telling me that something I had eaten contained wheat, gluten or both. I slid deep into the bed covers and must have fallen asleep. Turning over, I felt a heavy pressure.

I tried to get up, but Lamont prevented me. "Stay still. It's not necessary for you to get up." Lamont was sitting on the bed. "Are you sick?"

"I have to use the bathroom." Lamont moved as I got up.

Before returning to bed, I washed my face and brushed my teeth. As I headed towards the bedroom, I stopped. My stomach cramped up, forcing me to sit down on the toilet.

Lamont was at the bathroom door. "Lorraine, are you okay?"

My voice was weak and hoarse. "I'm fine. I'll be out in a minute." When I re-entered the bedroom, I was drained and weak. I climbed back into bed.

"What did you eat last night?"

"I don't know. I've thought about it and I can't remember eating anything I wasn't supposed to."

"Um…you didn't eat the snack you took, but didn't you have some mixed nuts?"

"I don't…oh, no, I did."

"That's what probably made you sick. You know certain brands of nuts are processed in the same place as wheat products."

"I know, but sometimes I forget and today I'm paying the price."

Lamont stood up. "Don't be so hard on yourself. You can't be perfect every day." He smiled. "Have you eaten today?"

A slight laugh escaped as I answered. "No and I'm not sure I can keep anything down and if I do, it's coming out the other end."

"Maybe, but you should probably eat something. You

have some gluten-free broth I could heat up."

"Okay, but I only want a little."

When Lamont went to the kitchen, I welcomed the quiet. I didn't want to talk or eat. All I wanted was rest.

CHAPTER 66

The next day, I felt better, but my legs were wobbly, making my movements slow and jerky and my head was still groggy. As much as I wanted to work on the book, I didn't have the energy. Furthermore, I knew Lamont would make me relax and would not let me do anything.

After I took a shower, I was surprised when Lamont had breakfast waiting for me.

"Good morning, Honey. How are you feeling?"

"Good morning."

My voice was hoarse. "I feel a lot better than yesterday." I sat down at the table. "This is a nice surprise. Thanks for making breakfast."

He smiled. "I still have my cooking skills. Once you've been a chef you're always a chef."

"Well, I would like to see those skills used a little bit more."

"You forget I did all the cooking when we were both working, and I swore after I retired I would cook when?"

I laughed. "You'll cook, but only out of necessity." We bantered back and forth and I was happy that I felt better.

When we finished breakfast, I sat on the sofa and turned on the television. Lamont cleaned up the breakfast dishes.

"What do you have planned for today?"

"Nothing because I want to make sure you do nothing." He raised an eyebrow. "Do you understand?"

Lamont stared down at me, making me feel as if I was a small child who had done something wrong and I was being issued my punishment.

"What we can do is discuss how we approach the next book chapter."

I sat up, a little surprised.

Lamont emphasized what he meant. "I said we can discuss what goes next. We will be doing nothing else but talking. No way are you going to sit at the computer, typing. Do you understand?"

"Yes, sir."

Lamont disappeared and returned with a binder. I reached for it, but he wouldn't give it to me.

"I'm in charge. You don't need the binder for our discussion."

I moaned.

Lamont flipped through the binder. "We finished the employment section. I must admit I'm not sure where we go from here."

"I guess we're finished then...."

"What do you mean finished?" Lamont stressed the word, *"finished."* Please explain what you mean."

"I was referring to the employment aspect. With that completed, maybe we can discuss Connellsville's Arts, Entertainment and Sports."

"Since we're using the alphabetical order system, I can guess where we'll begin."

My eyes twinkled and I didn't need to say what Lamont was thinking. He was right; alphabetical meant "sports" was last.

"I don't want to be cruel, but there are Arts in Connellsville?"

"All forms of art. You know music, writing, and painting."

Lamont was skeptical. "Is there anything noteworthy in the Arts? I never noticed a performing arts theater or anything in town."

"You may not think there's anything remarkable about the arts in Connellsville, but you'll be surprised."

"Okay, dazzle me with this information."

"For one thing, in the 1950's, Connellsville's Community Chorus was integrated."

"Where did they sing?"

"I don't know. I don't have any other information about the group except that the black members were Sara Pollard, Kathleen Walker, and Ruth Webster. Isn't there a picture labeled community choir?"

Lamont shook his head. "Surely, Ms. Elsie has a better picture than this. It's not clear and the faces of the black members can't be seen."

"Maybe I can get a better picture from her."
Lamont nodded. "That's a good idea."

CONNELLSVILLE'S COMMUNITY CHORUS

The photographer unknown, photograph courtesy of Elsie Webster Haley's private collection.

CHAPTER 67

Lamont wasn't impressed and I could tell. "Is there anything else?"

With attitude I said, "Yes. "Isn't there information about the Molinaro Band?"

"Here it is. It says the band was formed in 1913. Could that be a mistake?"

"I believe that information is correct. Anyway, James Betters was the first and only black member of the band. Primarily, they performed in parades."

"There's no picture."

I snapped. "If I had one it would be in the binder."

"Are you getting tired?"

I exhaled. "I'm fine."

"Is that it?"

"No. Why are you hurrying me?"

I didn't wait for a response. "I guess you're ready to move on to the sports chapter. You need patience."

Lamont rubbed his hands together. "I can't wait either. Okay, what else do you have?"

"The Mozart Club, and again, I have no idea when it was formed, but it was integrated in the early 1950's. The club's focus is performing a variety of classical musicals. The black members were: Mary Bonds, Letchrude Furman, Elsie Haley, Sarah Pollard, and Ruth Webster."

Lamont handed me a picture. "Did Miss Elsie give you this picture?"

"Yes, she did, and this is a picture of the Mozart Club"Isn't that Miss Elsie?"

"Yes, it is."

Lamont asked, "Who's the other woman?"

"The other woman is a mystery. I guess I'll have to find out who she is." It occurred to me that I needed to make a list of all the items I should follow-up on. My research had not ended.

Unidentified woman and Elsie Haley
The photographer unknown, photograph courtesy of Elsie Webster Haley's private collection.

"How are you going to distinguish between the arts

and entertainers?"

"What?" I threw up my hands in disgust. "Can we continue, please?"

Lamont pressed hard about the arts. What didn't he understand? Rather than answer his questions, I responded by closing my eyes.

"Are you okay?" I opened my eyes. Lamont's forehead was full of worried lines. "Can I get you something?"

"I'm okay." I didn't mention he was the source of my headache.

CHAPTER 68

Lamont's questions and off handed remarks had grated my nerves. Rather than continue, I told him I was going to take a nap. Connellsville may be small, but it did have culture.

Around twelve o'clock, Lamont woke me up. The food was on the table and I hoped we would resume our discussion after lunch.

"Did you do anything while I was napping?"

"No I napped too."

I had to laugh. Why wasn't I surprised?

"What's so funny? What because I had a nap? You know I take a nap every day. You're just jealous because you don't know how to relax."

"Whatever. Why don't we continue with the arts? I'm not sure how much more there is, but I don't think it will be much. The next person is Shanana Gales. She may be Connellsville's only African American poet."

"Isn't there a picture of her in the binder?"

"Did she graduate from Connellsville in 1932?"

"Yes. Can I see that binder?"

Reluctantly, Lamont handed it to me. I looked at her picture. "Writing poems was her God-given talent."

Shanna Gales

The photographer unknown, photograph courtesy of the 1932 Connellsville Year Book.

"Are any of her poems published?"

"Oh, over the years, she authored and published numerous poetry books."

Lamont suggested. "Maybe you should try to get one of her poems and put one in the book."

Again, Lamont was assuming I had made up my mind about writing the book.

"Have you ever read any of her poetry?"

"Yes, in fact you have too. At one of my class reunions, John Regis Taylor, read one of them when we were honoring deceased classmates."

"You really don't expect me to remember that, do you?"

Again, I didn't answer him.

"What? What's wrong with you?"

"Nothing is wrong. I'm tired." I rubbed my eyes and leaned back in the recliner.

Lamont took the binder from me and gave me a kiss on the forehead. Playfully, Lamont said, his voice breathy, "I'm sorry you're not feeling better because I have just what the doctor ordered."

CHAPTER 69

One o'clock a.m. and counting sheep was not putting me to sleep. Two o'clock, I was counting backwards from 100. My eyes were closed, but I was wide awake. After tossing and turning, I accepted defeat and realized that sleep was not coming. As I turned on my side, the hands on the clock read, three o'clock, I eased out of bed, hoping not to wake Lamont.

If it wasn't night sweats, it was insomnia. These were two evils of the many menopausal symptoms I suffered from and hated. Usually, lack of sleep meant my morning mood would be irritable, and weepy. Not to mention that Lamont would be my target for everything that was wrong in my world.

As I waited for the microwave to heat the cup of hot water, I sat at the kitchen table, thinking about the day. The schedule was busy, a doctor's appointment and the Florida Writers Association meeting. Lamont had two things on the calendar—bowling and the Sophisticated Gentlemen's dinner.

Holding the cup of herbal tea, I walked to the den. I closed the door, turned on the computer and sat down.

Since we're working on the arts, it will be easy for me to make some progress without Lamont. He can review everything later.

Thumbing through a few papers, I came across two pictures that should have been included in the high school chapter. I was about to type in the information when Lamont walked in.

"Are you sick? Why are you up so early? What are you doing?"

I took my time and answered slowly. "I'm not sick, thanks for asking. I couldn't sleep and decided to work on the book." That was the only explanation I gave him and then handed him two pictures.

"Where did these come from?"

"They were in this stack of papers. I'm glad I found them, but then again I think there will be a number of things I've miss and I have to accept that."

Lamont started laughing. I waited to hear what was so amusing.

"I guess Connellsville was no different than the rest of the country during the 1950's."

"What do you mean?"

"Back in the day, everyone was singing *"doo wop"* and lots of teens, especially males, wanted or thought they could sing. In the cities, young teens would stand on street corners, singing and Connellsville seemed to have been no different."

I threw up my hands and cheered. "Yeah!"

"What's that for?"

"Connellsville was normal in some aspects."

Lamont gave me a weird look. "It's hard to read these newspaper articles, but the high school Student Council sponsored talent shows. Is that right?"

"Yes, they held amateur talent shows. These are two different groups that won the singing portion of the show."

First and Second place winners of the Student Council Talent Show. L. to R. Sam Spotts, Don Sanner, Jim O'Donnell, Sandra Parrish, Fred Thompson, Les Wormack, Vivian Hart.

The African American students, left to right are: Sandra Parrish, Fred Thompson, Les Wormack and Vivian Hart

The photographer unknown, photograph courtesy of Patty White's private photo collection.

The Delrays

Left to right, James Hart, Wilbert Scott, Ralph Tennessee, Mike Johnson, Pete Bradley, and Les Womack

The photographer unknown, photograph courtesy of Patty White's private photo collection.

Lamont was curious. "Did any of these groups go on to the big time and make a record?"

CHAPTER 70

Lamont waited. I smiled and said, "Surprisingly, the Delrays made a demo record, but that was the extent of their singing success. The one person who made it big in the music industry was Harold Betters."

"Do I know him?"

"I think you met him, but you probably don't remember. Anyway, he is known as Connellsville's legendary jazz trombone player and celebrity. In 1947, Harold graduated from Connellsville's High School and studied music at Ithaca College in New York and the Conservatory in Brooklyn, New York."

"That's impressive, but in sports Connellsville has some celebrities." Lamont saw my face and returned to the subject at hand. "Tell me about his career."

"Well, in the 1950's, he played in New York City with several different bands and toured with the renowned Ray Charles. Shortly after that, he returned to Connellsville. During an interview, he stated that he did not like the road life."

"That might have been the case, but he continued his career."

"He did it locally in Pittsburgh. For over seventeen years, he played at a club named the Balcony."

"I hope you have a picture of him."

I gave Lamont his picture from the yearbook.

Harold Betters
The photographer unknown, photograph courtesy of the 1947 Connellsville Year Book.

"I hope you have a more up-to-date picture." I handed him the picture of Harold my sister, Patty had sent to me.

The photographer unknown, photograph courtesy of Patty White's private photo collection.

"Before you interrupted me I was about to tell you that during his career, he played with famous greats such as Louis Armstrong, Al Hirt, Slide Hampton, Ramsey Lewis, and Urbie Green. He also appeared on televisions programs such as The Tonight Show and Mike Douglas."

"Is he still playing?"

"He was when I began my research. Where ever he plays, he draws a large crowd, even here in The Villages."

Lamont jerked his head up. "What are you talking about?"

"Before we moved here, Harold played at Katie Belle's with Tony D."

"What a small world. Are there any other entertainers?"

"Yes. Cecil Cole…."

"Is that the same Cecil Cole…Cynthia's dad?"

"He's the one and the same. He graduated in 1937 from Connellsville's High School."

"Lorraine, you mentioned that before. You can't keep repeating information."

I responded, my voice not hiding my irritation. "Okay, remember we're organizing the data. If I write the book, I'll catch the duplications."

"Go ahead and tell me about his talent."

"While he served in the Army during World War II, he met a fellow soldier who was skilled in the art of magic and this solider introduced it to Mr. Cole. However, he didn't pursue magic until after the war. In the late 1940's, he began to perfect his magician skills. He was known as the Silent Knight of Magic by wearing a turban and cape. During his career, he appeared at parties and on local television programs."

CHAPTER 71

Something caught my attention. The clock on the computer read eight o'clock. The morning was moving too fast. We had made so much progress and I hated to stop.

"Lamont, I have to quit."

"Why, what's going on today?"

"I have a doctor's appointment and then I'm off to the Florida Writers Association Meeting at the Lady Lake Library."

We showered, dressed, ate breakfast and went our separate ways. For a change, my doctor's appointment was on time. I would make the meeting on time.

As I entered the meeting room and before I could sit down, someone handed me the sign-in sheet. Before passing it on, I was undecided as to whether to read. I signed in and marked the *"would read box."*

Instead of paying attention to the conversation, I was concentrating on the chapter I would read. My nerves were on edge and of all times, I was having one of those private summers, perspiration was running down my back. After glancing over the chapter I was going to read,

I made several minor changes as I heard my name being called.

My voice lacked luster as I read. On an occasion, I looked at some of the members, wondering what comments they might make. When reading the last paragraph, relief filled my body.

The leader asked, "Are there any comments for Lorraine?"

Comments were slow, but everyone made the same one. "There were too many statistics." Everyone agreed that the information was interesting, but the writing style didn't hold anyone's interest."

One man, sounded like Lamont. If I didn't know better, I would have said Lamont had put him up to making his comment. "Your heart isn't in this and you can tell. Why don't you want to write the book?"

"To be honest, this is my husband's story and I'm writing it for him."

The same man asked the same question again. "Why don't you want to write the book?"

I shrugged. The explanation I could give him wouldn't mean much so I didn't give him an answer.

He continued. "I think you need to find out why you don't want to write the story. Maybe then, you can tackle it from a different viewpoint. Does that make sense?"

Angry words almost erupted, but thank God I kept my mouth shut. This man was not Lamont. He was only expressing his thoughts. I reminded myself, not to take his comments personally.

I was relieved when I heard the leader's voice. "If there are no additional comments for Lorraine, then let's hear from Saundra."

A woman sitting next to me, leaned over and whispered, "I've read your other books and you know how to tell a story and that's what's missing. You're not telling a story, but quoting facts."

On my drive home, I kept hearing the woman's words, echoing, "Just write a story."

Maybe that's why I'm struggling because I don't know how to tell the story. "God, if I'm supposed to write this book, please give me a sign. I say this prayer in your precious Son's name. Amen."

CHAPTER 72

When I arrived home, Lamont had not returned and I was thankful. The meeting had left me mentally and physically exhausted. My jaw was throbbing and in a few minutes a headache would be in full force. To help ease the pain, I did something I rarely do; I took a nap.

Movement, why did I feel as if something was shaking the bed? Several blinks and opening and closing my eyes, I opened them. The room was dark. My mind didn't comprehend.

Lamont was sitting on the edge of the bed. "Are you okay?"

My response was a yawn. "I'm fine. The day was long and when I came home, I took a nap." I rephrased my words. "I guess I took more than a nap. More like a deep sleep."

"You must have needed it. I shook you several times before you responded. It's getting late and I'm about to leave. Are you going to be okay?"

"I'm fine." Lamont leaned down and kissed me. "I have the cell phone. I'm off to my dinner date. I'll be at the Golden Coral if you need me."

Thirty minutes later, I was still in bed, trying to make up my mind as to what I wanted to do. Finally, I sat up, on the edge of the bed. Tension filled my neck and upper shoulders. To relax, I moved my neck from side to side and rolled my shoulders backwards and forward several times.

The book entered my thoughts. For a minute, I wanted to work on it, but changed my mind. After I ate, I called a few friends, the girls, read a magazine, and watched television. Before Lamont returned, I was in bed, asleep.

The next morning, I felt refreshed. From Lamont's facial expression, I knew he was worried.

"Good morning. How do you feel?"

"Good morning. I'm feeling great."

"Maybe you should rest for the next couple of days. You've been doing too much."

I didn't say anything because he was probably right.

"What are your plans today?"

"I'm going to rethink the book."

Suspiciously, Lamont looked at me. "Why? Did something happen at the writers' meeting yesterday?"

"Well, I read two chapters and…."

Excitement filled Lamont's voice. "And, they liked it."

I chewed on my lower lip. I didn't know how to tell him that no one liked it. "Uh…Uh…"

"What did they say?"

I made a face. "Well…I received a lot of comments. I

mean they liked the overall concept, but they expressed that something was missing."

"Like what? Did they have any suggestions?"

"Not really…."

"I can't believe no one had a suggestion that would help you write the book. If anything, they reinforced your feeling that the book shouldn't be written?"

"No, they didn't say that. What they said was that there was something…. Wait, one woman recommended that I write a story."

Lamont shook his head. "And how does that help you?"

"I'm not sure, but at least it was a suggestion.

CHAPTER 73

The day couldn't have been more beautiful. The sun was shining and although the predicted temperature would be in the mid-eighties, the breeze made it feel cooler.

Lamont and I sat on the lanai, had breakfast and read the morning newspaper. As the morning faded, we were content at watching people take their morning walks and the passing golf carts and cars.

Rather than spend the day in the den, we decided to work on the lanai. Instead of bringing all the binders out, Lamont brought out the one containing the sports information.

Lamont could not contain his excitement. "The sports aspects of Connellsville are interesting because of its population. The town has produced many individuals who had successful careers, in football, baseball, and boxing. I find that amazing."

"I know. You tell me all the time. Let's start with Billy Carter."

"Is that the man who was the high school athletic trainer?"

"Yes, that's him. In 1919, he became a professional boxer. He was one of the leading challengers for the world lightweight championship, but declined the offer."

"I wonder why."

"I don't know and the newspaper article doesn't say. He also fought an elimination bout for the right to fight Eddie Leonard who was the world champion. During his fighting career, he won an estimated 30 to 40 bouts or 90 percent of his fights."

Lamont smiled. "He was good. How long did his career last?"

"He fought for 18 years before he retired from boxing and for a while he was a boxing instructor."

"Where's his picture?"

"This picture isn't very clear, but this is the only one I found in the newspaper archives."

Billy Carter

The photographer unknown, photograph courtesy of Elsie Webster Haley's private photo collection.

Lamont wanted answers. "I wonder why he didn't go for the big time."

"I don't know. Maybe the next time you see Cynthia Cole Griffin, you can ask her. Billy Carter was her grandfather and you already know that Cecil Cole was her father."

"Wait! I knew Mr. Cole was her father, but I guess I didn't realize he was the pitcher for the National Negro Baseball League, the Newark Eagles."

"That's him."

Lamont's face lit up. "Did you know he played with the Negro Baseball Hall-of-Famers—Satchel Paige, Larry Doby, and Monte Irvin?"

"I didn't know any of this until you told me."

Excited, Lamont continued. "Not only that! His team won the Negro World Series in 1946. That was the year the Negro Baseball League ended and the end to segregation in professional baseball."

"I bet I know something you don't know."

"What's that?"

"Mr. Cole continued his love of baseball by becoming a scout for the Pittsburgh Pirates."

Lamont's jaw dropped. "No, I didn't know that.

Cecil Cole

The photographer unknown, photograph courtesy of Elsie Webster Haley's private photo collection.

CHAPTER 74

"I think the most famous athlete from Connellsville is John Woodruff."

"I agree. I knew who he was, but didn't realize he was from Connellsville until I was reading the book titled, "First Blacks."

"Most people can't believe that a person from Connellsville won a gold medal from the 1936 Olympic Games that were held in Berlin, Germany."

"There's that western Pennsylvania mystery of producing highly-skilled and talented athletics."

"I know, you tell me all the time. The local newspapers have written many articles about John Woodruff and his views of what it was like during that period. Anyone can learn more about him if they go on the Internet. He achieved the high honor of becoming a member of the United States Track and Field Hall of Fame. I think the city did a wonderful thing when they named a park in his honor."

John Woodruff

The photographer unknown, photograph courtesy of Elsie Webster Haley's private collection.

PARK OF CHAMPIONS

The photographer unknown, photograph courtesy of Elsie Webster Haley's private photo collection.

"Has any other Connellsville athlete received a similar tribute?"

"You mean Connellsville naming a park in their honor?"

"Right."

"Not to my knowledge."

"You know Lorraine, Mr. Woodruff was the first American to receive a gold medal during the 1936 Olympics. The problem was that Jesse Owens, a black man, won three medals during the same time and that overshadowed Woodruff's accomplishment."

"You're probably right, but it doesn't matter because the town has honored him and he has done the same. Do you remember when we went to the high school?" I continued, "He gave the high school all of his medals for display at the school."

"I remember that wall."

"One last thing, when he returned to Connellsville from the Olympics he brought with him a tree that was planted and still remains at the stadium."

"I would like to see that the next time we visit Connellsville."

CHAPTER 75

The book was finished. Nothing else seemed relevant to discuss. What else could be written? My intuition told me that Lamont might disagree.

"Well, the sports chapter is done and that completes Connellsville's story about African Americans."

"I don't think so. Before I tell you what else should be included, you forgot to mention the city's Auxiliary and Volunteer Police."

"Where did you find that?"

"It was buried underneath these papers. According to the write-up, the auxiliary was integrated for years and the members assisted the police department when needed. Are any African Americans mentioned?"

"Miss Elsie gave me a picture and the names of the black volunteer police force. They were: James Baker, Sr., Tom Banks, Noble Hardy, George Johnson, Archie Taylor, James Meadows, and James Scott."

"I'm surprised there were no women."

"I'm sorry. Roberta McCargo was the first African American female member to serve on the Auxiliary and Volunteer Police."

CONNELLSVILLE'S AUXILIARY AND VOLUNTEER POLICE FORCE

The photographer unknown, photograph courtesy of Elise Webster Haley's private collection.

"What else is there to write about?"

"I don't think the book is complete until you tell what happened to the many high-achieving African Americans students who left Connellsville and those that remained."

I chewed on my bottom lip. "I guess."

"Come on, Lorraine. People want to know if you all were able to transfer what you experienced living in Connellsville into the real world. I think they would like to know the type of success you all had."

CHAPTER 76

With the completion of the early years, I came to realize that living in Connellsville might have been different. However, the town wasn't Utopia, but considering everything as a whole, Connellsville did produce some positive results. Just thinking about it put goose bumps on my arms. As much as I didn't want to admit it, Lamont had been right and sooner or later I would tell him.

His voice interrupted my thoughts. "Hey, why don't we go to the movies?"

I didn't have to think twice. "Okay. What do you want to see?"

"I don't care. Well, no chick-flick."

###

Instead of taking the car, we drove the golf cart to Sumter Landing. Before we bought our tickets, we ran into a couple we knew. After talking for fifteen minutes, we changed our minds about the movies and joined them for dinner at TooJays. Later, we walked to Town Square, listened to the band playing and watched couples, and others line dancing.

A slight breeze made sitting outside delightful and the conversation was light and full of laughter. As I admired the clean, smoke-free, Key West style decorations adoring the town square and surrounding buildings, I said a quick prayer. "Thank you God."

I couldn't speak for anyone else, but Lamont and I were blessed. Our retirement community, The Villages, was friendly, the lifestyle casual and affordable with hundreds of free activities, live entertainment and access to an abundance of doctors, churches, restaurants, and a hospital on the property.

Something triggered a memory or an event as my mind drifted from The Villages to my hometown. It was more about what Lamont said earlier. "You have to write about the blacks who left, stayed, or returned to Connellsville to complete the story."

The question that I cannot answer was whether the harmonious living conditions, especially the equality of education, had made a difference on the African American graduates. This was something that required additional study and documentation, similar to the questions regarding the large number of successful athletes from western Pennsylvania.

As Lamont asked, "What was the impact? Were the blacks able to succeed beyond Connellsville? For those that had returned, what had been their experience?"

A tug at my arm brought me back to the present. "Are you okay? You seemed like you were off in your own world."

I told a half lie. "I was thinking about The Villages and how blessed we are." I smiled. "Are you ready to go?"

We waited until our friends finished dancing and said our goodbyes.

Chapter 77

The hour was late, but I wanted to dive right into the material regarding the blacks who had stayed, left or returned to Connellsville. Trying to gather this information had not been easy.

The mistake might have been that I wasn't forthright when asking individuals what they had done after high school graduation. I had only hinted about my intention of writing a book. The response was laughter, questions about why write about Connellsville, and how I would use the information. Most of all, there was a general belief that no one was interested in small-town blacks, no matter what the success stories might be.

On all points I could identify with them. Most of all, I'm never anxious to share my story even though I've had a successful career. Another reason for their reluctance about sharing could have been the small town mentality, in that my interest was nothing but pure nosiness.

As I sat with my face in my hands, the same question kept nagging me. "Will anyone be interested in reading about black Americans from a small town?"

From time to time when I tested the waters by discussing some of the facts with people not from Connellsville, the reaction was mixed. Some were curious, others were skeptical, while some wanted to buy the book when it was published.

"What are you doing?"

"I was thinking about how I did not have that many success stories. Not to mention, my trepidation about explaining why people were omitted."

"As I've said before, I wouldn't worry about it. Don't stop now. You have more than enough success stories that will pique interest and cause surprise at the ones you do mention. You can apologize in the introduction or preface of the book to those not included."

"That's a good suggestion, but it's still bothersome."

"Come on, let's see what you have."

I let out a heavy sigh. "This is overwhelming." I scratched my head.

Lamont urged, "We'll use the same system of putting everything in alphabetical order? At least it's a starting point."

"Okay. The first will be Awards."

Lamont had a face of puzzlement. "What type of awards are you talking about?"

"Well, I have a person by the name of Robert Farmer." Here's his picture.

Robert Farmer

The photographer unknown, photograph courtesy of Payne A.M.E. Church Program Bulletin.

"Is that the best picture you have?"

"Listen, this is the best I have. I took this from a church program. After I scanned and cropped it, this was the result. I can always try to find better pictures later, but for now this is all I have."

"Didn't you mention this man before?"

"I don't think so. Besides I'm going to double-check everything when I finish."

Lamont was apprehensive. "Exactly what type of award did he receive?"

"He received his undergraduate and graduate degrees from Howard University in Washington, D.C. and...."

"No, no. Let's talk about the award?"

I pulled in my lower lip before answering. "I was getting to it before you interrupted me."

"I only wanted to keep you focused. You sound as if you were going all around the barn and back again."

"He was Connellsville's first black doctor to receive a prestigious award from the Gateway Medical Society. He was awarded the Dr. Oswald J. Nickens Physician of the Year Award." My ending was a glare.

"What's the look for? You did a great job with the write-up. Has anyone else received an award?"

"Arts and Entertainment is next."

"Excuse me, the arts goes before award." Lamont started reciting the alphabet, "a, b, c, d...."

I made a face. I didn't need him to recite the alphabet. "We're in the general area of the a's. William (Pete) Bradley graduated in 1958 and is a well-known artist who lives in Paris, France."

"That's impressive. Has he ever returned to Connellsville?"

"I don't know and don't have any additional information about him." I didn't give Lamont a chance to say what was next. "Let's move on to broadcasting. The radio station, WVLG, was located on Main Street."

"What type of music did it broadcast?"

"The music played was a mixture of the day. I do remember that not many black artists' music was played because we were always trying to listen to the radio station, WAMO, out of Pittsburgh."

Lamont asked, "Is that the same radio station that I tune into when we visit your parents?"

"That's the same one. Can we get back to Connellsville's radio station?"

Lamont held up his hand. "Wait a minute. What happened to the radio station?"

"It went out of business."

Lamont seemed annoyed as he stated. "Why can't you tell me the whole story? Instead, I'm dragging the information out of you. Now, what happened?"

"Fine, my best guess is that there probably wasn't enough money to sustain it. We're getting off the subject. The only reason why I brought it up was because Kevin Harrison was a Disc Jockey for the station."

"I hoped he played rhythm and blues."

"I couldn't tell you because I wasn't living in Connellsville when he was a radio station DJ, but since he was black, I'm sure he played a variety of music. Let's move on to the hospital employees."

"Wait a minute. You're not going to include yourself?"

"What do you mean?"

Lamont's voice was filled with irritation. "You're an award-winning author and you have six published books. In addition, you donate proceeds from the sale of your books to charitable organizations."

"Okay, I'll include it."

"What about a picture?"

The word, *"fine,"* was my response but for some reason it was full of anger.

Lorraine Mockabee Harris

The photographer Lamont C. Harris, photograph courtesy of Lorraine M. Harris private collection.

What's wrong with you? Why are you being so modest about your accomplishments?"

I knew he was right, but it felt awkward including information about me in the book."

"You're not going to mention your 2008 Author of the Year Award from Artists of America." Lamont stopped when he saw my face. He threw up his hands. "Okay, why don't we stop and pack for our fourteen day cruise."

"Believe it or not, I've been packing. Every day I've been putting clothes in my suitcase."

"Okay, but what about the Literary Book Festival the Saturday before we leave? Are you ready for the workshop you're doing?"

CHAPTER 78

Tension was the overall mood in the house. The cause was because of the cruise and the upcoming literary festival. To make sure we did not miss anything, I compiled a list.

The festival was approaching quicker than I had time to finalize everything. What had I been thinking about when I signed up to do a workshop? To participate as an author was stressful enough. The printing of the workshop binders and putting them together was taking longer than I expected. The problem was too much information for the forty-five minute workshop and it was too late to revise it.

"How's it going?"

"Slow."

"What can I do to help?"

Normally, I would reject Lamont's help only because he would find fault in my method of doing things. But, the reality was I needed him. I had two days to finalize all the workshop binders.

"Can you punch holes in these papers?"

"No problem, but how many binders are you making?"

"I've made twenty-five. All the printing is done, but now comes the hard part. All the pages need holes punched and then put into the binders."

"Okay, but is that it?"

I didn't want to tell him, but I heard my weak voice say, "I'm also working on a PowerPoint presentation." I chewed on my lower lip. "Well, I'm not really doing it. I'm putting all the information together and then someone else is putting it together."

Lamont's voice had raised a notch. "You don't know how to do it?"

My chest raised and fell. "No, I don't know how to do it. When I was working, my secretary did all of my PowerPoint stuff."

Lamont said nothing and worked at his assignment. As much as I hated to, we had to stop for dinner. After we ate, it was back to work. This was our routine until every binder was finished.

Saturday came too soon. My nerves were on edge because I wasn't as prepared as I would have liked. The book selling would take care of itself, but my concern was the workshop.

Lamont was encouraging. "Remember, no one knows what you're going to say but you. You'll do an excellent job as always."

I gave him a kiss.

Lamont teased, "We don't have time for that."

When we arrived at the festival, I was given a table assignment and workshop schedule. To my disappointment, my workshop was at the end of the day. My worries went from presenting the workshop to whether or not anyone would attend.

All of the books sold well attributed to Lamont's unusual sales technique. Despite my apprehension, the workshop was well attended and the participants found it informative and the material useful.

With the festival behind me, our focus shifted to the cruise. We had last minute errands, including paying bills, double-checking items packed, weighing the suitcases to avoid paying extra, and making sure we had our passports and cruise documentation.

We checked with the couple we planned to travel with and everything was in order. Before we left for the airport, I pulled out the documentation regarding our return trip.

"Lamont we have a problem."

"Why?"

I pointed to the bus receipt. "Look at the date. Cruise Connection, our bus transportation, from the Miami Port when we return from the cruise, had us coming back on the wrong date."

"Can you call them?"

I glanced at the clock. It was early and probably no one was in the office, but I dialed the number anyway.

After the third ring, a real live person answered. It was the bus dispatcher.

I explained my concern. He assured me that our papers were in order and our names were on the correct return date.

The repositioning cruise from Rome to Miami was an unbelievable experience. Since I suffer from motion sickness, I worried about the choppy seas and being on the ocean for seven days, but everything was perfect—the weather, the activities, and the nightly entertainment.

When we returned home from the cruise, the holidays were fast approaching. Our attention now was on decorating the house, attending parties, and entertaining. We were happy that our daughters, Nicole and Natalie, could join us. This holiday was more special than usual because we were celebrating Lamont's 62nd birthday.

CHAPTER 79

To bring in the New Year, we attended a party sponsored by the African American Club at one of The Villages' recreational centers. Partying on New Year's Eve was something we had not done in a long time. The party brought back memories of when we were younger and frequented house parties or cabarets.

Over the past several years, we had celebrated bringing in the New Year in Maryland. Although we had a great time at the African American New Year's Eve party, we missed not being with my family and most of all not attending my sister Patty's New Year's Day party.

The food would be in abundance. Patty would showcase her cooking skills by preparing what most blacks would call traditional New Year's Day food—black eyed peas, collard greens, pig feet, ribs, potato salad, macaroni and cheese, a variety of cakes and pies and anything else that family members might have her cook.

As with every New Year, Lamont and I discussed our goals for the year. My number one priority was to finish the Connellsville book. At least, progress had been made and I could begin to see light at the end of the tunnel.

In starting off the New Year, we decided to ease into it. We were not making any new commitments. That made me happy because that would free up time for the book. With the holidays concluded, Lamont and I were still recouping from eating too much and staying up to late.

Two weeks later, I decided it was time to get back into a productive mode, meaning, working on the book. The success stories Lamont wanted me to include were limited. Mentally, I recited the alphabet. C was next.

Lamont stood at the doorway. "What are you doing?"

"I'm going to put my energy into finishing this book. We started last year and this year it's a done deal."

Lamont grinned at me, but I didn't know why and I didn't ask. "Are you going to help me?"

"Sure. Where did we leave off?"

Lamont pulled out the binders and because of his organizational skills we had no problem identifying where we had left off.

"Here we are, people hired by the Connellsville Highland Hospital." I was surprised at the number of African American that had or still worked for the hospital.

"Your notes state they might have worked at the hospital as early as the 1950's." Lamont stopped and thumbed through more papers. "The information isn't…" Lamont had this forlorn expression as he uttered, "Oh, no!"

"What?"

"A list is necessary. There's no other way to provide this information, but to make a list."

"No problem. We can always omit the list later. Who are they and what did they do?"

Lamont handed me a sheet. I typed their names and their positions.

Name	Position
Bertha Baker	Dietary Department
Charlotte Fant	Supervisor, Laundry Department
Alberta Glass	Dietary Department
Anna Mae Harrison	Medical Records
Betty McMillian	Revenue Department
Jean Baker Searcy	Payroll/Accounting Department
Geraldine Smith	Health Assistant
Anna Bell Thompson	Housekeeping Department
Toni Walker	Procurement Department

"Is that it regarding the hospital?"

Lamont said, "No. Now, this is amazing."

"What?"

"Robert Farmer, the man you mentioned earlier that received that award." Lamont didn't wait for me to respond. "Well, he was the first black to serve as the Director of Radiology at the hospital."

"That is surprising. What else?"

"A man named Ellis Harrison." Lamont paused and handed me an obituary. He continued. "He was the first black to serve as a Trustee for Connellsville's Highland Hospital."

Lamont hesitated. "I believe that's everything in reference to people working for the hospital. Make sure you take his picture off his obituary program."

Ellis Harrison

The photographer unknown, photograph courtesy of the Harrison's Family private photo collection.

CHAPTER 80

That went fast, I thought. "What's next?"

"Entertainment, I think." Lamont was mumbling something. "We should have put the binder's information in alphabetical order.

"What are you talking about?"

"Nothing. Let's move on. I'm looking at a picture marked Gary Walker. Do you know him?"

Gary Walker

The photographer unknown, photograph courtesy of the Walker's Family private photo collection.

"Sure, I know Gary. I'm not sure, but he graduated from Connellsville and....look over there. There should be a newspaper article about him."

"Here it is. According to this, Gary started his singing career when he joined the Junior High West Chorus. Merle Stutzman was Gary's high school music teacher as well as his private vocal teacher. He credited him for his successful career."

Lamont paused. "Gary had a CD called, "Storybook" in Japan and produced commercials for General Hospital. He also opened for Ray Charles, Ringo Starr, and Christina Aguilera."

Lamont nodded his head. "He's had quite a career. He also produced records and won the Producer of the Year Award for his work at Newport Record Company."

"I didn't know that. When Gary visits Connellsville he usually does a benefit concert for Payne A.M.E. Church."

"That's nice. Okay, let's move on. I think we're getting confused. Why do you have Connellsville High School Teachers separate? Why didn't we include them earlier?"

"Uh…let me see that paper." I glanced over it. "I don't know. Let me take care of it now."

Lamont read my notes. "I think Cynthia Cole Griffin might have been the teacher hired after Jane McPherson. Cynthia graduated in your class of 1964."

"Yes she did. I believe she taught high school English."

"Okay. She graduated from Alderson-Broaddus College and taught at the school from 1972 to 1976."

"Where is Alderson-Broaddus College?"

"It's located in West Virginia."

"Lamont, let's not get distracted. Who else did I list as a teacher at Connellsville?"

"You have a Natalie Moon Cole?" Lamont smiled. "Wait! Is she related to Les Moon who graduated with you?"

"It's his sister."

"That's all the information I have about her. Another teacher is Andrea Michaux. She graduated from Greensburg, Pennsylvania's Seton Hill College. Andrea taught English in Connellsville and was the Yearbook Club sponsor."

Lamont couldn't believe it. "Didn't you have any black male teachers?"

"Yes, Kenny Washington taught English. In fact I believe he taught at the high school the same years as Cynthia. He might still teach there."

"Okay, that's it."

I slapped my forehead. "How could I forget Robert Anthony Lewis, Senior? When we were growing up, we called him Copie."

"Wait a minute, his name sounds familiar. Oh yeah, I met him at your church."

"That's right. Do you have his obituary?"

Lamont rifled through the obituaries I had gotten from my mom. I waited. "I can't find it. I think you have it."

My voice was firm. "Lamont, you have it."

He started laughing. "Here it is. He was born August 1944 and ...." His voice broke off. "I didn't realize he died in January 2004."

"I told you, but you don't remember. Anyway continue."

"He was the first black principal in the Connellsville Area School District. He received a football scholarship to attend California University of Pennsylvania."

He hesitated and let out a sigh. "This is pretty long. Anyway, he received a Master's Degree from the University of California in 1971. He taught reading from 1982-1992 for grades seven, eight, and nine. He coached basketball, football, and track. Before he became South Side Elementary School principal, he served as acting principal at Bullskin Elementary School and Connellsville Township Elementary School. He retired in 2001."

"I had no idea Copie did all of that."

"His career was extraordinary. I believe that's all the teachers that taught in Connellsville."

"Look at my notes and see if I mentioned the individuals that became teachers, but didn't return to Connellsville."

CHAPTER 81

Lamont didn't respond right away and then started chuckling. "I have them. Your sister, Nancy Mockabee Murrell is one of them."

"Let's keep to our system of using alphabetical order."

"Okay. Marva Cole DeBeary was a teacher, but you don't have anything else beside her name."

I could not hide my annoyance. "If there isn't anything else then I don't have anything." I exhaled. "She is ... I should say, was Cynthia's sister. She died several years ago."

"I'm sorry."

I didn't want to repeat information, but I wanted Lamont's opinion. "I don't know if Cynthia should be mentioned again or not. She taught in Connellsville and then she taught near Pittsburgh in Monroeville, I think."

"Maybe...I'm like you. It needed mentioning, but where?"

"Then, there's Maurice Moon. Yes, he's Les' brother. I don't have any other information about him except that he was a teacher."

Lamont sighed. "You really need to get some more information."

My voice was testy. "Well, I can't make people give me information."

I stood up and went to the kitchen. I tried telling Lamont that parts of the book would lack information. What did he tell me? *"Don't worry, just write it."*

I must have been in the kitchen too long because I heard Lamont yelling. "Lorraine, where are you?"
I went back to the den. "Let's quit."

"Let's quit, I don't think so. We'll finish listing the individuals who became teachers and then we can stop. Besides you don't seem to have much except for names anyway."

I sat back down at the computer.

"Nancy is next. She graduated in the class of 1965 and attended California University in California, Pennsylvania. She earned a Master's Degree from Bowie State University in Bowie, Maryland."

Lamont shook his head. "I remember Nancy when she taught at Oxon Hill High School in Maryland. She was a tough math teacher."

I cocked my head to the side. "Maybe she was, but her students loved her."

"Right! You forget I was the assistant coach for the boys' basketball team and she taught some of the players."

"No. If I remember correctly, Nancy wasn't the

problem. It's just that she wouldn't compromise by giving athletes a grade they didn't earn or deserve."

Lamont raised his hands in defense. "You're right. I believe Prince Georges School System lost a good teacher when she retired."

"I agree with that."

Lamont grinned. "Janet Scott, the class of 1966, and she's another relative of yours." He hurried on before I could get the words out. "She graduated in 1969 from the University of California in California, Pennsylvania, with a B.S. degree. She was the first black teacher hired at the Plansville High School in Plansville, Ohio."

"We aren't finished yet?"

"Well, this isn't about high school, but Janet, your cousin was the first black female hired at Memphis State in Memphis, Tennessee."

I added, "Until I researched my family's genealogy, I didn't know that."

"Okay, let's continue. Georji Lewis, class of 1989, graduated from Edinboro University in Pennsylvania with a B.S. degree in accounting and a Master's degree in Counseling/Student Personnel Services. For the past twelve years, he worked as the Dean of Students for the Georgia Southern University."

"Lamont, as a side note, this is Copie's son."

"Wow! Copie must have been proud."

"Can we go to bed now?"

CHAPTER 82

Another day in The Villages and both of our schedules were filled for the next several weeks. The last thing I should have done was to add another commitment to my calendar, but this was important. I joined a non-denominational Bible study group for women, the Community Bible Study, that met on Mondays.

Lamont knew how happy I was to join the group, but he also stated a concern, "Lorraine, Monday will be hectic for you. You'll be rushing from one place to another."

I knew he was right, but I wanted to at least give it a try.

When bowling ended, we rushed home. I changed clothes while Lamont made lunch. After I ate and was about to leave, I spotted Lamont with the binders.

Seeing him going through the papers made me uncomfortable. "What are you doing?"

"I thought I would organize the rest of this information."

"Okay, but don't do any typing."

We laughed. Lamont's idea of typing was using one finger from each hand. We kissed and I left.

When I returned home I shared with Lamont how much I enjoyed the Bible study group. I was curious. "Did you get anything accomplished?"

"I think so. I cooked dinner. Why don't we eat and review what I did."

While I was cleaning the kitchen, the phone rang.

"Hello. This is Lorraine." I didn't recognize the male voice and he was slow in providing me with his identity. After several minutes of going back and forth, the man finally gave me his name.

"What a surprise? How are you doing?" The man was from Connellsville. The last time I visited my mom, I saw him at church. He sang in an all-male chorus, along with my dad's brother, Uncle Albert.

"I understand you've written a book about Connellsville. Where can I buy it?"

"Uh…" I hesitated and tried maintaining a pleasant voice. "I'm working on a book about Connellsville, but I haven't finished it."

"Oh, well it was my understanding that it was completed."

"It's not, but I'll let you know when it is."

We talked for several more minutes before hanging up.

Lamont yelled, "Who was that?"

Rather than yell back, I went to the den. "It was someone I knew from Connellsville."

"Anyone I know?"

"You've met him, but you probably won't remember." I tried jogging Lamont's memory. "He belongs to the same singing group as Uncle Albert."

"You're right. You uncle introduced us to the entire singing group. So, there's no way I'd remember. What did he want?"

I exhaled. "Someone told him I had written a book about Connellsville."

"You're kidding?"

"No, and again I didn't ask who told him. This is getting out-of-hand and I wonder who's spreading this rumor."

Lamont smiled. "It's not a rumor?"

"It is until I decide whether I'm going to write it."

"Well, what have we been doing all these months?"

I held my ground. "We have been organizing information, making it easier if and when I make a decision."

"Well, if you're not writing a book, do you think someone else could be writing one and you don't know about it?"

The question hung in the air. "I don't know and I can't worry about it."

CHAPTER 83

According to Lamont, yesterday's telephone call was another *"sign"* as to why I should write the book. I didn't even argue with him.

One thing for sure, the end was near because there wasn't much more to write about. The last part would have probably included more if I had persuaded more people to provide me with information, but I couldn't worry about that now.

I hoped today would be the day we would complete the organizing of the data. Then, I could focus on the decision of what to do.

"Hey, Babe, what are you doing?"

I snapped. "What do you think?"

"I'm sorry."

"I'm the one who's sorry. It's just that I want this project finished. I'm ready to move on to another book I should be working on. People continue to ask when I'll be getting back to the Sunday Golf Series."

"And you will, but you have to complete this first."

"You don't have to remind me."

"Okay, where are we?"

"I guess we were on the letter "e." If not, we can change it later."

"Are you going to have chapter headings? If you do, you might want to name this chapter, Business Owners or Entrepreneurs."

"Why?" My patience was short, my head was hurting, and I was having a hard time concentrating.

"If you title it Entrepreneurs, you're fine. If you call it Business Owners then this would be an earlier chapter—remember the alphabet."

"Let's not worry about it now." Frustration filled my voice. "Please give me the first business owner."

"Gregory Gray graduated from Connellsville's High School. He is a master barber and opened his barbershop in 2003. It's located on Main Street on the West Side and the shop welcomes all races, genders, and ages. This picture isn't very good. Where did it come from?"

Gregory Gray

The photographer unknown, photograph courtesy of Gregory Gray's Business Card.

"I scanned it off his business card."

A slight laugh escaped Lamont, but he didn't say anything. I knew what he was thinking. *"I needed a better picture."*

And, he was probably right. "Who's next?"

Lamont was not responding. All he was doing was sitting with a goofy look on his face.

"What's wrong with you?"

CHAPTER 84

As Lamont began to answer me, it was as if he was trying to smother a laugh. "Here we go again. Your family, your cousin, Janet Scott is next."

"What's wrong with that?"

Lamont snickered. "Nothing is wrong."

"What does it say?" He paused and gave me her picture from my family photo collection.

Janet Scott

The photographer unknown, photograph courtesy of Janet Scott's private photo collection.

Lamont was reading and then said firmly. "You've already mentioned most of this. I suggest you don't repeat it."

"I don't mean any harm, but let me be the judge of that."

Lamont's voice was terse as he spoke. "Okay, but you're repeating yourself."

He began reading. "She was in the class of 1966, graduated from California State University, California, Pennsylvania with a B.S. Degree. In 1976, she graduated from Ohio State University, Columbus, Ohio with a PH.D in counseling."

Lamont stopped. "I'm telling you, you can eliminate some of this information."

"Please continue."

"In 1983, she established a business and is the founder of Janet Scott, PH.D & Associates. She is a National Board Certified Counselor and is a Tennessee Licensed Professional Counselor and a mental health service provider. Her services are offered to individuals, groups, couples and family therapy for diverse areas of emotional issues such as relationship problems, depression, alcohol/drug abuse, eating disorders, stress, women issues and abuse. In addition to her private practice, she offers private workshops, training, and consultation."

When Lamont finished, I said nothing. That information had not been stated earlier. He was getting as tired of this book as much as me. I thought we should stop before we say something to each other that will end in hurt feelings. "Do you want to quit?"

"No. We still have some other business owners."

I couldn't believe it. "Who are they?"

"Dr. Farmer is one busy man. He is the founder and President of Diagnostic Imaging Service, Inc. and the President of Highlands Ultrasound Associates. Then there's Rozella Canty, class of 1965. Did she graduate with your sister Nancy?"

"Yes, but I didn't think she was a business owner."

"Well, she was an Exercise or Fitness Expert according to your notes. She graduated from Howard University in Washington, D.C. and became a lawyer. She was a pioneer for full-figured women and appeared on the Mike Douglas television talk show in Cleveland, Ohio, demonstrating exercises for the larger woman."

"I remember that. In fact, she was discussing full-figured women issues before the subject was popular."

"Does she still do it?"

"I don't know. Who's next?"

Lamont cleared his throat. "I'm not sure if this belongs here or in sports." He cleared his throat again.

"Do you need a drink of water?"

He smiled. "No, the person I'm referring to is your cousin, Wilbert Scott, class of 1957. After his professional Canadian football career ended, he continued his love of the game as an owner of a Canadian Football Team."

Rather than make a comment, I asked, "Do you want to quit for the day or keep working on it?"

"Let's get something to eat and then finish up."

"It sounds good to me."

CHAPTER 86

After dinner, I decided that Lamont and I either didn't know the alphabet or we had created a new way of viewing A through Z. I couldn't believe we had glossed over Connellsville's City Government.

"What's wrong with you?"

"We somehow missed Connellsville's City Government."

"No, we didn't. We missed someone who belongs in that chapter. Don't make a big deal of it. You can easily put it where it belongs later."

"You're right. I'm tired."

Ignoring my comment, Lamont pressed on. "The person you're referring to must be Roy Taylor, class of 1956. According to this, he was the first African American elected to Connellsville's City Council. Here's his yearbook picture and a newspaper article about him."

Roy Taylor

The photographer unknown, photograph courtesy of the 1956 Connellsville High School Year Book.

The photographer unknown, photograph courtesy of Roy Taylor.

" Is there anyone else?"

"Yep, two African Americans served as police officers. Their names are Frank (Buddy) Barrett and Charles Mills."

"Do I have a picture of either one of them?"

"Here's a newspaper article. Charles Mills was being honored along with other fellow officers. He's in the second row."

The photographer unknown, photograph courtesy of Payne A.M.E. Church Program.

Lamont asked, "Is that it?"

"No, I have an idea. If I'm going to title the chapters, perhaps this one should be "City Government." Then all information about anyone who worked for a city government would be mentioned."

"Lamont, why do you want to do that?"

"Because the chapters should be about those that stayed, returned, or left Connellsville and had success stories."

"Okay, do you know of any other individuals who

worked for a city government?"

"Remember the woman who sent me an email? Well, her brother Allen Fant, Dunbar Township High School, class of 1961, served in the United States Air Force."

Quickly, I raised my hand because I could read Lamont's face. "He retired from the District of Columbia Metropolitan Police Department after twenty-five years of service in 1995."

Before Lamont could ask I added, "I think Marvin Griffin worked for the New York City Police Department, but I'm not sure. Anyway, that's it."

CHAPTER 87

The day had been long and Lamont and I had been less than loving. If it wasn't my words, then it was both of our nonverbal glares, stares and facial expressions. I prayed this book would end soon. The more I prayed, the more it seemed we had to do.

In an effort to keep our happy marriage, we agreed to stop. I wanted to continue only because we were nearing the end.

###

Upon opening the den door, I found Lamont stretched out on the sofa. His eyes were closed. Either he was sleeping or meditating. As I was about to close the door, he sat up.

Lamont's face was grave, his voice heavy. "I think we have a problem."

I entered and sat down, facing him. "What's wrong?"

"I'm referring to the book. I was watching the History Channel. A woman was discussing a book she had written about her hometown and how she was being sued. Many of the people stated she had not told the truth about them."

I interrupted him. "You must be talking about Peyton Place."

Through gritted teeth he replied. "This is serious. The novel wasn't Peyton Place. It seems the author didn't get permission or release forms or something like that for using the information she had included in her book."

"Wait a minute. Are you saying I can't write the book?" I hoped my voice sounded sincere and even a tint of disappointment to mask my true feelings of happiness.

"I didn't say that. I'm concerned about how you got your information and pictures."

I pondered over his concern. "Much of the information and photos came from Mrs. Elsie Webster Haley and she gave me permission to use the information and photos."

"That was your primary source?"

"No, do you remember Reverend Acquanetta Osborne?"

"Was she the last female minister assigned to Payne?"

"That's her. Well, she gave me some information and photos. The only stipulation was that I would give her credit for using the information and pictures she provided me. This was because she received permission to use everything during a display at the church during Black History Month."

"Okay, what about any other sources?"

I thought about it before responding. "As you know, many of the pictures came from high school yearbooks, my family genealogy book, public documents, obituaries, and from people who provided me with family information."

Lamont smiled. "I think we're back in business. Let's get started."

CHAPTER 88

When I turned on the computer, I was less than enthusiastic because we had made a mess of the alphabetical system that had given us our start and our sense of order. I didn't know why I was worrying about it because the book wasn't even a reality and it still required a lot of work. My nagging doubts continued to haunt me and still there were no answers.

"Lorraine, are you with me?" Lamont was snapping his fingers.

"What?"

"I've been talking to you and you haven't responded to anything I've said. You were sitting, staring at the computer as if you were in a trance."

"I'm sorry. What were you asking me?"

"I asked if we should include a chapter for Ministry."

"I guess we have to start somewhere, but do we have enough for a chapter?"

Lamont's tone was harsh. "What is your problem? I thought you were excited because we were almost finished?"

I exhaled, noisily. "I don't know what's wrong. I'm

sorry. We're wasting time having this discussion. I'm sorry."

"It's okay." He teased. "That's why I'm in charge." Ignoring his remark, I asked, "Who do we have regarding the Ministry?"

"According to your notes, there are two people to mention, Cynthia Cole Griffin and Eileen Davis Burton."

"I think Cynthia is an Evangelist and Motivational Speaker. I know she often appears on local television. What have I written about Eileen?"

"She graduated from Dunbar High School and that she is a minister in Detroit, Michigan." Lamont turned the paper over and added, "There isn't anything else."

"Let's move on."

"April Straughters, class of 1996, went to college and after returning to Connellsville, she became the first black hired as a Newspaper Reporter for the Connellsville Daily Courier. When she left the Courier she worked as a reporter for the Uniontown Standard Herald."

Counting to ten, I waited for Lamont's comment. I knew it was coming.

He chuckled, "I don't have to say it. I know and everyone else knows."

Indignant, I said, "Look, I can't help it if my family members are high achievers."

Lamont's twinkling eyes met mine. "I didn't say a word. You did."

I stood up, with my hands on my hips. "This is

another reason why I didn't want to write this section. I don't want people to think I'm bragging about my family."

Lamont stood up and put his arms around me. "It's okay. Everyone will understand. Small town—everyone's related to everyone." Playfully, I hit him.

CHAPTER 89

We took a break to shower, eat, and make a trip to our favorite store, Wally World. We had not gone in several days and we in need of items like milk, lettuce, and whatever else we would pick up that we wanted, but didn't necessarily need.

On our way home, Lamont patted my hand. "You probably don't realize it, but we're almost there."

"Are you making idle promises?"

"No, I'm serious. I bet we don't have ten pages to go through."

"Praise the Lord."

When we returned from the store and put away the perishables, we returned to our favorite project.

"What's next?" At times, I felt as if Lamont and I were on a long journey, not knowing where we were going, but I knew eventually we would reach our destination.

"Let's take a look at Pennsylvania State Government."

"Are there many employees?"

Rather than give me a specific answer, Lamont

replied. "You're beginning to sound like a child riding in a car asking every so often, "Are we there yet?" The difference is that you keep asking, "Are there many employees?"

If I said something, it would not be kind. Instead, I asked, "Can you please give me the name of the person?"

"John Regis Taylor, class of 1964, graduated from Alderson-Broaddus College. Hey, he and Cynthia went to the same college."

"Yes, they did. I can't recall the exact story, but it's interesting. John Regis was in the military and a man told him that he knew Cynthia. To make a long story short, the man was responsible for John going to Alderson-Broaddus College on a basketball scholarship."

"If you're going to include this story you should call John Regis and get the details."

"You're right. Is that all I have regarding John Regis?"

"No, he worked for the State for twenty years and retired."

"I think his wife worked for the State too."
Lamont was curious. "His wife, Sofie, is from Connellsville?"

"No, that was just a side note."

"I think we need to stay focused."

Under my breath I mumbled, "Oh, you're the only one that can ask irrelevant questions or make side comments, especially about my family."

With bass in his voice Lamont barked with a tease.

"What did you say?"

"Nothing. Let's not get distracted."

Lamont let out a slight laugh. "You're right. Brian Burton was the first black from Connellsville to serve as a State Police Officer. James Baker, Jr. was the first black to hold the position as a Supervisor for the Driver's Exam Unit in Western Pennsylvania..."

Before Lamont could finish his sentence, I threw my hands up and started going through some papers marked *"finished."*

I found what I was looking for and shouted, "Oh, My God, how did I forget this?"

CHAPTER 90

Lamont had a concerned expression on his face. "What did you forget?"

"Sylvester Parris was the first black tax auditor for the State of Pennsylvania. He worked for over thirty years and retired as a Senior Field Tax Auditor."

"I'm glad you remembered."

"I'm sorry. What else do you have?"

"There are two women who were nurses that worked for the State."

"Who are they?"

"Lilia Furman and Alise Milton."

"I guess I don't have any other information about them?"

"Nope that's it except for others who worked in the medical/health field, but it wasn't for the State of Pennsylvania. Do you want this information now or do you want me to hold it?"

"No, give it to me."

"Burnack Scott Dowell, class of 1954 was a Registered Nurse. In 1995 she graduated from Spring Arbor College in Michigan with a degree in Management

Health Service."

"Is there anyone else?"

"Marian Smith, class of 1959, was a Registered Nurse. There is also Roberta Scott Thomas, class of 1961. She attended Cleveland Community College and graduated from St. Alexis Medical School. That's all you have."

"Okay, what's wrong with that?"

"With regard to your two cousins, Burnie and Roberta, I would have thought you would have more."

Irritated I said, "Can we move on?"

Lamont pumped his fist, "Yes! The Connellsville's Sports Chapter is next."

"This chapter is not titled Connellsville's Sports. The title has to be more general like, Sports."

"You're right. I got excited because we're talking about Connellsville sports' facts."

I extended my hand and said, "Please enlighten me?"

"There's no call for the sarcastic tone. I mean with Connellsville's population and size of the high school, there have been numerous individuals who had successful football and baseball careers, both black and white."

"Tell me something you haven't already told me."

Lamont shot me a disapproving look. "There have been eleven football players who attended college and were drafted by the National Football League. Of the eleven, three were African American. Do you have any idea what the odds are for being drafted?"

I mumbled, "I'm sure you're going to tell me."
In a huff, Lamont stood up and left the den.

CHAPTER 91

When Lamont walked out of the room, I didn't stop him. We needed some time apart because tempers were rising and I knew I could not be responsible for anything I might say.

Besides, his time away gave me a chance to surf the Internet. I wanted to find out the odds of a college football player being drafted into the NFL. After ten minutes, frustration set in. The search was not providing what I wanted.

Out loud I said, "Be patient."

After several more tries, success at last. As I read the information, my mouth flew open. I thought, "This couldn't be right."

According to the website, there are thirty-two football teams with a total of 2,240 players, and if I was reading correctly, that included the injured reserved and practice players. Considering how many high schools there are throughout the United States, the odds were .5 percent.

I shook my head in disbelief. No wonder Lamont keeps pounding into my head that Connellsville was part of that western Pennsylvania mystique of producing an unusual number of NFL football players.

The Internet search had given me a new respect for what Lamont had been telling me over and over again. As I clicked off the Internet, Lamont walked in.

My voice was syrupy, "Hey, Sweetie."

His response was a glare as he sat down.

To make amends, I turned around in my chair and put my hands on his. "I owe you an apology."

His tone was cold. "Why is that?"

"I was on the Internet and discovered that getting drafted into the NFL is like winning the lottery or…." I let out a nervous laugh.

"A person might win the lottery before being drafted."

Lamont pulled his hands away and stared at me. "What do you think I've been trying to tell you?" He emphasized. "I don't throw out idle statements without doing my homework."

I threw up my hands in defense. "I'm sorry. I guess I needed to see the facts for myself." I waited for him to say something, but he remained quiet

I was curious. "Do you think the average high school and college football player understands the odds?"

With his head cocked to the side, his voice had a hint of sadness. "In reality, no, but the dream is the draw. I understand all too well. I had dreams of playing in the NBA. The reality for me was when my height stopped at 6 feet one inches and other guys were growing to 6 feet three inches and taller. They were taller and stronger, making them more suitable for the sport. Understanding that, I knew my chances of playing professional basketball were gone."

"But..."

"Let me finish. Most guys get stuck in the fantasy of playing in the NFL or NBA. Nothing is wrong with wanting to live the dream, but most football careers end after high school and college because of injuries or other guys are just better."

He stopped. His voice saddened. "As you have discovered, the odds are small even if the player is outstanding. When you think about how many talented players are competing for a limited amount of positions, it's close to impossible.

"I get it. Thanks for being patient with me. This chapter is special because these guys achieved the dream that so many are unable to do."

"No, the entire book will be special because your hometown gave everyone opportunities regardless of who they were or what they wanted to pursue."

CHAPTER 92

The room filled with an uncomfortable silence. I think Lamont thought that with my newfound appreciation of the sports' facts that I would be excited and shouting how the book should be written. Unfortunately, I was not ready to make that commitment.

The silence was broken by my words. "Where should we start with the sports facts?"

"Maybe we should begin by mentioning some outstanding college football...." I stopped and shouted. "Wait! Are there any black professional baseball players?"

"The only one was Cecil Cole. All of the professional baseball players that made the big league were white. I remember reading something about Connellsville having six or seven white professional baseball players. Before you include any of these facts you'll need to verify them."

"Lamont, you've forgotten, the focus is on black players."

"I'm sorry. When it comes to sports' facts, the color line gets blurred for jocks. We don't care about the color of someone's skin; we're only interested in the record or feat the person has accomplished."

He stopped and smiled. "Think about Tiger Woods and all he has done for golf."

My eyes bugged out. "We're getting off track and need to refocus."

"Okay, okay. Is there anything outstanding about someone who went to college playing football that should be mentioned?"

Going through the stack of papers, there was something notable. I handed Lamont the newspaper write-up.

"This is what I'm talking about. Where is his picture?"

I handed him the picture that came out of Payne A.M.E Church program and said, "This is Copie Lewis' son."

Georj Lewis
The photographer unknown, photograph courtesy of Payne A.M.E. Church Program Bulletin.

"I remember. He was Connellsville's first black principal. Well, I'm sure his dad must have been proud of him because he had a wonderful college football career."

"When I was growing up, Copie was a good football player. I don't think his records were as good as his son's, but he did play football."

"Okay, but right now we're talking about his son."
I threw up my hands. "I was only making a comment. What does the article say?"

"It states that his son, Georj Lewis, went to Edinboro University and was inducted into the Edinboro Hall of Fame. He was a two-time All-American and was named the team's Freshman of the Year after totaling 45 tackles, five pass break-ups, and two interceptions."

Before Lamont could continue, I asked, "Is it necessary to include all the statistical information?"
Lamont had a puzzled look on his face. With a cool calmness he responded. "This is important information because I believe this is why he was inducted. Now, let me finish." He continued.

"As a sophomore, Georj finished with a career high of 68 tackles along with two more interceptions and six pass break-ups. In 1991, he had up to 50 tackles and 11 pass break-ups. In his senior year, he had 66 tackles, three pass break-ups and a career high of three interceptions."

I waited for more statistical data when I realized Lamont was finished. I voiced my concerns. "I still say that it's too much information and no one wants to know all of that."

Lamont's lips curled in disapproval "Listen to me. It's not enough to mention that he was inducted into the Hall of Fame without giving information about how he earned it."

Again, we were at odds. Rather than continue the debate I closed my eyes and said a quick prayer.

"Are you okay?"

"I'm fine. However, I am concerned about this chapter. From what you've said Connellsville had quite a few football players who had outstanding college football records."

I paused, carefully choosing my words. "We aren't going to mention every student who played...."

Lamont didn't let me finish. "I understand your concern, but you have to agree that this was important." Lamont voice became loud. "Come on. He was inducted into the College's Football Hall of Fame."

CHAPTER 93

Once again, that uncomfortable silence invaded the room as if to suppress what could turn into an unpleasant disagreement. Lamont stood up and left the den.

My head was throbbing and I prayed that a headache would stay away, at least until we could get through this chapter.

When Lamont returned, he gave me a glass filled with lemonade and iced tea. I welcomed the cool, refreshing drink.

"While I was making you an Arnold Palmer, I thought about what you were saying and you're right." He held up his hand to stop my interruption.

"But, not every football player gets induced into their College's Football Hall of Fame or becomes an All-American. Believe me, this should be included."

"Like other areas, let's agree not to make the decision now."

With a smile, he said, "I agree."

"Who's next?"

"I believe Jim (Buddy) Braxton, class of 1967. Wow!"

"What?"

Lamont was surprised. "He died in 1986. Do you know from what?"

"No, I don't."

Lamont began reading. "He attended West Virginia University and had a successful college football career and earned honors of being an All-American."

Lamont waved his hand, stopping me. "In his junior year, he rushed for a team's best of 843 yards for the Peach Bowl Champion. He was a talented kicker and booted three field goals and was ranked as the eighth kicker in the nation. As a senior, he played tight end, catching 27 passes for 565 yards and eight touchdowns."

"Do you have a picture of him?"

"No, but I'll see what I can do about getting one."

"Okay and that ends all the outstanding college material."

"Can we take a break?"

"Sure, why didn't you say something before?"

Before I could stand up the phone rang. "Hello."

"Hi, mom, this is Natalie."

"Hi, Baby Girl, what's going on?"

"Nothing much."

We chitchatted for several minutes before she got to the real reason for her call.

"Remember the draft of your book about Connellsville?"

"Yeah, but why do you want to talk about it now? That was how many months ago I sent you that draft?"

"I know, but with my new job and other social commitments, I haven't had a chance to read it." A silence entered the phone.

"Are you still there, Natalie?"

"Yes. It's just that...you know I read all of your books before you submit them to a publisher and...."

"What's wrong?"

"Mom, there is no easy way to tell you, but something is missing from this book. I understand what you're trying to accomplish and there's some interesting facts about your hometown, but in its present form I don't think anyone would buy it, let alone read it. This book needs some serious work."

I laughed.

"What's so funny?"

"Have you been talking to Nicole?"

"Yeah and she told me that you and daddy were doing something with it. That's why I thought I better hurry up and review it before you get too far."

"I appreciate you calling and sharing, but as I told you when I sent it to you, I didn't think I was going to write the book and you confirmed what I've been saying all along."

"Mom, I said I didn't like how you put the book together. I didn't say don't write the book."

"Where's daddy?"

I handed Lamont the phone and left him talking to our youngest daughter. When their conversation ended, Lamont wandered into the kitchen, where I was cooking dinner.

"Did Baby Girl tell you what she thought about your first attempt at writing the book? I didn't even know you had a first draft."

"Yes, you did."

"Well, I must have forgotten. I want to see it because we could have saved ourselves some time. Instead, we started from scratch."

"I know. I wanted a new perspective. I thought if I brought out that first draft, we would end up with the same finished product and I knew I didn't like that draft any more than Natalie."

So, that's part of the resistance of writing the book. Your first try, your writing group and now Natalie, they all confirmed your fears."

"You could say that."

"Lorraine, you usually don't give up that easy. I still think there's something you're not telling me. Are you crying?"

"No, I wish…never mind." Tears were about to fall.

CHAPTER 94

During dinner, our conversation was strained. Everyone wanted the book written, but no one had a solution as to how the story should be told. Lamont and I were at odds about what and how much to include.

The last thing I wanted was to stop, but then I would be faced with making the decision. I wanted it done, finished, completed, the end. Lamont joined me and massaged my neck and shoulder.

"That feels good. I needed that."

When he finished, he patted my shoulders and said, "Okay, let's finish this baby. There are only a few more pages."

"Good. Where were we?"

"We finished college football and now we're at the professional level, the National Football League."

"Who's first?"

"Your cousin, Wilbert Scott, class of 1957, was the first black from Connellsville drafted by the NFL. He attended Indiana University and in 1961 the Pittsburgh Steelers drafted him as a Defensive Linebacker. When his NFL career ended, he played professional football for the Canadian Football League. Is that how he ended up living in Canada?"

We were not about to get into a conversation about my cousin. My answer was curt. "Yes. Let's stay focused. Who's next?"

"Your cousin...."

"You don't have to keep saying, your cousin. I know who my cousins are."

"Aren't we a little sensitive?"

"That's not it. You don't have to remind me who I'm related to."

Lamont cleared his throat. "Okay. Robert Scott is next. He's better known by his relatives as "Bo."

I turned around and threw a balled up piece of paper at him. "You're not funny."

Lamont laughed and after a few seconds, I joined him.

"Come on, Lamont. We need to stay focused."

"Okay. He graduated in the class of 1961 and graduated from Ohio State University, Columbus, Ohio with a B.S. in social work. He played professional football for the Canadian Football League before he was drafted by the NFL."

Lamont paused. "I didn't know that. So, he and Wilbert played Canadian football during the same time?"

"Yes, they did. What else do you want to include about Robert Scott?"

"Oh, any other time, you would have said Bo, but now you're being formal and referring to him as Robert

Scott."

"Whatever. What else do you have about Bo?"

"In 1965, he started playing football for the Cleveland Browns as a Running Back."

I interjected. "What I did enjoy about our family reunion in Cleveland was our visit to the Football Hall of Fame in Canton, Ohio. I was surprised like everyone else when we watched the football film. When we saw the football jersey number 35, none of the family could contain themselves. There Bo was, being tackled by Hall of Famer, Dick Butkus."

Lamont agreed, smiled and proudly said, "He might not be a Hall of Famer, but every time they show that clip, he's there."

CHAPTER 95

The conclusion was near and I was going to celebrate. Lamont was about to continue with the NFL when he stopped.

"When we were discussing college accomplishments I think this would belong in that chapter."

"What is it?"

"It's about Jim Braxton. After his death West Virginia University honored him by naming one of its residence halls after him."

"I didn't know that…" I paused. "Wait a minute. I did know something about that. When I went to the Spicy Ladies Luncheon, I met a woman who worked for West Virginia University and she mentioned it to me."

"Well, you had it in your notes, but you must have forgotten about it."

"I'm sorry. Continue reading."

"The information you took from the West Virginia University's website states there are four connecting buildings and one of the buildings is called Braxton Tower. In fact, the students refer to the buildings simply as the "Towers." A theme represents each resident hall.

Braxton Tower is engineering and science."

"Wow! What an honor. I'll go back and put this with the college chapter."

Lamont poked me. "I guess you know he played for the Buffalo Bills?"

"Yeah, I know that. Braxton played when O.J. Simpson played for the Bills. I understand he was known for his sensational blocking for O.J., although in college, I believe he was a leading rusher."

"Oh, you do know a little about football."

I teased, "I know more about football than you'll ever know. I'm just not a fanatic about it."

"I could say something, but I won't. As you would say, let's stay focused."

"Is that all the NFL players?"

Lamont opened his mouth, but closed it. "There is a Marcus Furman who graduated from the University of Pittsburgh in 2006. He played for the Pittsburgh Panthers as a tailback, wide receiver, and kick returner and...."

"Is this professional football or college?"

"If you'll let me finish reading the newspaper article, I'm getting to his professional career."

"If you ask me, I think you're trying to mention as many stats as possible and it's not going to happen."

"We'll see. Anyway, after graduation Furman worked out with several NFL teams including Indianapolis and the New York Giants, but was never drafted."

"Then, why are we including him?"

In a huff, Lamont said, "Because he plays football for the Arena Football League. The team is the Wilkes Barre/Scranton Pioneers."

"Oh."

"Don't sound so excited. He might not be playing for the NFL, but Arena football is big and for him to obtain a contract is an accomplishment."

"I didn't say it wasn't." It was amazing how Lamont and I could get off track so easily by a simple comment.

"I'm sorry I didn't demonstrate a little more enthusiasm."

"Now, you're being sarcastic."

"No, I'm not."

"Yes, you are."

We started laughing. We were kids at heart.

"Is that it for football? I asked.

"Yes, but we're not finished with sports.

CHAPTER 96

If it wasn't baseball, football or basketball, I couldn't imagine what else there was to include about sports. The room was quiet. The only sound was our breathing.

What was taking Lamont so long? The way he said we had one more sports item I thought he was ready to discuss it.

Finally, he handed me a picture from a newspaper article.

Anthony French

The photographer unknown, photograph courtesy of Payne A.M.E. Church Program.

I glanced at the picture. "Who is this?"

"His name is Anthony French. He participated in the Summer Special Olympics."

"Did you say, Special Olympics?"

"Yes, why?"

"I didn't know Connellsville even participated in the world event."

"Well, you've just learned something because according to this newspaper article, Anthony was best known for his track skills in running and jumping."

I chewed on my lower lip. "I don't want to...I think we should include this, but it would be nice if he had won...."

"If you'll let me finish, I was coming to all of his accomplishments. He competed against athletes from the United States and Great Britain. He earned his goal medals in the High Jump and Pentathlon."

"That's what I wanted to hear."

I didn't like Lamont's tone when he said, "You know, even if he had not earned any gold medals I think this would have been worthy enough to include."

I wasn't about to discuss this because I knew where it would lead us. I plastered a smile on my face. From Lamont's puzzled look, he didn't know what to make of my silent response.

CHAPTER 97

All of our months of laboring over the content of the book would soon conclude. I was elated. I believe the next and final chapter will be the United States Government.

"What were you saying Lamont?"

"I noticed there were quite a few of you that ended up working for the United States Government. That's rather strange, I would have thought that many of you might have sought employment in the nearest large city, like Pittsburgh, instead of going to Washington, D.C."

"You know, I never gave it a thought, but I think most of us went where our relatives were and of course where there would be employment opportunities. If you'll remember, back in the day, you only needed a high school diploma to obtain a decent job in the Federal government."

"Well, that was true with just about any of the major employers like transit, telephone, police and fire departments."

"From my notes do I have enough information to

write about those who worked for the government or will we be making a list of names?"

"You have a little of both." Lamont passed me my notes. "Why don't you go in alphabetic order?"

"Okay." I gave him back the notes. "Who's first?"

"Eileen Davis Burton and she graduated from Dunbar High School." Lamont stopped. "I think we mentioned her earlier and stated where she graduated from."

"I think you're right, but go on."

"Let's see. After graduation she served in the United States Navy and…."

"Why did you stop?"

"Okay…if I remember correctly, you saw her when you were on travel in New Hampshire. She was working for the Department of Transportation, Federal Aviation Administration."

"How did you remember that?"

"There were only two blacks there, you and her. You told me how you didn't recognize her, but she asked you if you were Lorraine Mockabee."

"That was a long time ago. I'm surprised you remembered."

"Yeah, but I did. Anyway, she retired after 20 years of service. I think the next person is Betty Fant Paige."

"Let me find the email message. Here it is." I handed it to Lamont.

"Betty graduated in 1957 from Dunbar Township High School. She worked for the Department of Agriculture. She started out as a Clerk-Stenographer, GS-

3 and was the only African American secretary for the General Counsel. After 38 years, she retired as a GS-9 Secretary to the Associate General Counsel." Lamont noticed I wasn't paying attention to him. "What's wrong?"

"When you were reading, I realized that unless you're familiar with the government grading system some of the accomplishments won't seem like much. I mean the grades start at the GS-1 level and go to the GS-15 level, with the top being the Senior Executive Service better known as SES."

"You're probably right. Therefore, an explanation is needed."

"Not only that, it's difficult to convey that even in the government, there was prejudice. In the beginning, there were very few black secretaries selected to work for the SES Managers. To be a secretary to an Associate General Counsel was not the norm."

"That is an important fact that you'll have to mention. Who's next?"

"Uh…Betty's cousin, Shirley Fant Ouzts graduated from Dunbar in 1959. She worked for the Department of Agriculture in the same Division of the Office of the General Counsel as Betty."

I slapped my forehead. "You may not know this, but when I was in high school, the government used to recruit graduating seniors from Pennsylvania to work for the Federal government in D.C."

"What do you mean?"

"Senior girls in the secretarial curriculum were given the clerk-typist and stenographer exams. If they passed, jobs were offered to them in various agencies in Washington, D.C. I think they even found or recommended places for them to live."

Lamont asked, "I wondered why they went to Pennsylvania?"

"It is my understanding that the government recruited from other states besides Pennsylvania. But, I have no idea why they did that. Did the agencies recruit in the D.C. schools?"

"I doubt it," Lamont said with confidence. "Are you going to include that information in the book?"

My answer was a shrug. "I would if I knew that was how many of Connellsville's black business students ended up in D.C., but I don't know if that was the case." I bit my lower lip.

"I know that the government wasn't the only ones that recruited in small towns. I ended up in D.C. because of the Chesapeake and Potomac Telephone Company. They came to Uniontown and gave the test. When I passed it, they offered me a job. They placed me in the Merriam Hill Hotel on Sixteenth Street, N.W. and paid for my lodging until I completed the training."

"We've been married how long and you never told me that."

"I guess with us working on this book, lots of things that you forget begin to resurrect."

CHAPTER 98

Lamont gazed at me. "Are you tired?"

I emitted a sigh of fatigue. "I think we've done enough."

"Yeah, but I thought you wanted to finish."

Whew. "Okay, will you fix me a cup of green tea?"

Before Lamont left the room he said, "But, you keep working."

My mind drifted as I looked at Betty's email, not wanting to miss anyone. Although I didn't remember her, I did know her brother, Allen, and I think I remembered her cousin, Shirley. I admonished myself to stay focused.

Her brother Thomas Fant worked briefly for the Department of Agriculture and graduated in 1960 from Dunbar. In 1974, he graduated from D.C. Teachers College and retired from Amtrak in 2004 as the Assistant Chief of Onboard Services. I'll include him in the government section, but he'll also have to be mentioned in another area since his entire service wasn't with the Federal government.

Lamont sat down the hot cup of tea. "Thanks,

Sweetie."

"How far have you gotten?"

"I'm on the last of the Fant Family, Sandra Fant Smith. I'm trying to remember their mother, Thelma Taylor and their dad, Napoleon Fant."

"Do you know them?"

"I must, but I can't remember."

Lamont cocked his head, his eyes expressing curiosity. "Is this conversation relevant to this chapter?"

"No, it isn't, but I was trying to connect, that's all. I'm focused, I'm focused."

"If you're ready, I'll begin to read."

I gave him a nod.

"Let's see, Sandra graduated in 1963 from Dunbar she also worked for the Department of Agriculture. She started out as a GS-4 Clerk-Stenographer and progressed to a Secretary for the Under Secretary of Agriculture."

"Did she mention whether or not she was the first black secretary to hold that position?"

"She didn't, but I would bet money on it. Anyway, in 1976, she was promoted to a Program Specialist and from there she went up the ladder and retired after 40 years as a GS-15, Staff Director."

"You can identify with her progression."

"Yes, and I know it could not have been easy. Let's continue. Please put this in the completed stack of papers."

Lamont said, "Wait. Did you see this note?"

"What does it say?"

"B. Smith, the restaurant owner in D.C., is from Mount Pleasant."

"I know, but I can't include Mount Pleasant or I'll never get this book finished. I concentrated on Connellsville and the surrounding area that has been incorporated into the town. That's not the case of Mount Pleasant. If I mention her then I would have to mention Scottsdale and who knows, even Uniontown."

"I'm sorry and you're right. But, that's something, especially since I know where Mount Pleasant is."

I couldn't resist. "Maybe you can encourage someone to write about Mount Pleasant and all the other small towns in western Pennsylvania who have success stories similar to Connellsville."

Lamont's lips parted to say something, but he changed his mind.

CHAPTER 99

I glanced at the clock; the eleven o'clock evening news was about to start. I wanted to stop. I was tired. I had hoped the tea would have given me a boost of energy, but it didn't. I yawned, raised my arms over my head, stood up and went to the bathroom.

When I came back, Lamont was excited. "Hang in there. It's almost over."

I sat back down and took a deep breath. "Where were we?"

"I think you're next or maybe your sister Doris Marilla Lee, class of 1959. She had several years of college and worked for the United States Post Office and retired after 20 years from the Veterans Administration. She started as a GS-3 and progressed to a GS-12."

"Okay, I'm next."

Lamont's voice held an edge of frustration. "And, I don't want you to downplay your accomplishments."

"Would you like to tell me what to include?"

"Okay. You attend the University of Maryland and received a B.S. from the University of California. You progressed from a GS-3 clerk to a GS-15 Supervisory Program Manager. After 34 years of service you retired from the Department of Transportation with the Distinguished Federal Employee Award."

I raised my eyebrows, but said nothing. "Actually, I think Veronica and Valerie Mason should have been before me."

"You're right. Are they twins?"

"No, but they're sisters. Veronica Mason graduated in 1961 and retired from the Department of Justice. Valerie was hearing impaired and retired from the Department of Health, Education, and Welfare. She died several years ago."

"What happened to Patty Mockabee White?"

"Alphabetical order, remember? She graduated in 1961."

"She was in Veronica's class."

"Yes, they were in the same graduating class. Patty progressed from a Clerk-Typist, GS-3 to an Administrative Assistant, GS-14 for the Department of Housing and Urban Development. I think that's it."

Lamont grabbed my hand as I started to shut off the computer. "Not so fast. For one thing, you forgot to mention that she retired after 37 years of service."

"Okay, I entered that information. Is that it?"

"You have one more person, Harold Robinson. He served in the United States Army for 20 years. After his military retirement, he went to work and retired after more than 20 years as a Mail Carrier for the United States

Post Office."

I waited for Lamont to make a comment since he had driven my parents to Hampton, Virginia to visit Harold Robinson, but he must have forgotten about me being related to him.

"You can now shut off the computer. We are officially finished. Now, you can start putting it all together and develop your story."

Lamont kissed me. I pulled away from him, not responding to his remark.

"What I want is sleep. I'm exhausted and it's late."

He grabbed my hand. "Let's go to bed."

CHAPTER 100

The next morning, neither one of us realized how late it was until we saw the morning sunlight. When I got out of bed, I glanced at the clock. It was ten o'clock. Even Lamont had slept in.

When I climbed back into bed, he was lying on his side, smiling at me. "Good morning, Wife. How are you doing?"

"I'm fine. How are you?"

He chuckled. "I'm doing great this morning."

"I didn't mean to wake you."

"Oh, I've been up, had a cup of coffee and now I'm back in bed. You snuggled up next to me and I fell back to sleep." He gathered me in his arms and nuzzled his chin on my head. "We have no place to go."

I knew he was waiting. I pulled away from his embrace and looked at him. "You want to know if I'm going to write the book. I'm still leery about the content and everything that might be excluded, but at least I feel better about the organization of it."

"Good! Admit it, when you started your quest to

document the accomplishments of your hometown blacks, you had no idea you would find out so much regarding them and their accomplishments."

"You're right, the achievements were more than I expected. Somehow, I would have to state that the book is not complete, but it's a start. At least, I've scratched the surface."

"Well, I believe it's imperative to remember and honor those who have paved the way for others."

I was shaking my head. "But Lamont, that's the point. I don't believe most blacks from Connellsville believe they have done anything extraordinary. If I find difficulty talking about my achievements what do you think about them?"

"I agree. You all are too humble. Believe me, and I know I say it all the time, but you and all the other blacks from Connellsville were privileged and prospered from your experience."

"I'm no longer arguing with you about that. The book will have to stand on its own merit and perhaps other blacks from small towns will take a closer look at their life story and gather enough information to think about writing their own book. I think you were right when you said I should have viewed this the same way I approached genealogy."

Lamont teased, "I didn't want to say it, but you're finally admitting that I was right."

"I eat humble pie. If I write the story, I still have to find a suitable title."

"What do you mean? I thought we had a title."

"The "Best Kept Secret"…I think…" My voice trailed off.

Lamont frowned. "What's wrong with the title?"

"If I keep that title, when the reader finishes, the question remains, what's the secret?"

"Come on honey. You know the secret."

"I do now, but how many others will understand and get it?"

"Well, let me put it this way. I would hope they would."

I let out a slight laugh. "If the reader wants more, a sequel could always be written. Are you ready to get up?"

"Not quite yet." Lamont kissed me. When he eased his embrace he said, "Now, we can get up."

As he started to climb out of bed, I shouted. "Wait a minute!"

"What's wrong?"

"It just dawned on me that the hard part of the book is done." Sweetly, I say, "I'll always be grateful for you helping and encouraging me to do the research and to put everything together. However, there's still a lot if I am to finalize it."

Lamont pouted. "You still haven't made up your mind. What about all the people waiting for its release?"

"That's still a mystery as to how so many people found out about it." Lamont started laughing.

"Come on, Babe. You're not that naïve."

"What do you mean?"

"You come from a small town. Each one told one."

"Who did I tell?"

Lamont sighed. "You told your mom, your sisters, Miss Elsie, the high school and public librarians, and all the people you were trying to obtain information from." Lamont stopped. "Should I go on?"

I started laughing. "How could I have forgotten?"

Lamont didn't comment as he gathered me in his arms and gave me another kiss. He released me and whispered, "Does that mean you're going to write the book?"

SOURCES

This book became a reality because of many and I deeply appreciate their support. Thanks to all that provided photographs from their private collections.

Although the story has been fictionalized, the facts can be verified through a variety of sources.

Information/Newspaper Articles

Connellsville Daily Courier Newspaper

Connellsville High School Library

Connellsville National Historic Society

Elise Webster Haley, Payne A.M.E. Church Secretary and Trustee

Reverend Acquanetta Osborne (Former minister), Payne A.M.E.

Photos

Connellsville Daily Courier Newspaper

Connellsville High School Library

Jackie Brown, Connellsville National Historic Society

Theodore (Ted) Davis

Elise Webster Haley

Reverend Acquanetta Osborne (Former minister), Payne A.M.E.

Roy Taylor

Patty White